ALWAYS THE QUIET ONES

OTHER TITLES BY JAMIE LEE SOGN

Salthouse Place

ALWAYS THE QUIET ONES

a Novel

JAMIE LEE SOGN

LAKE UNION
PUBLISHING

This is a work of fiction. Names, characters, organizations, places, events, and incidents are either products of the author's imagination or are used fictitiously. Otherwise, any resemblance to actual persons, living or dead, is purely coincidental.

Published by Lake Union Publishing, Seattle

www.apub.com

Amazon, the Amazon logo, and Lake Union Publishing are trademarks of Amazon.com, Inc., or its affiliates.

EU product safety contact:
Amazon Media EU S. à r.l.
38, avenue John F. Kennedy, L-1855 Luxembourg
amazonpublishing-gpsr@amazon.com

ISBN-13: 9781662520051 (hardcover)
ISBN-13: 9781662520068 (paperback)
ISBN-13: 9781662520044 (digital)

Cover design by Caroline Johnson
Cover image: © Jesse Morrow / Stocksy; © New Africa / Shutterstock

Printed in the United States of America
First edition

To Danielle, my Sea Star and my dearest friend

Chapter 1

Monday

Some days it astonishes me how much effort it takes to be alive.

It's my normal morning routine. Every day for years now, I've lined up the bottles in my medicine cabinet, then gone through them one by one until I have all the pretty pills in my palm. It looks like a lot, but it's not nearly as much as I used to take; now I can swallow them all in one go. I don't even get sick from them anymore; that is, unless I miss a dose, and I hardly ever do.

On my worst days, these little colorful ovals and circles simply prop me up and help me get through the hours so I can get back into bed as soon as possible. But on decent or even good days, when I think I might not need them, the medication reminds me that I've gone through a lot to get here.

I think today is going to be a good day.

There's something about being the first one up in the morning, that still, quiet calm of a day about to unfold. It's a mirrored surface of water that I can slowly slip my finger into before the ripples break up my reflection.

This morning, I take some extra time to tame my thick black hair, running my long locks through a flat iron. Normally, I would throw my unruly mane into a ponytail and call it good. After I straighten, I put some hair oil into my palms and then run my fingers through my hair for extra shine. As for the face, I only do a little mascara and blush, and I'm ready to go.

I stand in front of the coffee maker and listen to the gurgle in between the raindrops pattering at the kitchen window. It's a mess outside. It was storming all night, and there's no sign of it stopping anytime soon. Nothing unusual for Seattle in March, though.

I add a splash of nondairy creamer to my coffee and stand against the counter, cradling the drink and letting my brain boot up to the sound of a rainy Monday morning. Normally, I would be annoyed if I had to leave the house for the office; this would be a perfect day to take this coffee and curl up in front of the TV and catch up on my latest shows. This morning I can't wait to get to work.

Down the hall, I hear a door crack open.

"Bea?" a voice calls. "Is that you?"

I smile. There goes my quiet morning. "Who else would it be, Mom?" I reply. "Besides Dad, I'm the only other person living here." I pop out the spent coffee pod and throw it into the smelly counter compost canister, then reload the coffee machine. "Coffee's almost ready."

Mom comes into the kitchen, followed closely by Dad. "Morning, Buzz!" he says, using the nickname I've had since I was a toddler, when I spent two weeks straight in August refusing to wear anything other than a bumble-*Bea* costume. "Hey, you look nice today."

I'm a little pleased he's noticed. "Thanks. I think it's gonna be a good day at work. I kind of wanted to dress up."

"What's going on?" asks Mom. She's wearing a fluffy robe; her shoulder-length black hair is already brushed; the odd gray cluster of hairs peeks through. She's not wearing any makeup, but her natural high cheekbones and flawless skin would fool most about her age.

We share the same round face and big eyes, shaped like marquise diamonds and as brown as the coffee I'm drinking. We share the same body shape, too; when I cried at eleven years old and wished I was as bone thin as the white girls in my class, she told me I would be thankful when I got older that I had hips and a backside that curved like the mountains of the nearby Cascades. She was right. Though neither of us could have accounted for the Kardashians happening.

I smooth my hands over my high-waisted black pants, which hug said curves—it's the nicest pair I have. "My boss *might* have hinted at something special happening this week," I say, looking down. "Like a promotion . . ."

Mom squeals, and Dad, not a foot away from her, winces, then smiles. "That's my girl!" he says.

"Finally," Mom laments. "You should have been promoted years ago, Bea! That it took this long to give you credit—"

"Well, it's only because a senior associate just left, so now there's a spot open."

Mom raises an eyebrow. "Hasn't he promised you the promotions before, when other spots came open? Like . . . for the last five years?"

Dad moves closer to Mom and puts an arm around her, a silent signal for her to bring it down a notch. She wrinkles her nose and looks up at him, while he simply smiles softly back. "Let her have her moment," he says.

"Well, Landon has a lot of good attorneys in the office to choose from. Besides, he's really busy, and maybe I'm not as flashy or vocal about my wins." I'm not sure why I'm defending my boss, since she's 100 percent correct. "But this time he told me I would be promoted. He promised. This is going to be an exciting week. Granite Holdings is coming in for our final bid presentation tomorrow, and we've been trying to steal them away from Saul Group for ages. If they end up hiring us and ditching Saul Group, it's going to be a huge deal."

My phone dings, and I check my texts. It's Greg Farrell, my colleague: Thanks again for finishing up that memo for me last night!

I type back quickly, Sure thing! How'd the date go?

Three bubbles appear and then a quick response back. Good! And she made a mean scramble for brekky this morning if you kno what i mean.

I get it yeah. So second date plans?

Wut. no, she's not my type. Btw, did you get those most recent numbers for the Granite presentation incorporated into the deck? Hope it wasnt a pain!

Not at all!

It was a bit of a pain. Honestly, I didn't mind finishing the deck by myself. The truth was that even if Greg had done his slides and given them to me, I would have been up late proofreading and correcting his work anyway.

"Bea?"

I snap back to attention and put my phone down. "Huh?" I say.

"I said once Granite hears about the brilliant newly minted senior associate, I know they'll be asking where to sign," Dad says.

Mom claps her hands. "I know! You should call Allegra and go out for celebration drinks! She'll be over here this evening anyway."

My mood instantly sours. "Why is *she* coming over?" I ask. "Besides the need to spread her endless propaganda on how amazing pregnancy is?" Allegra is a childhood friend of the family—her family and mine grew up going to church and school together. She's also Filipino, so we were basically contractually obligated to hang out together.

Mom clicks her tongue. "She's coming to help make the lumpia for the church fundraiser this weekend! And, Bea, I don't know why you always have to make that face about her, huh? You two used to be such good friends."

"Yeah, in high school, Mom." I glance at the clock. "I have to go." While I genuinely like her, we have grown into different people, and Mom constantly trying to rekindle our girlhood friendship is irritating. While I'm single and still live with my parents, Allegra curates an Instagram-perfect life. Though if I thought she was annoying before, I couldn't have prepared myself for how insufferable she would become when she got pregnant. I'm convinced Allegra would stay pregnant for the rest of her life if she could. She is one of those uncanny women who actually does *glow* during pregnancy.

I imagine Allegra with her grown-up life, and I can't relate at all. I try not to think about it and insist to everyone and myself that I don't care. But how can I not care? How can I not be hurt when she is living this perfect life and sharing it with, of all people, Caleb?

It's true, Allegra and I were good friends a long time ago. But that was before . . . everything. Before the pills, before Caleb Crown, before my family lost it all trying to save me.

When it was all different.

"Go get 'em, girl!" says Dad. "Big things!"

I give a wave to Mom and Dad as I leave the house and let the bright-red door of our small home swing shut behind me. I step lightly down the porch stairs—the third one down has been broken for months.

Just like I'm not the person I used to be, we live in a different house now from the one I grew up in.

I still remember it: a two-story brick Tudor, and an entryway with a hanging lantern that always looked so big to me as a little girl. Mom grew roses outside that house, and we were always throwing parties. That house had a red door too. But then we lost it. I mean, I lost it for us. Unable to afford the mortgage anymore, we moved. When I left for law school, my parents moved into our rambler, with a dirt driveway that my parents have been meaning to pave ever since.

I remember when we painted the door here red, too, maybe in a bout of hope that we could re-create what we'd had in the Tudor. Mom has tried growing roses here, but they've never taken, even though Father Cristobal came and threw holy water and prayers at all her garden tools and each square inch of soil. I think Dad still looks at Zillow estimates for the Tudor, which is well over a cool million now thanks to Seattle real estate.

Now the neighborhood we live in is somewhere in the middle of the gentrification that's overtaken Seattle and all its suburbs. The three houses on the corner were bought up last year and demolished, to be replaced with stylish condo buildings. They stand in cold geometric opposition to the humble single-family homes surrounding them. A spin studio is opening down the road, which Dad claims is the official beginning of the end. Beginning of what and end of what, he's never actually specified, but the increase in the property tax bill last year made us all do a double take.

Once I got the job at BCC, I took over most of our mortgage. It seemed the least I could do for my parents. We still have medical debt from the accident, and debt from the loans they took out to pay the lawyers. Not to mention my law school loans on top of it all.

Things are different. Sometimes Mom and Allegra don't see that, or won't. I don't blame Allegra. I made my own choices, which turned me into who I am today. I blame Caleb Crown a little, though—maybe a lot. And the fact is that I would have never met Caleb if it hadn't been for Allegra Montoya.

◆ ◆ ◆

I feel the blast of cold and wet air long before I reach the top of the staircase at the downtown University Street station. Behind me and back past the line of morning commuters, groggy eyed and clutching their morning coffees with desperate fingers, the Seattle Link light-rail train speeds away with a groan. I shrug off the past and get back to the present.

Walking along the busy downtown sidewalk of Fifth Avenue, I'm not sure which will sweep me away first, the rain or my own excitement. Because today, all my hard work and my parents' sacrifice will finally be paying off. Sure, the promotion means a bonus and a salary increase, but what the promotion means most is validation that I'm no longer the person I used to be.

I get to my office building, a new glass skyscraper that looks like a crescent moon cutting into the sky. In the elevator, I push the button for the fiftieth floor. The doors open up to a lush modern lobby with a bronze plaque front and center as you enter that reads "Bellingham, Charles & Chan."

The receptionist greets me. "Congratulations on the award, Bea! We saw in the morning email announcements." I beam.

"The morning announcements?" I repeat.

She nods. "Yeah, it's exciting."

"Thank you!" I breathe. It's done. It's already been announced.

I've gotten a little past reception and into the lobby when I notice the crowd gathered in the normally vacant space. Every inch of cream-colored faux leather seating is taken up by suits, and I can't even see past the sea of black and gray to the normal panoramic views of Puget Sound. I'm taken aback when I see my own boss, Landon Laurie, at the head of the room, speaking. I catch the tail end of a sentence. "I can assure you, nobody is more deserving."

Is this all . . . for me?

I move past a couple of people, and they glance to me, then back to Landon; I'm not even sure these people know who I am . . . and they don't seem to care about my arrival. No, whatever this is, it isn't for me. I backtrack to the reception area.

"Sorry," I say. "What were you congratulating me for?"

She blinks. "Oh, it said you're getting some pro bono award." She reads my clueless face. "At the Legal Aid gala next week?"

"Oh right," I say, remembering I did receive some email about that a while back. Nothing special, I just clocked fifty hours of pro bono work through the Seattle Legal Aid offices. "So why the party?" I ask, gesturing to the crowd.

"Greg's getting promoted! Landon just announced he's the newest senior associate!"

My mouth drops open, and I turn just in time to see Greg standing to join Landon at the front of the crowd. Landon shakes his hand, and they both dole out shit-eating grins to the group, which bursts into applause.

Greg. Who was just chatting with me and didn't say anything.

Greg. Who never gets his work done on time and is constantly leaning on *me* for help.

And Landon. My boss, who just last week promised me that I would be getting the promotion. The boss who's overlooked me for five years is now patting the back of a mediocre man who joined the same time as I did.

There *is* someone more deserving than Greg.

It's me.

At the announcement of celebratory donuts in the break room, the crowd disperses. Except for me. I stand in the lobby and watch Landon and Greg walk together right toward me. They're talking and laughing and don't even notice me. I step aside to let them pass me by. "Congrats, Greg," I say quietly. They don't even hear me.

I'm so disappointed I could cry.

I'm so angry I could kill.

Chapter 2

I sit at my desk and stare at my inbox. I can hear Monday-morning chatter spill in through my glass office walls; from the other side of my office window, I can hear the rain, which hasn't let up outside. The drops pelt my window with a useless kind of anger. I usually have a view all the way to the water, in between buildings at least, but right now I can barely see the building next door to us in the rain and fog.

On my screen, I've been staring at the morning announcement email for who knows how long now. Greg's promotion is top billing, with a write-up with his picture and a quote from Landon about how Greg is "promising, a brilliant legal mind, and the only golfer who's come close to beating me at Pacific Dunes at the BCC Summer Men's Retreat!"

I feel ill.

I scroll down to find my own name in bold under a section titled "Other News."

> Save the date for the annual Legal Aid gala, sponsored by Bellingham, Charles & Chan. Junior Associate Bea Ku to accept an award.

A buzz from my phone jolts me back to the present. A text from Mom on our family group chat. CONGRATULATIONS Bea!

It's followed quickly by one from Dad: That's my girl! He adds a GIF image of a dancing bumblebee.

I leave them on read and bury my head in my hands. Do I talk to Landon? Greg? What do I do? I decide my best strategy is to wait for a sinkhole to appear under my office chair, but after nearly twenty minutes of waiting, I accept it's no longer an option.

"Are you okay, Ku?"

I nearly jump as Landon Laurie comes into my office.

"Sorry." I quickly click out of the announcement email. "Uh, didn't hear you knock."

"I didn't." He takes a seat in the chair across from my desk and casually leans back, propping his feet on my desktop and tipping the chair back precariously. I wish for a sudden breeze to come through the office and knock him over.

As with the sinkhole, no such luck on the breeze.

"Uh, how was your weekend?" I hate myself for asking that as soon as I say it. *How was your weekend?* What about *How was it robbing me of my promotion?*

He ignores the question. "Congrats on the pro bono award," he says. "Was that because of the voting project that took you away from your real work last fall? We lost a shit ton of billable hours because of that."

"You mean the voters' rights project I chaired? Well, I figure the firm requires its attorneys put in so many pro bono hours a year, I might as well do work I'm interested in and that makes a difference—"

He yawns and begins scrolling on his phone with one hand, rubbing his clean-shaven jawline with the other. Landon is in his midforties, and he's kept a trim physique, as revealed by the unnecessarily formfitting tailored shirts he sports.

"Um, is there something I can help you with?" I ask.

"Actually"—his blue eyes glance up from his phone screen to me—"there's something you can help Greg with." He runs his hands through perfectly slightly messy russet hair.

I ignore the charm offensive. "You mean our newest promising senior associate?"

Landon smiles. "Actually, yes, one and the same."

I can't help myself. "What could such a brilliant legal mind possibly need my help with?"

"Ku," Landon says, still grinning. "Do I sense some professional jealousy? Not a good look, I should warn you."

"It's not jealousy," I say, measuring my breath. "It's just that I thought you said . . ." I trail off.

"Said what? What did I say?"

"Last week. After the Peterson matter was resolved, you said—you told me . . ."

"What?"

"That I was overdue for a promotion and you were going to make things right." I almost whisper it. *He did say that, right?* I find myself asking myself.

"Oh, sure I said that," he says. "But I didn't mean *now*. I didn't mean *this time*. Shit, Ku, did you think you were gonna . . . did you think you were going to get the promotion that Greg earned?"

"The promotion Greg earned"; the one I didn't. I want to shrink away to nothing. "I really thought you meant the promotion was mine since the spot was open and I've been passed over before . . ."

"Passed over? Look, I haven't passed anyone over for anything." He's not smiling anymore. He swings his feet off the desk, and they land on the carpet with a thud; in one swift manspreading motion, he sets his elbows on his knees and leans in earnestly. "If you weren't promoted, it's because you weren't ready. There's nothing else to say."

I'm quiet now and just holding back the deluge of tears I can feel pushing at the backs of my eyes. I nod and stare down at my keyboard, wanting the conversation to end. My cheeks are burning, and I know I must look like I just ran a mile.

"But." Landon's voice is also quiet. "It is the end of the fiscal quarter, and if Granite should end up hiring us as their official counsel of record, then I might be able to look at the budget for an additional senior position."

"That's if Granite signs?" I ask.

"Only if they sign. And if they do and I can find the resources for the additional role, which I'm sure I can . . . you might just be next in line."

"I might?"

"You will be. I promise."

I sniff and nod. "I just don't want to misunderstand again."

"Dammit, I'm telling you, stop it with the impending waterworks, and the next promotion will be yours if we secure Granite. Does that work for you, or can you at least go cry in the bathroom like a respectable lawyer?"

"As long as you're promising . . ."

"Great." He leans back. "Hey, you look like you could use some coffee."

I attempt a smile at the peace offering. "I can always use coffee."

Landon stands and pulls out his phone again. "Perfect. Can you make mine a hemp milk latte? And get it from the cart downstairs, not that trash from the break room. Thanks, Ku, you're a rock star."

◆ ◆ ◆

The lobby coffee cart is busy; it's a Monday, and the people need their caffeine. Since I already had coffee at home and there's free coffee upstairs, I decide I'm just going to get Landon his ridiculous order. I wait for a long time, more time than is reasonable, but the people of this city take their caffeine intake seriously. The beanie-clad, tattooed baristas make each matcha latte or pour-over with care. I finally make it to the front of the line and am about to order when a blond woman butts in front of me.

She waves a coffee cup in front of the barista. "You gave me the wrong order!" she snaps. "My boss freaked out on me. I need a new one."

"That's what you ordered," says the barista.

"It is not," the woman argues.

"Sorry, you'll just have to get back in line," says the barista, unaffected.

I give the woman a sideways glance and silently agree she can't be cutting. Not in front of me, anyway.

She turns and looks at me. To my surprise, there are tears in her eyes, and her face is a mottled red and white. "Can I please get in front of you?" She sniffs and wipes at her nose. "I don't want to get in trouble. Well, in even more trouble . . ."

"Tough boss?" I ask.

She nods. "It's been the worst day ever, and it's not even nine a.m."

I take pity on her. "I understand the feeling," I say. "It's fine if you want to cut."

"Thank you!" she says. She reorders her coffee and then asks me, "What are you having? My treat."

"Really? Thanks! Just one grande hemp milk latte."

While we wait for the order, the woman thanks me again. "I don't even work in this building, but my boss likes the coffee from this place the best."

"Well, it's rare when you can actually taste the snobbery in the beans," I say.

She laughs. "It's funny because it's true. Hey, thank you again."

"Us girls have to stick together, right?"

The barista calls out our orders.

"Absolutely. Have a good day!"

◆ ◆ ◆

I drop Landon's order off at his thankfully vacant desk. Unfortunately, my own office isn't as empty when I return.

"Greg? What are you doing in here?"

Greg is standing behind my desk and looking at my photos. He turns. "You're back. Landon told me you said you wanted to help me out with some last-minute Granite presentation fine-tuning."

"I don't remember saying that at all."

"I already sent you the case studies. Just integrate them into the deck as best you can."

"Why didn't you tell me you were getting the promotion?" I ask.

He pauses. "Huh?"

"We were chatting this morning, and you didn't even tell me about it. I had to walk in on your little party."

"Look, I'm sorry. I probably should have said something, but I didn't want to make you feel bad."

"You wouldn't have made me feel bad," I lie.

He cocks his head. A curl of brown hair falls perfectly across his forehead, and I want to smack it off. "Come on, Bea. Everyone in this office knows you've been gunning for a promotion since the day you first walked through this door."

I sigh. "Everyone except Landon. I am excited for you, Greg." I lie again. "It's just that I keep feeling like I'm getting ignored here."

"So go somewhere else," he says. "You've put in your time here, God knows."

I've thought about it many times. But part of me has invested too much in this firm, five years of my life—it's all I've known since graduating law school and passing the bar exam. To start over somewhere else seems, in a word, terrifying. I think about Landon's newest promise. "Maybe things are finally going to turn around," I say. "Especially if we get Granite."

"That's the spirit," says Greg. "And why I need you to go over these presentation numbers with a fine-tooth comb. I want it all perfect for tomorrow."

"Me too."

"Then I'll leave you to it." He checks his watch. "I gotta go. Landon and the other partners are taking me out to a celebratory lunch at the

George. You know," says Greg, pausing just before leaving. "You could avoid all this hard-work nonsense and just sleep with Landon if you want to get promoted."

I don't react. "That's what they say, isn't it?" That is what they say about at least the last three female associates from Landon's team that earned promotions before I was hired; they've all since left the firm. I've never believed the rumors, and Landon has never been more than your average amount of work flirty with me, though I've seen him be more shameless with younger and newer women. The fact that there's even an acceptable amount of "work flirty" from my boss should be a red flag, but this is a law firm, and sometimes I feel like we're still *Mad Men* adjacent.

"So," Greg says. "You're not going to sleep your way to the top."

"Don't get me wrong—I see the appeal. But I think you're just jealous because you can't sleep your way to the top," I retort.

Greg laughs and leaves, calling behind him, "What makes you think I'm not?"

I roll my eyes.

I put all my work for the day aside to focus on Granite. I finish up when the lights are out in every office except mine. Well, mine and one other. I walk out of my office and turn to look back at hers down at the end of the dark hall, like a glowing yellow beacon. She's head down and writing something, but I give a wave anyway. Olivia Oxford is a junior partner, like Landon, and the only woman to hold the title. When I originally interviewed for a job here, I requested to be on her team. I was assigned to Landon's instead.

Unlike my boss, Olivia is quiet and thoughtful. She has a reputation as a shark, or as a bitch, depending on who you ask; she's known for being brilliant at what she does.

Legal nerds like me usually have our idols in the field, those whose careers we want to emulate; Olivia Oxford is mine. But she has a lot of fans, and if I've been semisuccessful in getting Landon's attention, I don't think Olivia has ever looked my way before.

I wonder if she ever had to sleep with someone to get promoted. Immediately, I feel ashamed of even speculating. I also wonder why we always blame and then gossip about the woman who takes the opportunity, rather than calling out the man who makes it the only option for her.

The train is empty and quiet, much like downtown Seattle after hours. I speed through the underground and arrive at my park-and-ride lot.

I don't remember until I pull into the driveway that I never responded to my parents' texts and never told them I didn't actually get the promotion. I step out of my car and groan at the sight of the silver Audi parked there too.

Allegra is here.

This day officially wants to murder me.

Chapter 3

I'm barely in the door when I'm pounced on. "Well?" Mom asks. "You didn't respond to my texts all day! Did you get the promotion? I've been telling Allegra how you said today was the day!"

Allegra waves from a barstool at the kitchen counter. In front of her and Mom is an assembly line of lumpia production. "Hey, Bea, I can't wait to hear the news!" Allegra is in a pair of leggings and an oversize T-shirt, but she still looks effortlessly glamorous, even with her dark-brown hair in a side braid, old faded caramel highlights twisting in and out of her natural color.

"Well?" Mom presses again.

How can I tell them the truth? So I don't. "You're looking at the newest senior associate at BCC," I say.

Mom jumps up and down. "Praise the Lord!" she says, clapping her hands.

Allegra gets up and gives me a hug, her hard pregnant belly pushing against me. "Congratulations, Bea!"

"Dad is stuck at work, but I have to text him right away! Right after I pour a glass of wine!" Mom fills up glasses for her and me, and Allegra holds up a can of LaCroix.

"Cheers!" We clink our drinks.

I nervously drink. It's just been delayed a couple of days, I rationalize. Landon said I would get the promotion if Granite signed—and they will. It won't hurt to say I got the promotion a teeny bit ahead of when I actually get it. It's called faking it till you make it.

Mom gets on her phone to text Dad the good fake news.

"So how are you feeling?" I ask Allegra.

"Oh my gosh, Bea," she gushes. "I have to tell you, I love being pregnant. It's been so easy, and now that I'm in the middle of the second tri, I've just gotten a rush of energy! We just finished painting the nursery, and you'll never guess the name of this paint color—Lemon Bar Yellow! How cute is that?"

I hold a smile while she details her nursery decor.

It's not that I don't like Allegra. She stands in my kitchen, and there's something about her; she talks with my mom in an easy way like I never could. But of course she does—our families have always been close. Our moms were like sisters, and we grew up knowing them as aunties. She even puts the accents in the right spots when saying Cebuano words, since she is used to speaking the language to her own parents. She's fit and slender; her round pregnant belly is like a beach ball attached to her petite frame.

The fullness of her body makes the emptiness of my own ache. I think about another world where I made different choices: I never drank, I never got in the car, I never ended up in the hospital, and I never left. I never hurt Caleb. In this world, maybe *I'm* the one carrying Caleb's baby.

While Allegra talks, I watch her quick fingers scoop up the lumpia filling and shape it just right. Then she envelops it in the rice wrapper, rolling it up and sealing it with a quick dash of egg wash. Then on to the next. My clumsy hands tear a wrapper nearly in half as I try to stretch it over the filling.

"No, Bea, fold it," Mom instructs me. "Ah, it's okay. Try another."

"It's easy once you get into a rhythm," Allegra offers, unhelpfully. Mom nods in agreement. "Try it like this." She demonstrates, and then they both watch me try to re-create it. I focus and successfully roll up a decent, if a little overfilled, lumpia roll. Allegra pokes the plump piece. "I feel as stuffed as this one!"

"I remember when I was pregnant with Bea," Mom says. "I didn't know how I could be so hungry all the time and never be full!"

"Well, it's because you were growing Bea's big brain." Allegra winks.

Allegra and Mom continue talking about pregnancy, and I roll the lumpia in silence. Sometimes, I wonder if Mom wishes she had a daughter more like Allegra.

In time, Mom finally announces we have enough, and we wrap everything up for Allegra to take home and store until the church sale. I help her out to her car with the trays and pack them securely in the trunk. "Thanks for helping Mom out," I say. "I know she loves when you come over and do all the things I'm not as good at."

She frowns. "Why do you say that? You were great. And we've been doing this all our lives, remember? The three of us plus my mom making goodies for church? It's a time-honored tradition. Trust me, my mom will be over as soon as she gets back to the US for the birth." Allegra rubs her palm over her stomach while talking, but gently, as if she doesn't even realize she's doing it. "Your mom thinks you work too hard, Bea."

I feel my defenses flare up. "If I'm not working too hard, I'm not working hard enough. She's never happy with what I'm doing."

"She just worries. I see it too."

"See what?"

"You seem worn down. I know you just got the promotion, so maybe now is a good time to slow down and find some work-life balance. Or you know . . ."

"I don't."

"We just don't want another . . . episode."

"Thanks for your concern," I say, looking up at the night sky.

"We just want you to be healthy."

"*We*? Who's this *we*? You're not a part of my family, as much as you'd like to be."

Allegra stiffens. "That's not true, Bea. I'll always be here when you need me."

"Yeah, it was me you were really there for . . ." I mutter. I don't say his name—I don't have to. He's there between us like a ghost. When I look at her, Allegra is frowning, holding her belly and looking like she is miles away. I feel a pang of guilt, but whether or not it's for my own lies or for our lost friendship, I'm not sure.

"I'm sorry," I say. "That was mean. You're right. I am stressed lately. But I can't imagine how stressed you must be . . . about to have a kid! It's kind of wild to think about. Do you think she'll be half as bad as we were?"

Allegra laughs. "I'm sure she'll be worse. It's my punishment for causing my own parents so much grief." She raises an eyebrow. "Not as much as you, of course."

"Oof," I laugh. "I guess I deserve that." She isn't wrong. We wave goodbye, and I feel the urge to smile.

Back inside, Mom has almost finished cleaning up and offers me a refill of wine. I wave her away. "No thanks, I think I'm actually going to go to bed."

"Of course. You must be exhausted! It was a big day!" She bangs some pans against one another as she stacks them in the cupboard. "You know," she begins.

Here it comes.

"You could try to be nicer to Allegra."

"I was nice!"

"I saw your eyes," she says. She laughs, an awkward high-pitched lilt, her telltale sign she's annoyed and being passive aggressive. "She's just done a lot for you."

"Again with this," I grumble. "I don't owe Allegra anything."

"She was really happy for your big news, and you couldn't even act interested in her pregnancy."

"It's fine. Her and I are all good. It's just . . . like this with us."

"Well, good. Because I promised you would help with preparations for her baby shower next weekend!"

"Wait, what?" I huff. "You didn't ask me if I was busy or anything?"

"Oh, Bea, you're never busy. You're just home all the time with us, so I thought you'd enjoy helping her. We'll go over to her house and help—"

"It's at her house?" I ask, wide eyed. "I really wish you would have asked me first." Before she can respond, I go into my room and close the door before immediately unbuttoning my pants and flopping onto the bed. Even when I get a promotion, Mom finds something to harp on about. Well, even when I get a fake promotion.

If they only knew the real story. If they only knew that I wouldn't have even gotten in half the trouble I did when I was younger if it weren't for Allegra.

When I was in high school, every Sunday after church, our families attended the postservice potluck. Though completely voluntary, the potlucks were highly encouraged, meaning gossip and shaming would ensue if a family missed a potluck or even turned up with a subpar food offering. The ringleader of the Filipino church ladies was LaCrista Montoya, Allegra's mom, and she organized all the highly recommended (read: mandatory) Filipino activities. Even when Mom came home exhausted each day from her shift at the nearby Residence Inn front desk, she feared being seen as an unsatisfactory community member more. This meant we attended church, the potlucks, the block parties, the dances, and the Mariners' Filipino Heritage Appreciation Day game, all the community events.

All I can say is Filipinos roll deep.

What Mom understood all along was that as an immigrant she couldn't afford a single misstep. Even though she was married to my white dad, anything less than perfect wouldn't do; she would be dubbed a green card chaser or a gold digger, despite the fact that there was no gold to dig in my dad's empty bank accounts.

It was this drive for the chance to be seen as equal, mixed with a natural pride, that caused Mom to push me hard to embrace the same ambition. Beginning in all-day kindergarten, my days consisted of essentially the same schedule: school, sports or whatever after school activity I had been signed up for, then studying, then family dinner around the dining table, then sleep. Repeat.

Weekends were more sports, tournaments or such, church, potlucks and Filipino party times, and more studying. She said she wanted us to have a community, but it was just exhausting.

My trajectory was clear. Graduate from high school with a 4.0, get into the best college I could, then get into the best law school or med school I could, then be the best lawyer or doctor I could. Somewhere in there, there was some hope I would eventually get married and have kids too.

By my junior year in high school, my world was a small one, but I was happy. Or I assumed I was. As the end of high school was creeping ever closer, I was beginning to feel the pressure of graduating. I had excellent grades, but my classes were getting harder. I was having to spend longer studying, and I felt like my brain was filling up to the brim with the processes of cell division, the major dates leading up to World War I, and the main existence theorems. I was running out of energy. Did other seventeen-year-olds feel this way?

Allegra and I manned the surimi salad station together at one October Sunday postservice lunch, and I complained about an upcoming AP history exam. "I'm not going to have the time and energy to study for history when there's a calculus exam the same morning. I basically have to choose which one to fail, because I can only focus on one."

"Who says?" said Allegra, who had been twisting her long hair into small braids, then combing them all out with her fingers again.

An older man came over and pointed to the surimi salad. "Hi, Tito Sonny," I greeted him, and scooped a spoonful of the fake-crab-and-avocado mixture onto his already overflowing plate. Allegra smacked her gum. I looked back at her. "Do you think you're ready for both exams?" Of course I knew the answer was a resounding *duh*. Allegra was one of those girls who was effortlessly good at everything she did.

In the cruel yet unavoidable high school caste system, Allegra was relentlessly popular. She was beautiful, smart, a great athlete, and nice too, so you couldn't even have the satisfaction of hating her. A family friend since childhood, she didn't even hold it against me that I was a bona fide member of the nerd caste.

"No," she replied. "But it's all good. I'll just call Jill."

"What does Jill have to do with anything?" I asked. "She's not in either of those classes."

"Yeah, but it's the first of the month. Which means she just got her Ritalin refilled."

I shook my head and lifted the corner of my upper lip. "What are you talking about?"

"You don't know about Jill's Ritalin thing?" Allegra asked.

"Why are you asking me that like it's common knowledge?"

"It is. For certain special people who have the hookup, she gives us a deal on extra pills."

"Extra pills? Doesn't she need all her pills?"

Allegra shrugged. "She knows what to say to her doctor to make it seem like her symptoms are worse than they are. That way they prescribe her more than she needs."

"Is that legal?" I whispered.

"You are such a rule follower," Allegra groaned. "Anyway, when I need to, I take one of those babies, and it helps me focus while studying and gives me energy to study longer. Then I take another during the exam, and the recall is bomb, Bea—you wouldn't believe. It's a whole other level."

"That's how you do so well on tests? That's how you get straight As?" I felt a strange jealousy and a righteous anger flicker on in me at once; how was it fair that I worked my ass off to get the As I got when Allegra was using someone else's prescription drugs to give herself an advantage? I didn't know how I felt about it. Maybe I wanted it for myself too; maybe I just didn't want to work so hard all the time. "Is that, like, cheating?" I asked.

"Why would it be? It's still your mind. Just better."

That sounded right. And it wasn't like it was a competition. "Do you think Jill would give me one? Just the one, one time."

Allegra smiled. "I'll ask."

I aced both exams. It was a fluke, I thought, a placebo effect. But it did help me focus when I studied, and I liked the way it helped me block out everything during the tests and only see what was in front of me. I joined Allegra and became a regular customer of Jill's.

Now, looking back, I know I was so naive to think those pills were my golden ticket. They were only the beginning of the end.

◆ ◆ ◆

My phone buzzes. It's Greg.

Check ur email. I added some slides.

My stomach sinks, and I pull up my inbox and swipe through the attached deck from Greg. I instantly spot some errors and groan. Even though I just want to go to bed early, I pull out my laptop and revise his work. *This is the last time I have to do this,* I think. Because tomorrow Granite will sign, and for real this time, I'm getting that promotion, just like Landon said.

He promised.

Chapter 4

Tuesday

The next morning I'm in the office early, and for the second time in two days, I've dressed up. I have my trendy wide-leg gray sack pants on and another crisp collared shirt, this time black with gold buttons. I've even worn my highest black heels, which make me almost five feet, five inches; of course I wore sneakers on the train and then changed into the heels once I got to the office.

I PDF the revised deck I finalized last night and email it over to the wider team, then send it over to our mail room for printing into a nicely bound handout. I balance the stack of them, literally hot off the press, and manage to stuff a protein bar in my mouth on my way to Landon's office.

"Collated and good to go." I set the stack on his desk.

Landon picks one off the top and flips through, nodding. "Looks great, Ku. These new case studies are fantastic. They really demonstrate the value BCC will be able to bring Granite. Nice work."

My lungs expand, and I take a deep breath. My chin rises as I smile. Despite his unending prickdom, it's embarrassing how much I still crave his validation. "Thanks, boss." I give a thumbs-up.

Landon frowns. "Don't do that. And is that what you're wearing to meet Granite?"

"Yes. It is." I clear my throat, which feels glued up with dry protein-bar bits.

"Hm, can you undo a button, for Chrissakes?"

My hands flutter to my collar. "Um, sure? Anyway, I'll see you at the meeting." I pick up my stack, and I'm almost out the door when Landon speaks again.

"Ku, about that."

I stop cold. "About what?"

"The meeting. You know, I was thinking that having two presenters just cuts up the flow, don't you think? I'm going to go ahead and have Greg present the whole thing. But don't worry, your name is still on the deck."

"Oh. Right. Of course. I understand." I don't understand. Greg doesn't know the presentation like I do. "It's just that I was going to speak to the case studies—the ones you said were really good. And I compiled all the financials—"

"Greg's a big boy; he'll be okay."

I nod and hold the stack higher. Please let me disappear. "Sure. Just glad I could make the deck."

"Thanks for being a team player, Ku." Landon turns to face his computer and clicks rapidly on something. I linger for just a moment and consider asking about the promotion, but I don't want to make him upset. I give up; the conversation is over.

Back at my desk, a message pops up on my screen.

Greg: Hey just heard im doing the whole preso??

me: yah heard that too

Greg: sorry I had no idea. LL just dropped that on me.

me: it's fine. you'll do great.

Greg: I'll try to find a way to kick you some questions or something during the mtng

me: thx. Let me know when you're walking over to conference room

My mind wanders to Landon's comment on my outfit. Is that why he pulled me off the presentation? Or was he never intending to have me speak at all?

Greg walks into my office, wearing a perfectly fitted black suit. "Marnell and the Granite team just walked in, and reception is leading them into the conference room now."

"Let's head over." I pick up my laptop and notebook and follow Greg out.

We arrive at the conference room, where the Granite team is shaking hands and chatting with the BCC partners, including Denny Chan, the managing partner and the only named partner who is at the firm on a daily basis. Denny nods at me. Though I don't interact with him often, Denny has always seemed friendly; I interviewed with him for this job, in fact.

Denny introduces an older man to Landon, who enthusiastically shakes his hand. I recognize him from the website as Mr. Marnell, the CEO of Granite Holdings.

Greg walks into the conference room, and I follow before being motioned to by Landon.

"Ku? Hey, this is exciting." He tilts his head, and I follow him hesitantly back out to the hall. "What's going on?"

"I hate to do this," he says. "Granite ended up bringing a couple more people than we were expecting." He pauses.

"Okay?"

"We just don't have enough seats."

"Sorry?" I blink.

"There's no room for you in the meeting anymore."

"Oh? Oh!" I feel my cheeks turning hot as realization spreads. "I see."

Landon smiles, that charming and sickeningly sympathetic smile. "I knew you'd understand."

I stare at the carpet, still holding my computer and notebook to my chest, and hear the male chatter suddenly silence as the conference doors shut. When I look up again, I see Greg at the front of the room, my presentation projected on the wall behind him and the rapt faces all looking at him and listening to his words.

Words that are really mine.

Landon sits at the head of the table, next to Marnell. He turns and looks at me looking at him. My breath catches, and I walk quickly into the lobby, out of the line of sight from the conference room. In a strange way, I don't want to go back to my office—it's too far away. It's as if I can still be a part of the meeting I've been kicked out of if I keep in close proximity. Maybe there will be a question no one has the answer to, and they'll realize, *Bea would know the answer*; I don't want to be hard to find.

I help myself to a glass of lime-infused water from the refreshment table that's always in the lobby, next to a table with a fresh-flower arrangement that is delivered weekly. The vase is slightly off center, so I correct it. I rearrange cushions on the lobby sofas before I plant myself in the armchair nearest the windows while I wait for the meeting to end.

My hands shake slightly as I take a sip of water.

Damn it, I think. I turn my face to the storm outside and feel my eyes well up with tears. I blink them back, but I'm really not sure how long I can hold it together.

Why wasn't it enough?

I take a breath and wipe my eyes. Laughter breaks up the somber silence, and I look up. I'm surprised to see Olivia Oxford standing at the reception desk, exchanging words with the receptionists. If Landon is an overgrown frat boy, Olivia is his polar opposite. She stands poised and graceful in sky-high black heels and a black jumpsuit with bell sleeves, her light-brown hair pulled up into a sleek bun. I admire Olivia for all her success as a good lawyer, but even more as a woman climbing up the ladder. Maybe one day I can get her to spill her secrets.

She sees me and gives a smile. I give a meek wave in return. She doesn't return the wave, but instead looks to the conference room, where my team is gathered without me. I look away. I pretend not to notice her approaching. "Bea," Olivia says. "Why aren't you in the Granite kickoff meeting?"

I send a silent prayer for the pleather love seat to swallow me whole. "I was, but plans changed."

She chews on the inside of her cheek. "That's too bad. Weren't you the one putting together the presentation?"

"That's right." I'm surprised. "How did you know that?"

She shrugs. "Granite was a huge acquisition from the Saul Group. Everybody's been talking about it. BCC has had our sights on them for a long time now. Denny will be rubbing this in Franklin Saul's face for years to come." I notice she doesn't actually say how she knew I was the one working on it.

"I'm just happy to have been part of the bid. And it's not like I won't be on the account at all," I say.

She glances around us and lowers her voice. "Just be careful, Bea. This is how it starts."

"What starts?"

"First, you get pushed out of a meeting here or there, then maybe left off a couple emails. But before you know it, they'll be excluding you from bigger matters. Don't be afraid to stick up for yourself. They're just big bullies; fight back, and they'll see you're not such an easy target. Besides, didn't you know? Bullies are always just scared little boys. I'll see you at the reception."

"What reception?" I ask.

"The welcome reception for Granite across the street." She considers my blank face. "I'm sure your calendar invite went to the spam filter."

She leaves me dumbfounded; the solid beats of her red-bottomed heels echo down the hall.

I haven't even considered it. Is this only the beginning of Landon pushing me out completely? This morning I thought I was up for a promotion; this afternoon I didn't even get the invite to the client happy hour. Have I been that oblivious? And where is my reception invite?

◆ ◆ ◆

I remember the interview for BCC. The first couple of interview rounds were with HR and some managers who I wouldn't be directly reporting to, but the final interview was with Denny. I wore the same suit I had worn to all the other interviews because it was the only suit I owned, bought on sale from Old Navy.

While other interviewers stared at my résumé and law school grades while pummeling the usual questions—"What makes you think you can excel at our firm?" and so on—Chan looked me straight in the eye. The desk in front of him was clean, no résumé. But he knew me.

In those days, my résumé reflected my full name, Bea Milner Ku. This was before I legally dropped Milner as a way to distance myself from Bea Milner and everything she stood for, which was nothing good.

"I called the University of Oregon School of Law," he started. "You took a leave of absence for almost three months during your third year. What happened?"

The floor dropped from beneath me. That wasn't reflected anywhere in my law school records, the doctors and administration had assured me. He'd called them personally to check on me? I quickly thought of my normal lies, the ones that formed and rolled so easily off my tongue after months of my telling them to colleagues and professors and nosy friends of my parents. But I knew he would know.

This was a golden rule of lawyering: never ask a question you don't already know the answer to.

"I had a nervous breakdown," I said. "I got off my meds, not for any real reason, just because I got lazy. I started thinking I could do life without them, but I couldn't. Then I started self-medicating with alcohol."

"Are you an addict?"

I shook my head. "No, I just have anxiety and depression. I got it under control. Once I got my meds stabilized, I returned to school and finished with extremely high marks." I steered the conversation back to my assets, not my past.

"Has that happened before law school?" he asked. "Any other . . . episodes, that is?"

I paused. If I answered and he called me out, that was it—no job. Despite each muscle in my body telling me not to lie, I was compelled to save a little privacy for myself, a little dignity. He had called my law school, sure—I was applying for a legal job at his firm. My records before that were sealed for a reason. "No," I answered.

He raised an eyebrow. Then smiled. "Well, that's good."

Maybe he knew I would lie about it, and simply wanted to see me do so with confidence. He offered me the job on the spot. I registered with HR as Bea Ku only.

◆ ◆ ◆

But if I should be listening to anyone, it's Olivia, who knows the realities of often being the only woman in the room. Granite and the Legal Aid award aside, if I'm never going to be promoted here at BCC, then maybe it's time for me to move on to somewhere else.

Chapter 5

Greg finds me as soon as the meeting ends. "It went great. Brilliant work, Bea!" He lowers his voice. "I would be shocked if they don't dump Saul today and sign us as new counsel of record."

I sigh with relief. "Thank God."

"By the way, you know I had no idea he was going to give the whole presentation to me, right?" Greg asks.

I bite my tongue and say, "I'm just a junior associate, Greg." *But not for much longer.* He raises his eyebrows, but before he can respond, Landon approaches me with Mr. Marnell.

"Ku," says Landon. "What a coincidence you're standing here. I'd like you to meet Mr. George Marnell. Mr. Marnell, this is Bea Ku, one of our brightest attorneys and the mind behind the presentation you just saw."

"Nice to meet you, Bea." Mr. Marnell extends a hand.

"Nice to meet you too! Oh, and it was nothing." Nothing, just hours of work and sleepless nights.

"I wanted to introduce you because Mr. Marnell had a note about the analysis on page fifteen."

Mr. Marnell flips through the paper copy in his hands. "That's right. I see you used last year's figures."

"This year's weren't available publicly," I say.

"Correct, but we have them available for you now as our new counsel of record. I emailed my team to have them sent to you all this afternoon."

"Perfect. I can have those updated figures to you tonight."

Mr. Marnell pauses. "Tonight? No need. There's really no rush—"

"Not at all," I insist. "It's really nothing at all."

Landon nods approvingly, his eyes shining. "Thanks, Ku. I knew I could count on you. Now, George, you know Greg here. Let's all talk about the game plan for that acquisition."

Greg looks at me. *Sorry,* he mouths.

As promised, they've included their current year's numbers. If I can turn around the report with the updated values, Mr. Marnell will see how hard I can work.

◆ ◆ ◆

The day has flown by, and by not pausing for anything else, I've produced an updated report.

"Oh no." I check the time and realize I'm over an hour late to the reception. I hope Mr. Marnell is still there. I grab my things and race downstairs. The cocktail reception is just across the street in the Fairmont Olympic Hotel's Georgian bar. Just through the doors and up the escalators into the lobby, I spot Greg near the bar.

"Hey, you," he says. "Where have you been?"

"Finishing up something. Where's Mr. Marnell?" I crane my head over the crowd.

"You're not going to give him a report right now, are you?" Greg points skeptically to the bundle of papers against my chest. "Kind of a buzzkill, don't you think?"

"He'll want to know his business isn't going to stop just because it's happy hour," I retort. Over the din of conversation and smooth jazz from the speakers, I hear an irritating cocky laugh. Landon. I follow the sound and spy him; sure enough, Mr. Marnell is right next to him.

I push through the crowd and wave the papers. "Mr. Marnell," I call. He looks at me, and I hold out the report. I'm just about to reach them when I feel an elbow in my back and someone stepping on my feet.

I trip.

And fall forward.

Directly into Mr. Marnell and his drink.

I grasp on for any kind of support and gasp as an ice-cold liquid splashes across my chest. The room goes silent, except for the lo-fi jazz over the speakers. I am hugging Mr. Marnell, and with one arm, he's holding me so I don't fall; with the other, he's holding what's left of a broken cocktail glass. My report is all over the floor.

Pushing off him, I try and fail to somehow gracefully regain my balance. "I am so sorry," I stammer. "Uh, are you okay?"

"I'm fine, yes. Are you?" He lets a waiter take his broken glass and helps to steady me. "What is that?" He looks at the papers on the wet floor.

"It's . . . nothing." I kneel to gather the papers, but a black leather shoe stomps down on them. Landon looms above me as he attempts to wipe down Mr. Marnell's sleeve. "We owe you a shirt now, George. Send us your measurements, and I'll personally pick you out a new one." Then he glances down to me and nods his head toward the door. "A word, Ku?"

The murmurs begin in the crowd, and I slowly pick myself up before anyone can offer a hand; I don't want anyone's sympathy right now. I leave the ruined report where it is and follow Landon.

Just outside the entrance, in an alcove next to the restroom doors, Landon blows up. "Are you fucking serious, Ku? What are you thinking?" His voice grows and swells, and even though we are outside the bar, I know he's being loud enough that everyone is listening to him telling me how stupid I am.

"But . . ." I attempt. "I finished the report—"

"Nobody gives a shit, Ku," hisses Landon, looking around, probably now conscious the client might be listening to him yelling. "Seriously, who gives a shit? Nobody! Nobody told you to finish the report tonight! This is exactly why you can't be in client meetings. Just leave. I'll deal with you later." He straightens his jacket and runs his fingers through his hair. He returns to the bar, and not knowing where else to go, I slink into the bathroom.

With scratchy paper towels, I try unsuccessfully to sponge off the alcohol from my shirt.

What was I thinking? I open a stall door and lean against the wall; I kick the door closed and lock it. I'm too angry to cry, too exhausted to scream. I wonder how long my shirt will take to dry and hope by the time it does, most of the people outside will have left so I can sneak out and just go home.

The door opens, and a pair of women come in, chatting loudly.

". . . how wild was that? Spilling a drink on a client, can you imagine?"

"Bea Ku," the other says. "She's such a bulldog. And not in the good way."

"She thinks she's a guy or something." *Okay, rude,* I think. What does that even mean?

"Even guys know when to play hard. All she does is work hard, and she wonders why nobody likes her."

"Do you think that means there will be an opening on Landon Laurie's team soon? He's such a big name. Having that on my résumé would be huge. I would give anything to work under him."

"Or on top of him, am I right?" They giggle and squeal, and I suppress a gag reflex.

"Are you going to Greg's party tomorrow at Solo? I think it's to celebrate his promotion, so Landon will definitely be there."

"I want to, but I have a birthday thing I have to get to in Belltown."

The rest of their talk turns to some television drama, and soon the bathroom door slams shut behind them.

They aren't wrong about Landon being a big-shot lawyer; as much as I loathe Landon, he is damn good at what he does. He is a partner for a reason; the clients love him, and he knows the law. When I got the job at BCC, I was thrilled; when I got assigned to Landon's team, I was in disbelief. He only took the best, so I was sure it was a mistake at first. But he took a liking to me, at least in the beginning.

He gave me important assignments, took the time to explain things, and included me in cases that a new associate probably didn't have any business being on, to be honest. I absorbed it all; I knew an opportunity when I saw it and wouldn't let this one get away. I can't say when things began to change. After the first year or so, he would let snide remarks sneak in, so casual and quick I was unsure if I'd even heard him correctly. Then a comment here or there: *Why would you do it that way?* or *I can't believe I have to keep telling you . . .*

Then it just continued like that; I didn't know any better. The worst part was, he was always perfect in public; it was only when we were alone that he would scold me.

Until tonight.

I can't wait until my shirt dries; I slink out of the bathroom and out of the hotel. Nobody looks at me on the train. When I get home, it's quiet and dark. A note on the counter tells me my dinner is in the microwave and Dad is asleep; Mom has another late shift. In my damp clothing, I eat my dinner cold in front of the TV, watching a mindless reality show for just the time it takes me to finish my food. In the dim glow of the TV, I wash the dishes by hand and dry them before putting them away.

Something has to change, I decide as I throw the dry-clean-only blouse into the washer. Who can afford dry cleaners?

I dread work tomorrow. How can I keep begging Landon for this promotion? Something has to give.

◆ ◆ ◆

In the morning, it's Olivia who knocks on my door. "How are you?" she asks, with a smile like a truce. Except it's not her I've been wanting to offer one.

"Fine," I say. "Why wouldn't I be?"

She tilts her head. "Are you the first?"

"First?"

"First lawyer in your family."

I nod.

She comes in and sits down in the chair across from me, leaning forward with her elbows on her knees. "Me too. So I had to learn this whole game from square one. And it is a game, Bea."

"So why does it seem like I'm the only one playing honestly while everyone else is cheating?"

"Because they've had the advantage of either growing up with lawyers or knowing how the corporate game is played. They've already had the rules explained to them. And sometimes that also means cheat codes, sure." She waves her hands. "Maybe this isn't the best analogy, forget it. What I'm trying to tell you is that you're doing fine."

I scoff. "It doesn't feel like I'm doing fine."

"It's not a career for the fainthearted, that's for sure."

"I'm the first person in my family to ever go to undergrad, let alone a grad school. I didn't know about college advisers or anything. All I could do was fill out the applications and pray."

"Really? So you got scholarships and stuff?"

"Some, but not a lot. I mostly got loans."

"It's admirable," she says. "You must have really wanted to be a lawyer."

"The funny part is I didn't. What I wanted was to be a different person from who I was."

"And that was?"

I accuse my parents of being scared of the truth; but I'm just as scared of judgment. I smile. "An uninteresting person."

"I doubt that." She stands. "I just wanted to come in here and give you a bit of a pep talk. Or at least tell you to keep going and don't give up. It sounds cliché, but you're too good to think about quitting."

"What makes you think I'm thinking of quitting?"

"Because I've seen that look before. I've seen it on myself a few times. Keep taking advantage of opportunities that come up—you never know what might present itself. Don't be afraid to take what you want, Bea. Even if it's scary."

"Thanks, Olivia."

With a small nod, she leaves. This is the second time in two days Olivia has given me a push of confidence. While a part of me wonders why Olivia is showing me this attention, the other part knows she's right. I need to do something and show my confidence again, prove to the firm I believe in myself.

I've worked too hard and too long at remaking myself to go backward now.

Chapter 6

Wednesday

I'm in the lobby of Denny Chan's office, two floors above the main floor where most of the offices are located, including my own. I have to swipe my employee badge to even get the elevator to access the floor. When the doors open, unlike in the large lobby on the main floor, here I'm met with a small and dimly lit reception area covered in dark wood paneling. The receptionist takes my name and gestures for me to sit in one of the plush chairs lining the walls. Instead, I stand and read one of the many framed articles on the wall touting the accomplishments of the BCC partners.

I've read them many times, but I like seeing the history of the firm as news. Soon, I'm called into Denny's office. The large corner suite affords unencumbered views of downtown Seattle and the glittering water of Puget Sound. In the background, snowcapped mountains peek over the horizon.

"Come in, Bea. Have a seat." Denny is already sitting on one side of a sectional sofa.

I take the opposite end, where a cup of steaming coffee waits for me on a clear glass coffee table, so it appears to be floating. His desk is made from the same, so at a glance, his laptop and folders also look to be levitating in front of the ocean view.

I pick up the coffee and take a sip; it's the perfect temperature. "Thank you," I say. There's a reason—there are many reasons, in fact—Denny is the managing partner. His ability to know what a person, namely a client, needs is a big reason.

"Of course," he says, leaning forward, his reading glasses perched at the tip of his nose. "So tell me, what can I do for you? My admin tells me you emailed for some time on my schedule late last night. Everything okay?"

I take a deep breath. "I wanted to talk to you and see if there was any chance I could transfer to another team?"

He keeps my gaze and makes no visible reaction. "I see. What's going on?"

I think back to my interview with Denny, and though I know he has no idea of the circumstances, I decide to spill all the tea. "The short version is I believe I've been passed over for a promotion, and even though Landon promised me it, and even though I deserve it—I don't believe I'll ever be promoted if I stay on Landon's team."

Denny nods. "That's quite something, Bea."

"I know, and trust me, I did not make the decision to come to you with this lightly. I've tried to work it out with Landon, I really have. He finds all the excuses not to promote me, and just last evening—"

"Is this about the spilling-drinks-on-the-client thing?" he asks.

"You"—I gulp—"know about that?"

"I may have heard a whisper or two."

I shake my head. "It's not just about that. It's just that I think I can be more successful on another team."

He nods. "I'm actually happy you came to me. Because you know what? I believe anything can be worked out through good old-fashioned communication." He stands and walks over to his door, opens it and speaks to the receptionist. "Can you call Landon Laurie up here?" he asks.

I freeze. "What? No, please don't," I plead.

"I'm sure it's just a misunderstanding."

My grip on the coffee mug is so tight I feel like it could smash in my hands. I can feel pinpricks of sweat dancing on my scalp. What have I done?

Denny sits back down. "While we wait, why don't you give me some details?"

Unprepared, I begin to ramble about assignments I've aced, empty promises to bait me, and Greg getting promoted before me. By the time Landon arrives, looking genuinely confused, I have a feeling Denny has already made up his mind.

"Landon," he says. "Glad you could join. Bea has brought up concerns. Did you promise her a promotion and then renege on it?"

Landon looks at me dead on. He's no longer confused; he clearly sees I've gone behind his back. He turns back to Denny. "No, I never promised anything."

I don't even hear the rest of the conversation, because I'm clearly not a part of it anymore. Landon and Denny talk at me and tell me that they're sorry I feel this way, it was just a misunderstanding, and Landon will find a way to communicate his expectations better in the future; all different ways of saying it's my fault.

"So, Bea, I hope you can take this as a promise that we at BCC take career planning seriously and look forward to having more conversations with you about how you can get to the next level here!" Denny smiles.

A crisp wave of cold air blows through me, and I can barely breathe. "Yes." I stand, using all my strength to keep from sagging back down to the chair. "Thank you."

"I'm satisfied if you are," says Landon. "Oh, Denny, I wanted to ask you quickly . . ."

I leave the office and drift to the elevator. When the door opens, I step in and lean against the wall. What have I done?

Just before the doors close, a hand juts in; the doors creak back open. Landon steps in and straightens his tie. I straighten up and try to stop my lips from quivering. He stands next to me. We both look straight ahead. "You need to stop being so sensitive," he says.

"You lied." My voice shakes as I turn to face him.

He leans in ever so slightly. "Whenever it comes to your word against mine, I will always win. Don't do that again, Ku. Or else I'm really going to start not liking you."

"What do you mean?" I ask. "You already clearly hate me."

He rolls his eyes. "That's just like you to make it personal. I don't hate you. I couldn't spare the energy to hate you."

"So what is it?" I demand, breaking. "I complete every task I'm assigned. I've always tried my hardest, worked the longest hours. There is never anything wrong with my work. Why are you snubbing me? Why do you keep insisting on bullying me?"

Olivia's words come back to me . . . *Bullies are always just scared little boys.*

Then the truth comes down like a guillotine's blade. I take a deep breath and step back. Of course. It's so clear now. "You're threatened by me."

A flash passes across Landon's face, so fast I almost miss it, but I know what to look for now and so I see it as clear as day: fear. He's been called out, and now he knows I know. He composes himself and returns seamlessly to ruthless form. "You really are crazy," he says. "Maybe you were right to ask Denny about a change. Maybe what you need is a change from this firm."

"Are you threatening to fire me?"

"I can fire you . . . or you can leave. One will look better, of course, than the other when you try to explain it to future employers."

I set my jaw tight. "You can't fire me."

"I can do whatever the hell I want. You just saw it."

The doors open with a ding. Landon walks out, leaving me frozen and my ears ringing with his words. After a moment, the elevator closes again and sits idle, waiting for a call to movement. I stand inside; it's as good a hiding place as any.

My shoulders are rolled forward, and I fold my arms in front of me, placing my elbows into my palms. Maybe he's right. Maybe it's just time to go somewhere else. Is this worth it?

I jump as a ding rings out and the doors open. It's Greg, who also starts at seeing me revealed inside. "What are you doing in there?" he asks.

"Nothing." I try to straighten up.

"Are you okay? You look flushed."

"I'm fine, just too much coffee this morning, I think." I step out and try to hurry to my office. I feel his hand on my arm; I stop in surprise and turn. He's never touched me before.

"Sorry." He lets go. "I want to make sure you're coming out tonight."

"Oh, your party thing? I'm not sure. I think I have something going on at home . . ." The thought of being somewhere with Landon right now makes me queasy.

His face drops. "No, you gotta come! You never come out for these things. Come on. Look, I know there's tension with you and Landon—"

"No, there's not!"

"Uh, okay, well, I was going to say maybe show everyone you're not all business and a stick-in-the-mud. Maybe just show up, get some face time in, and you can duck out after one drink."

I wave him away. "Maybe next time."

"Suit yourself!"

◆ ◆ ◆

Back in my office, the morning emails begin to flow in earnest, and I can't focus on a single one. A meeting invite comes in, and I don't even look at the details; I click "Will Not Attend," then delete.

Read the writing on the wall, Bea, I think. *It's over for you here.*

I pull out my phone and do a quick LinkedIn search for senior associate jobs; there are hundreds of results, including one at the Saul Group. Now that might be interesting. I went to law school with someone who's at the Saul Group now. I look up Amy Carren in my contacts and send her a quick text asking how she's doing and if she'd be open to grabbing lunch or something soon.

I save the search and make a decision: I'm going to tell my parents tonight that I didn't actually get the promotion, and in fact I've decided to begin looking for another job somewhere else. I can get more pay and, more importantly, more respect at a new firm, I know it.

To make sure I don't chicken out, I call Mom.

"Hello?" she answers.

"Hey, I wanted to let you and Dad know that I kind of have some news I want to share at dinner—"

"What? I can't hear you," Mom says, speaking too loudly into the phone. "I'm at the grocery store. Allegra is coming over tonight for dinner."

"Why?" I ask, annoyed. "Can we ask her over another time, because I wanted—"

"No, I invited her, and I'm not taking back my invitation. What's the matter with you?"

"I just don't know why she's coming over, and besides, I wanted to talk to you and Dad."

"Don't get defensive, Bea! I know she's not eating as well as she needs to, and I'm going to cook her some soup with a healthy broth. She's pregnant." As if we have to treat her like a porcelain doll in her condition.

"Pregnancy isn't an illness. And I'm not being defensive," I say. "Wasn't she just over?"

"I'm not doing this in the store, Bea." She huffs. "I'm so busy. What is it you needed?"

I give up. "You know what?" I say. "I called to say I won't be home for dinner. Tell Allegra I'm sorry I missed her." I hang up and text Greg.

Hey, I think I'll go tonight after all.

He responds right away: attagirl

At least if I'm leaving BCC, I can enjoy a couple of drinks on Greg's expense account before I go.

Chapter 7

By holing up in my office all day, I manage to avoid work and conversation. At 5:00 p.m., Greg texts me that he and a bunch of people are going out to get happy hour drinks and apps, but I tell him I'll see him at the lounge later. Once I'm sure they are out of the building, I go downstairs and get a prepackaged Caesar salad from the lobby deli. To pass the time, I research open associate jobs and get my résumé in order, all on my phone, of course. I switch my little LinkedIn profile toggle to "Open for Opportunities," which LinkedIn assures me won't be visible to anyone except recruiters.

At almost 8:00 p.m., I admit I'm getting sleepy. Maybe I could just sneak home and go to bed; is Allegra even still there?

A knock on my office door. Olivia waves through the glass. "What are you doing here still?" she asks after sliding the door open.

"Working late on some deadlines."

"I hear you. I was just finishing up a couple things myself before heading over to Greg's thing."

"Oh, yeah," I say. "I was going to that too."

She tilts her head. "Really?" she says, then smiles sheepishly and chuckles. "That didn't come out right." It occurs to me I've never heard her laugh before.

"It's okay," I say. "I get it. I'm a stick-in-the-mud, is what Greg called me earlier. But I figured I could show up and at least say hi, since he's on my team and this is really a group win."

She nods. "How sportsmanlike of you."

I pause. "What do you mean?"

She glances around, even though nobody is here but us. "Well, since he basically robbed you of your promotion and Granite."

I laugh nervously. "Oh, that's just . . . a misunderstanding."

"It always is. Want to walk over together?"

I sweep up my coat, and we go down to the lobby together. Olivia says she knows the way, so I oblige and follow her, wondering how often my coworkers go out to Solo Lounge without me. *It's not like I want to join them,* I think, *but it would be nice to be invited.*

The night is heavy with mist, illuminated commuters crossing beneath the streetlights. We crisscross streets and step around unhoused individuals camped on the sidewalks, an unfortunate feature of downtown Seattle these days, where the city council and the Not-in-My-Backyard Seattleites clash. We vote for tiny-house villages to go up to provide affordable housing alternatives, but nobody wants them in their neighborhood. So they never get built, and progress is never made.

We all have our growing pains, I suppose, and Seattle is a place where I still run into people from high school occasionally, and immediately turn and walk the other way. It's one of those places that's still small enough for a person to be remembered, but just large enough for a person to disappear.

As we walk down the steep sloped streets toward the piers, a small detail tugs at me. "What did you mean?" I ask Olivia. "When you said that Greg robbed me of my promotion and Granite? Landon put him as lead in the presentation because he was newly promoted, and I think he wanted to give him some responsibility—"

"That's not what I meant," she says. "Landon was telling people you're off the Granite account, with Greg as the sole lead now." She watches my face drop. "Oh shit, you didn't know?"

"I'm discovering there's a lot I don't know," I say.

Olivia looks up at the sky. "At least the rain stopped."

We get to Solo Lounge and find our cover has been paid for. "Your party's in the back VIP corner," we're informed as we leave our coats at coat check. Inside, we're met with loud music and a semiempty dance floor, considering it's Wednesday and the early hour.

Olivia looks at her phone. "My goal is to make it out before the crowds show up. Want to find Greg and show our faces?"

Sidestepping through the crowd, I scan the handful of bodies silhouetted against the multicolored lights splashing across the room and notice more than a few BCC people having a good time. We make it to the VIP section and spot a whole gaggle of BCC folks sitting and drinking on an elevated platform with lit glass tables and dark couches set back against dark curtains. Landon is right there with some woman on his arm, a junior BCC paralegal, if I'm not mistaken, and I see Greg talking with some other associates.

"You made it!" Greg yells in genuine excitement when he spots me.

"Yeah, Olivia and I just got here." I turn to her, but she's already gone over to another table where her team is sitting. I suddenly feel very alone without her next to me.

"Where's your drink?" Greg invites me to sit next to him. The rest of the table nod and raise their drinks to welcome me. Greg flags down a server walking by and asks me what I want. "Glass of pinot noir," I tell him. He squeezes his brows together in confusion, but relays my order anyway. While I wait for my drink, Greg continues to tell a story, and the group listens raptly. Even I find myself laughing; when my drink arrives, I find it goes down smoothly. In fact, it's not long before I find myself with an empty glass. I get up.

"You don't have to go," Greg says. "I can find the server."

"It's okay," I say. "I was going to chat with Olivia too." I don't want to miss her before she leaves. Besides, after some liquid courage, I've decided I'm going to tell her I'm thinking of leaving BCC. She might have connections, or even be willing to write me a letter of recommendation, because God knows Landon won't.

But I don't see her anywhere in the VIP section. Craning my head, I finally spot her. She's near the bar and speaking with someone, a blond woman who looks vaguely familiar somehow.

I begin to head toward them. In the darkness and with the wine and bass pumping through my blood, I completely miss the stairs. I try to catch myself, but feel myself falling through the air. Until I stop.

I look up and find Landon gripping my arm, with my own hands pressed against him. I leap back. Landon stares at me in genuine surprise. "Is this a problem for you?" he asks. "I mean, walking without falling on your ass? If you'd had a drink in your hand, that would have been two disasters in two days, Ku. You're lucky I'm around to save you every time."

I feel my skin burning. I can't be mad at him, though; he did actually save me this time. "Thanks," I say, sheepishly. "It's so dark . . ."

"And you're drunk," he finishes. The paralegal next to him giggles.

I shake my head. "I'm absolutely not drunk." I look around. "I was looking for Olivia . . ."

"Why? So you can talk shit about me to her too?"

I'm hot and brave from the wine. "Did you tell her I was off of the Granite account?"

He grimaces. "You're wasting your time, Ku."

"Why couldn't you tell me to my face? Why do you hate me?"

"Fine, Ku. Fine. You want to know why you're off Granite and why you're not getting promoted? Come here," he says as he tilts his head. I lean in, and he presses his cheek close to mine. His breath is hot against my ear. "You're a bitch."

My body jolts back, but he grabs my arm and pulls me back into him. "You're a bitch, and everyone knows it. Nobody wants to work with you, because you're an anal-retentive psycho, and until you get the stick surgically removed from your ass, you are not getting a promotion while you're on my team."

I step down the stairs in a fog, barely noticing the strangers jostling me as I reel on the dance floor. Olivia called it exactly right. And I didn't see it coming at all. What now?

"Hey, what was that?" Greg is next to me, his face unnervingly close and his breath reeking of alcohol.

"You got me kicked off Granite?" I ask.

He shakes his head. "You're off Granite? Did that happen just now?"

"Stop playing stupid, Greg," I snap. "First you have no idea when you take over my presentation, and now you're completely surprised when I get taken off the biggest client we've ever had? A client that I was instrumental in signing?"

He throws his hands in the air and sneers. "Hey now, don't blame me. Maybe I can put in a good word for you with Landon?"

"You? Put in a good word for me? Ha!"

"Okay, I think you're getting a bit emotional here."

"Screw you, Greg."

"Hey, I'm sorry, Bea." He places his hand on my shoulder. "Let me get you something—"

"Leave me alone." I brush off his hand and squeeze through an opening in the crowd before he can follow me.

I try to get the bartender's attention, but Greg follows me, and in the crush of bodies, he pins me against the bar. "You know what, you're right. Landon sucks, and the vibes in here suck too. You want to get out of here or something?" he says, his words slurring.

My hands push back against his chest. "You know what, it's fine. I'm sorry I snapped at you."

"Let's go somewhere else, and I'll take care of you, Bea, if you let me."

Grimacing, I look around for a way out.

"Hey, hi!" I turn to the female voice calling out. A woman next to me waves, and she extends a hand. Surprised, Greg backs away, releasing me. "I thought it was you!" the blond woman continues, moving in and giving me a hug. "How are you, girl?" She pulls me close and whispers into my ear, "You looked like you needed rescuing."

"You have no idea," I reply.

"Come on, I have a table over here." She leads me to a small high-top. I glance behind to see a confused Greg eventually retreat back to the rest of the BCC group.

I sigh. "Thank you again," I say. "That was getting a little dicey. He's usually a nice guy."

"Aren't they all?" She rolls her eyes. Now away from the bar and able to focus, I recognize her. She's the woman who Olivia was just speaking to. And then I look closer and realize I know her from before too.

"Hey, you're the girl from the coffee cart the other day. What's your name?" I ask.

"I'm Kelli Stewart," she says.

"I'm Bea Ku." I look around, but Olivia is nowhere to be seen. "Were you just talking to Olivia Oxford?"

"Who?"

I shake my head. "Never mind. Nice to meet you."

"But don't you remember, Bea Ku? We're old friends! Now, how about we catch up over a drink?"

"Old friends, right. And sure, I can do one more, I guess. Why not?"

Chapter 8

"Can I ask you something? Are you a lawyer?"

"Yeah," I say. "What, you don't usually wear a cotton button-up and slacks to the club?" I joke.

"It's not that." She smiles. "I actually noticed you before, talking to those guys over there." She motions toward the VIP area. "I thought I recognized some people from BCC. Is that where you work?"

I sit up. "You know BCC?" I notice her own clothing, a black pencil skirt and silky tank top; I see a black blazer hanging from the chair behind her.

"I'm an attorney with the Saul Group," she says.

"No kidding. I'm happily surprised to run into another female lawyer here. Is Saul Group having a thing here too or something?"

"We had a happy hour down the road, and I was supposed to meet a date here, but it seems like he's stood me up."

"Classic," I say, though I can't imagine who would ever stand her up.

"What's the celebration with BCC then?" she asks.

I pause, deciding not to mention it's a party to celebrate Greg's promotion. "Same," I say. "Happy hour that never ended."

"Work hard, play hard, right? You're empty handed."

"It's fine. I was getting ready to leave anyway. I don't really drink."

"Oh shit, are you sober?"

"Not exactly. I don't do it often, but I can have a drink or two. For special occasions or for epically bad days."

"So what's tonight? A special occasion or an epically bad day?" I raise an eyebrow. Kelli laughs. "It has to be one or the other. Someone who doesn't drink in a nightclub on a Wednesday?"

"Fair," I admit. "It was supposed to be a special occasion. A work thing. But it definitely turned into a bad day."

"There you go. You're allowed a drink on a bad day—you said so yourself. Now, I'm getting another. Can I treat you to one?"

I study my new companion. She's refreshing, this stranger. "Sure. One more."

◆ ◆ ◆

"It was toxic as hell," Kelli yells over the thundering bass that's crept up louder and louder without me noticing, until suddenly it's almost impossible to hear anything at all.

Moving some of our empty glasses out of the way, I lean toward Kelli to hear her better; she is talking about the first legal assistant job she had straight out of law school.

"How was it toxic?" I ask.

She swirls her vodka martini and crosses her legs, drawing my eyes to her nude heels and then up to the black pencil skirt that has shifted up her thighs. Under the glow of the strobing DJ lights, Kelli is jarringly beautiful.

I drink the twinge of jealousy down on my overpriced vodka sour and try to look like I belong at the chic club as much as my companion does. Never mind that I really want to go home and take off the high-waisted pants that are cutting into my tummy.

"Everyone was determined to undermine you," Kelli says. "And the ones who weren't trying to trip you up were trying to fuck you." She shrugs. "Tale as old as time, right?"

"Did you ever tell anyone there?" I ask.

She looks at me quizzically. "Now why would I do that?" Her eyes turn wide and glassy, like she has suddenly gone somewhere far away.

She sips her drink and gazes out onto the dance floor. The crowd has grown massive in the time since I arrived, and the throng of sweaty revelers moves in time to the music like a wave. "I was swimming in debt from student loans; I needed the paycheck while I studied for the bar exam. And it wasn't anything I hadn't put up with before, you know?" She shakes her head. "I was twentysomething."

She says it like an excuse, and I know it kind of is. I never know whether it's through willful ignorance or a kind of glorified main character syndrome—or maybe simply that we don't know any better and can't—but twentysomething women are always making excuses for badly behaved men.

"Funny the things you tell yourself to convince yourself shit is okay," I say.

Kelli slides her fingertip around the edge of her glass. "The really sad part is I'm still in that position."

"What do you mean?"

"I've got a shitty boss, and I'm too scared to do anything about it."

"I can relate. No, really," I say when she raises an eyebrow. "My boss just now told me I was never getting a promotion, even though I deserve it."

"Are you serious?"

"Dead serious. He called me a bitch to my face."

Her jaw drops. "What? That is . . . beyond fucked up. Why would he do that?"

I nod. "Yeah. An understatement. He's trying to get me to quit or something because I embarrassed him in front of a client, I think."

"Jesus. I am so sorry that happened to you."

"It's so maddening. I keep my head down, I do my work—in fact, I do more than my fair share. I don't make waves; I'm quiet and I do my job and I'm damn good at it, so I don't get it. What does he want?" My chest deflates, rant over and the hot air mostly out of my lungs. It feels nice. "I'm sorry you're dealing with someone like that too."

"He's never called me anything to my face before, but I'm sure he repeats all sorts of things in his head." She raises what's left of her drink. "To men in charge," she sneers. I raise my glass and we clink.

"But seriously," I say. "Are men, like . . . okay?"

Kelli snorts. "You made vodka go up my nose—ouch!"

Lights flash, the beat changes, and the crowd gives a cheer. Kelli grabs my hand. "I love this song!"

Before I can protest, she leads me onto the dance floor.

We push through the crush of bodies; I hold on to Kelli like a lifeline.

We sway to the beat; I let a smile slip.

"There it is!" Kelli squeals. "I see you having fun, Bea. And—" She suddenly looks around at the floor frantically. "Did I see a stick just fall out of your ass?"

I fake a dramatic gasp. "Don't you dare tell anybody!"

"Are you kidding? I'm sending a company-wide email and then replying all to myself."

For a second, the mention of work jars me back to the real world, and I wonder what time it is and how I'm getting home. Around me, younger people are dancing and throwing away their worries and caution; I feel like the oldest person here, and I'm suddenly self-conscious. I was never one to go out clubbing or partying; the temptations were too fresh and the consequences still too real. And it's not like I had a group of girlfriends to go out with.

But then I lock eyes with Kelli in front of me. She throws back her hair and flashes her white teeth, which glow even brighter under a rotating black light. I sway unsteadily and hold my hands out at my sides, not sure what else to do with them. Kelli leans toward me and takes each hand in hers, intertwining her fingers through mine; we raise our hands together, and when she begins singing along to the song, I join her. A strange familiarity rises in my chest. A half-forgotten memory of Allegra and me, dancing and singing together in my bedroom to the KISS 106.1 top-ten countdown before poring over a stolen issue of *Cosmopolitan* and laughing over sex articles that we didn't even understand.

When Allegra and I had a bond you could lose yourself in.

In the dark and dancing now with Kelli, I can't help but want that back. For the rest of the song and the next one too, we dance together and belt out the words. I close my eyes and let the vibration of the crowd swell into my skin until my bones themselves thrum to the hypnotic rhythm.

Once the song ends, I'm sweaty and happy. Kelli mouths, *I. Have. To. Pee!* and we make our way to the women's restroom.

We each go into a stall. I brace myself against the graffitied stall walls and lower myself unsteadily onto the toilet and lean my head against the door. It's equally hard getting up. Washing my hands at the mirror, I feel the ground sway slightly beneath me.

A gaggle of girls enters the bathroom, the chamber filling with the echo of the music as the door opens before muffling again as it closes. The girls are chatting loudly and surround us, touching up their makeup and pulling out vape pens. "Want a hit?" one of them asks. Kelli nods and takes one.

"Thanks," she says. "You are all so pretty! How's your night going?" I watch her with envy; she's so at ease with these girls. Like another species of woman I never understood.

The girls fawn. "Aww, thank you, you're so gorgeous too! We're taking our friend out because she broke up with her boyfriend!"

They erupt in a chorus of whoos and squees. "He was the worst, and she's going to do so much better now without him!"

Kelli lets out a whoop. "Damn straight! You don't need him, girl. My friend Bea here is in a toxic relationship too, but she doesn't know how to get out of it."

Gasps and looks of pity turn my way. "Uh, I mean, it's not really like that," I say.

"That's what they always try to say," the newly single girl says. "I was just like you. You have to think about what you want and what's best for you. Are you happy?" she asks. She takes my hands in hers. They're warm. "Like, really, are you happy?"

I shake my head, tears suddenly appearing. "No," I whisper.

"Then fuck that guy!" her friend yells. They all loudly agree. The newly single emancipated female squeezes my hands and gives me a sad smile. "I hope you find your truth," she says. One of her friends tugs on her arm. "Ohmygod, we should do shots!"

This is hailed as a genius idea, and they leave in the same fury as when they came in; Kelli and I are alone again. But I don't feel so good anymore.

"You okay?"

I lift my heavy eyelids. Kelli is staring at me.

I nod and straighten up. "Yeah, just . . . having a good time."

"I'm so glad! As soon as I saw you, I had a feeling we'd get along."

"You did?" I ask, incredulous.

"I did." Kelli pops her tongue. "I have an idea."

She sounds a hundred miles away, my head suddenly cloudy. "Huh?" I drag my fingertip along the bottom of my eye, removing smudged eyeliner. My heart beats in time with the muted bass seeping in from the speakers outside.

"I'll kill yours if you kill mine."

I think I mishear her at first.

"What did you say? Kill who?" I speak deliberately so each slippery vodka-soaked syllable can be heard above the low base drone from the dance floor just beyond the doors.

She laughs, her voice as fizzy as that last glass of prosecco, or was that the second to last? Wait, when did we even order prosecco? "Our bosses, remember?" She looks at me—rather, my reflection in the mirror—and stretches her long bare arms around my shoulders, nestling her crown of soft golden hair against my neck. I stare at us in the mirror of the ultrachic lounge, standing under the artificial-golden-hour ladies' room lights that always make everyone look beautiful.

We look beautiful. And invincible.

I tilt my own head toward her, and she strokes my long black hair, loose and freed from its normal ponytail.

"Oh yeah, I remember." I don't remember, but I don't want to admit it. How many drinks have I had tonight anyway? She twirls my hair around her fingers, nails expertly manicured, with barely visible crystals stuck to the tips.

My fuzzy mind is caught up in the thought now—lighting up every serotonin receptor in my brain: "Landon Laurie . . . gone?" I laugh, the drinks catching up with me and rising in my brain, soaking up all the sounds and softening all the edges. "There's an offer I can't refuse."

I steady myself against the countertop. Making a Very Serious Lawyer Face, I hold out my hand. Kelli matches my look and also extends her hand; we shake on it.

Then, unable to keep our Very Serious Lawyer Faces any longer, we fall over ourselves laughing. The bathroom door opens and lets in the techno beats like a cold wind, along with a group of women loudly chatting. We straighten ourselves up until they all file into respective stalls.

The door swings shut and the bass notes muffle again; now the only vibrations are in our bones.

Kelli holds a finger to her lips. "Shhh. It's our secret then, right? You shook on it. So that means it's a deal."

"It's a deal." I nod.

She squeals, her voice gin rich with vocal fry. "I'm so glad we met tonight." Then she points a finger gun at the mirror, at her and me. Bang, bang.

Chapter 9

I don't know what time it is anymore. What I do know is that I'm long past the point of a fun buzz or even the deliciousness of a delirious drunk; I'm beginning to feel ill, and I want to go home. Kelli convinces me to dance to one more song, and we decide to call it a night. We huddle under the club entrance, dodging raindrops with our blazers on top of our heads. Kelli orders a car on her phone, and she groans. "It's fifteen minutes away. This is going to take forever."

"I can walk to the train and take it back," I say. "It'll be faster."

"No way," she protests. "There are hardly any trains running at this hour, and I'm not letting you walk through downtown alone in this rain." She has a point; the storm that's lasted all day is continuing into the night as a proper torrent. The rain and the mist coalescing under the streetlights seem to my glazed eyes like a painting; the yellow headlights and red brake lights sweep by like brushstrokes in the darkness.

"Where do you live, anyway?" I ask. "How do you know if we're going the same direction?"

"I'm north. You?"

"Same."

"There you go. I'll put in your address as a second once we get into the car."

"Thanks, I'll Venmo you the difference."

She fixes an errant piece of hair on my face, brushing it behind my ear. "No need to do that. Don't you have girlfriends? You can make it up to me by getting me a mimosa at boozy brunch next weekend. Here, give me your number so you know I'm good for it."

I humor her, and we exchange numbers; I don't have the heart to tell her this whole getting-wasted thing was a onetime deal. I'm not looking for a girlfriend.

She leans against me and yawns while watching her phone. "I think the driver is lost. They keep circling the same block." She gives up and sticks her phone in her purse. "Do you see a blue Prius?"

"Yeah, several. It's Seattle." I pick up each foot and wiggle my aching toes in my boots.

"Hey, check this guy out." She nods to a Tesla parked near the front of the club, where a man is slumped against the passenger-side door, repeatedly making a motion like he's giving the car a high five, though nothing is happening.

"Is that how you unlock a Tesla?" I ask, after we watch him continue the fruitless motion for a good minute.

Kelli shrugs. "I actually have no idea. They could run on telepathy for all I know."

I peer through the rain and watch the man attempt to stand, then completely fall over onto the sidewalk. "Jesus," I say. "Should we . . . help him?"

Kelli giggles. "Can you imagine the things these cameras catch on a nightly basis out here?" I glance behind us at a lens fixed directly above the club door and pointing out to the street, no doubt recording the current slapstick routine in progress. The man manages to claw his way to an upright position, and then, miraculously, the Tesla door opens. He attempts to climb in, but not before he falls over again.

I look over at the bouncer who's leaning against the club door, scrolling on his phone. "Really?" I say, pointing to the guy. "Should you stop him?" The bouncer looks up and back down without a word. But before I can do anything else, Kelli is off and running. With a groan, I adjust my blazer over my hair and follow her. To my surprise, when I get to her and the drunk guy, they're both laughing.

"It was pretty funny," Kelli is saying. "I'm glad you're not hurt."

The very drunk and very wet man gazes up at me from his spot on the pavement. "Ku!"

I suddenly feel ill.

"Landon?" I grab Kelli and pull her back. "He's fine. Let's leave him alone," I say. "How far out is the car, did you say?"

"You know each other?"

"Yeah, we know each other."

She squints her eyes in the rain. "Well, we can't leave him here. He's wasted, and he's trying to get into his car to drive."

"And clearly failing. Can we leave, please?"

"We can't let him get in the car."

"Okay, so let's steal his keys and give them to the bouncer or something."

Kelli looks over my shoulder. "That guy will one hundred percent steal this Tesla if we give him the keys."

"Ku!" Landon calls from the sidewalk. "Come here and introduce me to your friend."

"Does he work with you?" Kelli asks.

I sigh. "He's Landon Laurie. He's the boss that I was telling you about earlier."

Kelli balks. "Him? You're kidding me!" She looks back at Landon and at me again. "You didn't tell me he was cute."

I throw up my hands. "Seriously? Do you not remember all the shit I told you about him?"

"Okay, okay," Kelli says. "Well, it doesn't matter. We definitely can't let him drive away drunk if he's your boss. Besides, he doesn't seem to remember any of that mean stuff he said. Maybe if you help get him home safely, he'll only remember that part?"

"He's an asshole, and I don't really care what happens to him."

"You don't mean that. If it was anyone else, you would want them to be safe."

Maybe it's the drinks or the state of near exhaustion, but I feel like I really meant it. It's so typical: Landon Laurie completely unbothered and smiling like an idiot, while once again, it's somehow my job to solve his problems.

"Fine," I say. "Since you're calling us a car on your phone, I'll call him a car on mine." I'm about to reach to grab my phone when a blue Prius pulls up in front of Landon's Tesla. The window rolls down, and the driver shouts out, "One of you Kelli?"

Kelli waves. "Hi, one second." She turns to me. "No time. Our car is here now. Let's share ours with him. What's a little detour?"

"No," I protest. "Come on, I just want to go home."

"Bea," Kelli snaps suddenly. I straighten at her abrupt change in tone. "If you leave him here and he drives and dies in an accident, how will you feel knowing you could have stopped it?" She steps closer. "And what will you tell people when these cameras show you finding Landon Laurie here on the street, then walking away when you knew he was too wasted to drive?"

My stomach turns. She's right. I stand there, my blazer long soaked through, the water now dripping through to my hair. I follow her back to Landon and shut his car door. She kneels down and asks him where he lives.

When he says he lives in Belltown, she claps her hands. "Perfect, that's not far from here at all. You want a ride?"

Landon's eyes light up. "Let's go." We help him into our car, then buckle in on either side of him. Kelli informs the driver she has a new destination address.

"So how do you know Ku?" Landon asks Kelli. He practically reclines on me; I elbow him in the ribs, but he doesn't move. I lean against the cold car window and cool my skin on the glass.

"Friends having a girls' night." Kelli purses her lips together.

Landon runs his hand through his wet hair and manspreads his legs, taking up almost the entire space in the back seat. "I had no idea

Ku had such . . . interesting friends." He spins around to face me. "Ku, why have you never told me about your interesting friends?"

I grimace at the smell of pure alcohol coming off him. "Are we almost there?"

In the rearview mirror, the driver's eyes squint at us. Most likely assessing the possibility of one of us puking all over his upholstery. It's a fair suspicion. I was already feeling woozy, and Landon and Kelli's flirting might take me over the top. But finally, out of the noise and heat of the club, my mind relaxes, and I feel myself floating with the movements of the car driving along the night streets.

It's suddenly quiet, and I turn to my companions. I'm not even surprised when I see Kelli's hands in Landon's hair and his mouth against hers. His hand slides up her skirt, peeling it up to reveal a milky thigh, and a gentle moan escapes her while she spreads her legs slightly.

I watch them the rest of the way.

◆ ◆ ◆

At our destination, Landon pushes me out of the car so he can exit. We climb out in front of a luxury condo building right on the Seattle waterfront. The building entrance faces a panoramic unobstructed view of the water, and even though it's night, I can imagine it in daytime, the water with the mountains in the background . . . This is where Landon Laurie lives? Just when I thought I couldn't hate him any more . . .

"Wow!" Kelli exclaims.

When I have to stand again, my stomach rebels. I awkwardly wave. "So good night, I guess. Kelli, can you put in my address as the next stop?"

"Wait," Landon says. "You're not coming up?"

Kelli smiles slyly. "Bea, you have to."

"I really want to head home, but you can stay if you want—"

But as I turn back to the car, it drives away. Confused, I watch it turn and disappear.

"Oops," says Kelli. "I forgot to put in we had another destination, so the ride ended."

Goddammit. "It's fine. I'll call another." My vision spins, and my stomach jumps up into my chest. I slap my hand to my mouth.

"Are you okay?" asks Kelli.

"I really hate to ask, but, Landon—can I go upstairs and use your bathroom before I go?"

It's not that I don't appreciate the millennial-white entryway to his high-rise condo, but I'm determined not to ruin it, so I push by Landon and Kelli as soon as he opens his front door. "Bathroom?" I ask and run to where he points.

I barely make it to the toilet before losing it. Afterward, I sit on the tiled floor and trace the grout with my fingers in order to keep my mind focused on something other than how sick I still feel. Beyond the door, I hear Landon and Kelli chattering, then music beginning to play from speakers. Once the room quits spinning, I pull myself up and open his medicine cabinet.

"Yes," I sigh in triumph and pull out a bottle of mouthwash.

After cleaning up as best I can, I feel better. I replace the mouthwash and look through the bottles in his cabinet. There are upscale skin-care products, a couple of hair serums, and a Costco-size bottle of melatonin. Then a row of orange bottles. The first one is a half-empty bottle of hydrocodone, the next is Xanax, and the last is Prozac. Huh, Landon needs Xanax and Prozac?

My stomach feels much better now, but my heart is still racing; I hold myself over the sink and look at my reflection in the mirror, only my sheer force of will keeping the dizziness away. *What are you doing?* I ask myself. I breathe and focus. I study my eyes, my mouth. *Keep it together. What are they doing out there?* I wonder.

Never mind—I actually don't want to know.

I have to get the hell out of here as fast as possible.

◆ ◆ ◆

When I emerge from the bathroom, Landon and Kelli are in the living room, sitting on the white leather sectional sofa in front of a square glass coffee table. There are three glasses of wine next to a huge stack of coffee-table books because I'm sure that's how Landon saw it done at Restoration Hardware, or wherever he bought this furniture.

But as I round the coffee table, I see what the big art books were hiding—next to the wineglasses, an open metal cigarette case, a razor blade, and powdered lines on the glass.

I freeze.

"Ku, come over here," Landon says. His eyes are glassy, and his smile is like a shark's—a predator's smile.

Kelli looks at me and smiles. "Want a bump?" she asks.

Despite the mouthwash, a sour taste rises up in my mouth. I shake my head. "No, I'm thinking I need to leave."

Kelli hands me a glass of wine. "One more, then we'll head out."

I shrug. "You can stay as long as you like." But I take the wine anyway and have a sip; I need something to calm me down, I think. "I need to get home."

"Both of you are welcome to hang," Landon says, eyeing Kelli. She giggles.

Heat flares across my skin. I take a drink; it's smooth going down. "Did you know you're sharing your coke with an associate at the Saul Group, Landon?"

"You're a lawyer at the Saul Group?" Landon pauses for a split second. "Ha, we just stole Granite from the Saul Group," he teases Kelli. "Losers."

"Unbelievable." I roll my eyes.

"You know," Landon continues. "Ku here was a killer in signing them. She did great work, really. No, you did, Ku. So *ku*-dos to you! Ha! I just made that up!"

Kelli laughs wildly.

"Wow, what a thanks I get." I gulp down my wine; it's the only thing that can make this tolerable now.

"And I didn't offer my coke," Landon continues. "It's hers."

I stop and glare at Kelli. "Seriously?"

She shrugs. "A little fun, that's all."

I can't think of anything else to say, or maybe I can't find a way to say it—my tongue is fuzzy and feels big in my mouth. I close my eyes and try to stop the spinning that's suddenly begun again. When I open my eyes, my view is distorted, and I can barely make out Kelli and Landon in front of me. I don't like this. I should have known. I should know better.

Close your eyes and breathe.

I remember now; this is what it's like to almost lose control. I remember how much I used to love it, the feeling of being on that cliff edge and looking down into the unknown. And then the jump. It was what I lived for. God, how were we so stupid? This feeling? Nothing is worth feeling like this, I decide. How could I forget?

I've worked too hard to lose control like this now.

I stand up. I'm leaving. I try to say it out loud, but I don't even know if I form the sounds.

My feet fail me, and I flop back onto the couch.

Kelli's face comes into view. "It's okay," she says. "You're fine. You stood up too fast. Shh, it's okay. Close your eyes . . ."

I do; it's warm.

It's not so bad here after all. I also remember now how it's so much easier to give in. I let my body and mind relax into the current, and I'm swept away.

Chapter 10

Thursday

My eyes snap open.

It wasn't a dream.

It takes me a moment, but I'm in my own bed, staring up at my own ceiling. How did I get here? I try to think back, but there's a block, and I can't remember anything after arriving at Landon's last night. A big, pounding, screeching block in my brain . . . Even though my body feels like it's mired in quicksand, I roll over and sit up, my legs swinging over the side of the bed. I'm still wearing my outfit from yesterday.

Wait. I remember Landon and Kelli. Kelli.

They were doing lines, and I had one more glass of wine, even though I didn't want to. Why did I do that? At the very thought of wine, my stomach lurches, and my throat cries for any kind of nonalcoholic liquid. I tenderly place my fingers on my temples and gently rub in an attempt to get the jackhammers to quell.

Finally, my thirst outweighs my body's desire to stay put; I stand up, wavering for a moment. In the bathroom, I drink straight from the tap, then splash water on my face and rub away the smeared makeup. I check the time, and I'm already running late, but I can't show up to work like this. I turn on the shower with the temperature almost too hot to stand.

Soon I'm in the kitchen and staring at the coffee maker.

Mom comes in. "Bea, what was going on last night, huh?"

I start at her entrance. I rub my palms together; they're sweaty. I don't know if I'm still slightly drunk from last night, but my skin is buzzing. The blank space of the night before weighs heavy on my aching head. "I know I was really late coming home." I twist the lid onto my thermos, avoiding eye contact. "Sorry I woke you."

I worry she can still smell the drinks on me, even after the scrubbing, because I can still smell them myself. The molecules have embedded themselves inside my nostrils, and I can't get the sticky-sweet poison out of my brain now. "I'll be home at normal time tonight," I promise her.

Before she can argue or ask anything more, I hurry out the door, ignoring the look of worry I know she's wearing. Who knows what condition I showed up in last night?

I keep my head down on the train, along the street, and all the way through the office lobby. I don't even bother putting up my hood in the gathering morning mist; droplets of water cling to my hair and hang off my eyelashes.

When I arrive at work, there's a group of people gathered in the lobby, all listening to a muffled voice speak. I stop. "What's going on?" I ask the receptionist. Then, I add, "Is Greg getting another promotion?" I think it's funny, but she only stares at me with wide eyes. She opens her mouth, but nothing comes out, and then she abruptly walks away, leaving the reception desk empty.

I hurry into the lobby and push through. The TV is on and tuned onto the news. The reporter talking into their mic is in front of a building where an ambulance is parked and police can be seen gathering; they part as a gurney with a black body bag comes into view.

My breath hitches, and I feel dizzy. I know that building.

I was there last night.

I can't hear the reporter over my own heartbeat screaming in my ears, but the headline is written in all caps at the bottom of the screen: PROMINENT ATTORNEY FOUND DEAD. CAUSE OF DEATH UNDER INVESTIGATION.

My lips curl into a smirk. *Is this a sick joke?* Someone behind me whistles. "God, it's horrible."

"They said his house cleaner found him this morning," says someone else. "Could you imagine?"

The lobby suddenly shrinks, and I back out of the crowd, needing air. Pressing my fists into my sides, I walk to my office and shut the door, then lean against it lest I crumple to the ground. *What happened last night? What did we do?*

A wave of nausea racks me, and I bolt to grab the trash can from underneath my desk. I dry heave into it, but nothing comes out. I drop the trash can and wipe sweat from my neck and forehead. *Keep. It. Together.*

"You okay?"

"Oh my God." I jump in my chair.

Greg is standing in my doorway; I didn't even hear him come in. "Are you sick or something? I don't blame you . . . It's insanity, isn't it? We just saw him."

Swallowing, I can only look down at my desk. "Yeah." My voice cracks.

"Wanted to make sure you were okay."

"Do they know what happened?" I ask.

"No, too early, I think." A pause. "Do you feel bad?"

My face turns up at him, and we lock eyes. "Why would you say that?"

"No, nothing. Only . . ." He hesitates. "You and him did get into it at the lounge."

"I don't know what that's supposed to mean," I snap. "We didn't 'get into it,' by the way. He grabbed me and called me a bitch, if you want to know what really happened."

Greg grimaces. "Of course. I'm sorry—shit, I don't know why I said that. I think I'm in shock."

"Me too," I say gently. "It's fine."

He runs his fingers through his hair. "Besides, you guys must have made up, right?"

"What do you mean?"

"As I was leaving, I thought I saw you and your friend talking to him by his car. Didn't look like you guys were still fighting is all."

I shake my head. "I honestly don't remember; it was so late." I shake my mouse and pretend to be distracted by something on my screen. "Greg, I have to work."

"Sure, yeah, I'll just . . ." He leaves and shuts the door behind him. As soon as I see him disappear around the corner, I go for my phone.

Looking in my contacts, I find her and begin a new text.

What the hell happened last night? I search and easily find a news article about Landon. I send it to Kelli.

The reply doesn't come immediately. It doesn't come at all. For a moment, I panic and wonder if she gave me a fake number. She was a stranger, after all. How could I have been so stupid?

I stare at my computer screen and wish I could go back to the person I was twenty-four hours earlier.

I get no work done. The office is like a tomb. There's none of the usual banter or the charged hustle. We're all in shock, and sure, he was an asshole, but we are all in mourning. I stay in my office and only see Greg pass by once more; he avoids looking at me.

I open my Uber app and look at the history. No rides home last night. Maybe Kelli or Landon ordered the car for me. No texts or photos reveal anything either. I go to the Saul Group's website and look at the associate directory. I realize I don't even remember Kelli's last name or the department she works in; I scroll slowly through the list of all associates and don't see a single Kelli listed. But it's possible the website isn't up to date; I know the BCC site still lists interns from last summer. I go to LinkedIn next and search for Kellis in the greater Seattle area working at the Saul Group. Still no results.

At exactly five o'clock, I shut my computer and leave the office. The storm is gone, and the early dusk is settling over the city in a golden-hour haze.

My feet take me past my train stop. I need to keep moving, need the fresh air. I can walk to the next stop and go home from there.

What happened to Landon?

But I know what happened to Landon. He died.

At some point between me blacking out in his living room and Landon's housekeeper arriving, he died. So what did we do in those lost moments, those hidden memories? And what happened to Kelli?

I keep walking as the sky gets darker. I pass the next train stop and the one after that. Finally, I stop, and my heart drops; I'm standing across the street from Solo. Landon's Tesla is still parked outside. A traffic cop stands next to it and inputs something into a handheld device. A ticket pops out, and the cop places it on the windshield. He looks up at me, and my breath hitches in my throat.

But he doesn't point at me and yell "Stop right there!" He doesn't even give me a second glance. I keep walking. Backtracking, I take the next train-tunnel entrance down to the platform, eyes cast down the whole way. When I exit the station and my phone gets service, a text pops up. Kelli. Her reply is four words long.

We have to talk.

◆ ◆ ◆

Kelli's apartment is in a historic brick building on Capitol Hill, in contrast to Landon's ultraluxury condo. She tells me her apartment is 500. I look at the nameplate on the front door buzzer and see the name: **K. STEWART**. I walk up five long flights of stairs to get to her front door, which is already cracked open. "Hello?" I call inside.

A voice responds, "Come on in. I'll just be a minute."

I walk into the small space, in the style of older apartments from the '30s and before open floor concepts were all the rage. I'm sitting in her cozy living room and admiring the high ceilings, plaster walls, and original-wood crown molding. It's sparsely but fashionably decorated. Shelves are populated with artfully designed vases placed just so in between aesthetic book stacks.

I notice a small side table against the wall and a pile of mail on top. I get up, and after checking to make sure I'm alone, I thumb through it. Utility bills, grocery store ads, all addressed to Kelli Stewart. There's even an office key card with the Saul Group logo on it. *At least she is who she says she is,* I think, a little relieved.

No family photos, I note. Nothing personal at all, actually. Besides a small powder room that I can see from the couch, there are two closed doors leading to, I can only assume, a bedroom and closet—maybe there are more personal things in there.

From a narrow hallway, Kelli comes in from the kitchen. She takes a seat at the opposite end of the couch, tucking her legs under her. She's wearing leggings and a sweater, no makeup, and has her hair in a ponytail. She looks as though she hasn't been sleeping. I can relate.

"I called in sick today." She swallows hard and runs her fingers along the coffee mug handle repeatedly.

My right hand rests in my left, and I take my thumb and begin to draw circles in the middle of my wrist. "I can't remember anything."

Her eyes look up at me, wide. "That's the problem, Bea. I remember everything."

I shake my head. "Then tell me what happened."

She covers her face with one hand and grips the mug so tightly with the other, I'm afraid it might shatter in her fist. "Because I didn't believe it at first, I thought I was . . . confused. Or dreaming."

"Confused about what?" I insist. "Kelli, you have to tell me what you saw. What happened to Landon?"

"You did."

"What do you mean?" My limbs feel frozen, and I don't feel like I'm in my own body—it's as if I'm floating outside myself.

"I mean I saw you." Kelli says it directly, matter-of-factly. "I'm sorry, Bea. I didn't want to tell you."

"Tell me exactly what happened."

"We were partying, having a good time." Kelli stops and opens her phone, scrolling. She stops and then holds her phone out to me. I stare down at the photo open on the screen. It's a selfie from Wednesday night: Kelli with her white teeth bared in a seductive smile, Landon with a slack-eyed grin, and between them both, me. In the background, I can see Landon's living room and his arms around us reflected in the window.

"Why are you showing me this?" I ask.

"It was just all fun. Or at least I thought. At some point you and Landon began arguing. Something stupid about a promotion. You were both yelling at each other so loudly. I begged you both to stop, but you kept on going at it. I went to the bathroom because I was really starting to feel anxious. I don't even know how long I was in there, but then I noticed it was silent out in the living room. And when I came out . . ." Her voice cracks, and she shudders.

"Go on," I say.

Shaking her head, she looks at me, almost apologetically. "He was lying on the ground, Bea. And you were . . . on top of him, straddling him. Your hands were around his neck."

My hands fly to my mouth, and I feel sick. I don't remember any of this. Could I have really gotten that angry? Enough to kill him?

"I yelled at you to get off him, and you finally did."

"But he was alive after that, right?" I ask.

Kelli nods. "Yeah, we checked his pulse."

I let out a gasp. "Thank God!"

"But then he started shaking and seizing. Like he was overdosing. He was high and drunk, Bea." She holds back a sob. "I told you we needed to call 911, but you told me not to. You said we would both be incriminated."

My brows furrow in confusion. "I did?"

Kelli continues. "He just kept shaking and then began making these horrible noises. But you said he would be fine. I just sat and held my hands over my ears. And then—"

"And then what?"

"He stopped."

My insides are knots. This has to be a dream. "I honestly don't remember any of this . . ."

"I wanted to check his pulse again, but you said we shouldn't touch him. You said he would be fine. I think I knew the truth, but I just wanted to believe you and just wanted to leave. At that point, you were so out of it, I called an Uber and made sure you got home okay."

"We can call the police now," I say. "I have to tell them what happened."

Kelli sets down her glass and scoots over to me, putting her hand on my shoulder. "But nothing happened."

"But we can let them know we were there and—"

She nods slowly. "And did nothing to save him?"

I swallow and try to keep still.

"I told you this because I couldn't bear it if I did something like that and didn't even know. I had to tell you the truth. But I didn't tell you so you could turn yourself in! For now, you're safe. Nobody suspects anything. What good will come if you turn yourself in? What will the firm think?" Her voice lowers. "What will your parents say if they know you just sat there and watched someone die?"

The mention of Mom and Dad hits me in the chest, and I can barely breathe. "You're right," I admit. "I can't do this to them."

Kelli nods and grins awkwardly. "Let me help you through this," she says. She reaches for my hands and holds them; her grip is warm.

"Okay." I nod, trying to still my shaking shoulders. We sit there, hand in hand, and hold our smiles with false hope.

What have I done? It makes sense now. The lost time, the nagging guilt in the back of my mind. I see the night replaying now the way Kelli has described it, and I can't make it stop. Each time I run through the timeline, I see another mistake I made, another way I'm going to get caught. The cameras, of course, but the bouncer at the club—he saw us clearly help Landon into our Uber—the Uber driver, the cameras at Landon's building, my DNA all over Landon's place. Not to mention the things I can't even remember because I was so drunk.

How could you be so stupid?

I regret the last drink, whatever it was—I can't even remember. But as I think back up the chain, I know I shouldn't have gone to the club at all.

I let my ambitions get the better of me and put everything in danger. And my parents can't save me this time—I'm a grown-up now. Even if they wanted to, they wouldn't be able to help me, and not just because they don't have anything left. An entire lifetime spent making up for the sins of my youth, and now my parents and I are going to pay for everything all over again. Everything remade has been broken anew.

At home I tell my parents I'm not feeling well. I strip off my clothes and cover myself in my blankets. Then I break into quiet sobs. For Landon and for myself.

Chapter 11

Friday

The air in the office is still one of grieving. People speak in hushed murmurs, appear to walk in slow motion. We are all still in shock. And if they only knew it's all because of me.

It's late morning, and I've barely finished my first coffee when an email appears from all three of the partners. The subject line is "Remembering Landon Laurie."

The email announces there's going to be a memorial for Landon at the Rainier Club tomorrow afternoon. My empty stomach roils, and I hover the cursor over the "Decline" button.

"Good morning." Olivia pops her head in. "Got a moment?"

I nod, swallowing back dread. I close the email. "What's up?"

"Walk with me?" Something in her voice tells me it's not a question.

I follow her to the elevators. I'm thinking we are going to go for coffee or a snack, but she presses the up button. Seeing my confusion, Olivia says quietly, "Going to Denny's office. Nothing bad, don't worry."

"Sure," I say. This can't be good.

There's no receptionist when we reach the partners' floor, and Olivia puts her hand on the door handle, then pauses and turns back to me. "Don't be scared," she says. "It's routine."

"What's routine?"

She doesn't answer me. She opens the door, and we walk inside. Denny is sitting where he was the last time I visited, on the far end of the sofa. But there's a new person here too.

The woman is middle aged and stands with her hands clasped behind her back, displaying a stick-straight posture and dressed in an ill-fitting suit. Her hair is pulled into a tidy bun, and her no-nonsense demeanor reminds me of a school principal. Then suddenly I realize it's much worse than that. I know exactly who this woman is.

Olivia takes a seat on the sofa and nods to the spot next to her, like a supportive parent. I oblige and sit, as if I have a choice.

"I'm Detective Judith Branson," the stranger introduces herself. "I'm here to get some details on the death of Landon Laurie. I understand he was your manager?"

I breathe in, but can't talk—my tongue isn't working. *What did they find?*

Mistaking my hesitation for nervousness, Denny chimes in. "Don't worry, Bea. Detective Branson is talking to everyone on Landon's team. The more information you can provide, the better."

"Of course." I nod. "Yes, he was my boss."

"How would you describe your working relationship with Mr. Laurie?" Detective Branson asks.

"Fine," I say. "He was a good attorney."

She squeezes her brows, and my breath hitches in my throat. What have I said wrong? I ride it out and don't say anything else, don't make it seem like I'm second-guessing my answers, even though I am.

"Not really what I asked, is it?" she finally says. "Did you ever quarrel with your boss?"

"Sure," I say. "We had an argument the last time I saw him, actually. I feel really bad about that." I feel like I'm going to throw up.

"What was your argument about?" Detective Branson asks.

"We got a new client, and I wanted to be more involved. Landon disagreed." *Keep it short and simple, Bea. Stick to the facts. Don't try to lie . . . just omit the truth.* I look over at Denny, and he's smiling thinly and nodding.

Detective Branson reaches inside her coat and produces a small notebook à la a BBC police procedural. She flips through some pages and then looks back at me. "You were seen having quite the public fight with Landon on Wednesday night at a club. Then, you were seen outside with him shortly before the club closed. If that's true, you would have been one of the last people to see him, Ms. Ku."

I blink. It's no mystery who supplied this information. I think back to Greg's loaded question, *Do you feel bad?*

"I did have a fight with him at Solo. There was a disagreement as to whether I deserved a promotion or not."

"How did the argument end? Did you resolve it?" Detective Branson asks.

"Yes," I say. "In fact, my friend and I saw him outside as we were about to leave and noticed he was really drunk. We didn't think he should drive, so we offered to share our Uber. But we dropped him off at his condo building."

"You didn't go in?"

"Sorry," Olivia interjects. "She said they dropped him off."

I lower my head. "Well, we did go in." I pause. Olivia's eyebrows rise. "Just for a nightcap," I add.

The detective looks at me. "We're just establishing a timeline, Ms. Ku. What you do in your free time doesn't interest me." She holds an emphasis on the *do*.

I nod, resisting the urge to clarify I wasn't *doing* anyone or anything.

"Who was your friend?"

"Oh, someone I ran into while dancing, named Kelli. I think her last name is Stewart. I actually didn't know her at all. We dropped off Landon and had a couple more drinks. Then I went home after that."

"If you happen to remember anything else, you'll contact me right away, yeah?" Detective Branson hands me a card, and I take it, sliding it into my jacket pocket without looking at it at all.

"Is that all you have for Ms. Ku?" Denny asks.

Detective Branson nods. "Thanks for your time. I might be in touch for any follow-up items."

Olivia and I stand. "Right, nice to meet you," I say. Olivia leads the detective to the door and holds it open as she walks out. Once she's gone, Denny clears his throat.

"Bea, I know this is a hard time, so please don't hesitate to come to us with anything on your mind. This is a great loss for everyone. Unfortunately, business has to proceed as usual, especially with the recent Granite work. They came over in large part because of him." Denny glances away, swallowing hard, revealing a bit of anxiety himself.

"But not to worry." He claps his hands together and smiles thinly, ever the fearless leader. "Olivia will be taking over as your managing attorney in the interim."

"Really?"

"Last thing," Denny says. "With Olivia now managing her own team plus his, it will really be all hands on deck for Granite. Olivia will give you the details, but we're putting you on a big due diligence project for a possible acquisition target for them. You'll be working with one of their analysts, Simon. I'm talking to Greg next, and I'll let him know to give you all the resources you need. Does all that sound good?"

"It all sounds perfect."

Denny walks me to the door and holds it open.

I take one step out, then turn. "Wait," I say. "Denny, I . . ." My words stop cold in my throat.

He tilts his head. "Yes?"

I shake my head, my mouth hanging open and the heavy confession stuck like rocks at the bottom of my throat.

Denny steps a little closer and asks again, a little softer. "Yes? Do you have something to tell me, Bea?"

But I can't say it. I choke. "I'm really sad about Landon."

Denny nods. "We all are, Bea. We all are."

Back in my office, I stare at the wall. I think to myself that Landon will rupture his spleen when he comes back and finds out I've been promoted without him. But Landon won't be coming back, and it's precisely because he's gone that I've now gotten what I wanted. And he's gone because of me.

I try to push the sick satisfaction down, but it floats on a new layer of guilt that's settled in my chest. How much can I possibly live with? Or maybe the question is, How much am I willing to live with if it means getting what I want?

◆ ◆ ◆

An email comes in from Greg. I freeze before opening it. But I shouldn't worry. It's not a tirade or an all-caps death threat—it's simply an email introduction to the analyst Denny mentioned earlier.

The email has cc'd the analyst, Simon, and a Zoom meeting invite from him quickly follows the introductory email.

When the time comes for the meeting, I join. In the grainy laptop video, my face looks gray and sunken. I rub my finger underneath my eye to wipe away some smudged mascara, then try to smooth my hair down. A chime indicates Simon is about to join, so I stop fidgeting.

The square on the computer screen appears, and I'm surprised to be looking at a young and attractive guy. His brown hair is shaggy in that Seattle-outdoorsy way, and even through the computer, his green eyes are piercing. He sips coffee and waves.

"I'm Simon," he says. "Nice to meet you virtually."

"Hi, I'm Bea. Nice to be working with you."

He begins talking about Granite, and even though I'm trying my best to focus on his words, my mind drifts, and I stop hearing him altogether.

"Are you okay?"

I snap back to attention. "Uh, sorry, yes. Can you repeat that?" I ask. "Sorry, it's just . . . I'm a bit distracted. I don't know if you saw the news . . ."

He pauses, and then the horror of recognition appears across his face. "Oh God, I didn't even realize that the guy was at BCC." He raises his hands and interlocks them on top of his head while leaning back in his chair. "Are you all all right over there?"

"Um, it's shocking to say the least." I bite my lip. "But I should be thankful for something to distract me. Sorry, let's try this again."

"Only if you're sure? We can reschedule."

"It's fine. Really, I can focus."

"Okay, I was saying that Granite has a small pharmaceutical company portfolio at the moment, but they'd like to explore expanding in this space. Actually, one of my friends is a scientist at a pharma start-up, and I think that could be a good relationship to explore for acquisition purposes."

After that, we make good headway. Simon is smart and knows all the ins and outs of Granite; he's been there since the beginning, it turns out. He's easy to work with, and we get into an easy rhythm and make a road map of where we need to go in our future sessions to most efficiently get our project done and generate a useful report. I breathe a sigh of relief at having an assignment, some kind of normalcy, to focus on for the first time in days.

As we wrap up, we schedule another meeting.

"See you Monday, Bea."

I wave to my camera and hit the red "Leave" button. The screen goes black, and a survey of how my call went appears. I exit out without rating. My heart is still racing, but I don't feel like collapsing anymore. While I was with Simon, I genuinely forgot about Landon. How can that be?

◆ ◆ ◆

When I arrive home, Mom is on the phone and Dad is glued to some TV show, so I easily make it to my room with a quick wave. Once the door is shut and locked behind me, I sink down to the floor; it's the first quiet moment I've had to process since it all happened.

I quickly strip off my clothes and stuff them into the hamper. I start the shower in my en suite bath, extra hot. I climb into the tub and let the water fall over me, standing there under the water until my skin shines bright pink. When I can't stand the prickling heat any longer, I sit with my knees pulled up under my chin, and I wrap my arms around my legs. I lay my head down and close my eyes.

The shower patters on my hair and on my face, like rain.

My eyes snap open and I stand, shutting the water off.

I put on a robe and wrap my hair in a towel before walking out to the kitchen. Mom has set the table, and Dad is filling water glasses, placing them at our usual spots.

They're both quiet until Mom says, "We heard about your boss, Bea."

I nod. "Yeah."

"They said it was an overdose," Dad says. "Just now on the evening news."

My heart sinks, even though I think this is good . . . for me. "They did?"

Mom clicks her teeth, never one to let a moment of judgment pass. "Imagine being that successful and still needing to find fulfillment in drugs."

"You know, I'm not hungry," I say. "I'm not feeling well. I'm going to go to sleep."

Dad looks up, concerned. "It's tough news. I understand."

"I'll make you salabat," Mom says. She loves making the Filipino ginger tea and will use any excuse to boil up a big pot of freshly sliced ginger. She reaches for the fresh root she keeps in the fruit bowl.

I wave my hands. "No, no. You don't have to. I'm going to get some rest."

"Fine." She frowns and puts back the ginger.

But there's no way I can sleep.

◆ ◆ ◆

A knock at my door. Shit. I wipe my eyes clear of sleep and roll out of bed. "One second," I call. I look at my phone and am shocked to see it's barely 9:00 p.m. God, will this day end?

I crack open my door and look down an empty hallway. Then I see on the floor, still steaming, a mug of salabat. I pick it up and inhale the spicy ginger scent. I sit in my bed, gathering the sheets around me, and hold the small offering from Mom.

I sleep in short fits, and my mind is filled with nightmares. I sit up in bed as soon as the sun comes up, thankful the darkness is over for a little bit, at least. With shaky hands, I wash my face and brush my teeth, then dress in yoga pants and a sweatshirt. I take my multivitamins and meds and place the containers back in the medicine cabinet. I turn each orange bottle to face outward, their names displayed like a menu.

A wave of shame and embarrassment floods my chest. All this time I thought I was better, but I haven't changed at all.

Chapter 12

Saturday

The face in the mirror can't be mine, I think. I look like a shadow, somebody using my skin and simply passing through.

The orange bottles stare at me, willing me to begin the morning ritual. I need extra support today. I pour the pills into my palm, then add another dose of Xanax. Something to take the edge off.

I help cook a chorizo scramble for breakfast. I'm on eggs on the left burner while Mom makes hash browns on the right. At the table, I push the eggs around the plate. I don't have the stomach for food.

Dad, however, is on his second helping. "How are you doing?" he asks me.

"Landon's memorial is later this afternoon," I say.

"Ugh." Mom grimaces. "It's all so horrible." She pauses and sniffs the air. "Do you smell that?" She hurries to the kitchen, and I follow. She turns the stovetop knob, the one I already turned off, and a bright-blue flame leaps up before I hear a click.

"Shit, I thought I had turned it off all the way," I say. "I usually remember, but I guess I was zoned out. I'm sorry!"

"It's fine," Mom says. "But you know that knob is sticky. Really make sure it's turned all the way—otherwise it just leaks gas. I don't know why I just don't get a new stove!" She yells the last part toward Dad.

He grunts. "Put it on the list of things to do!"

Mom and I return to the breakfast table. Mom clears her throat. "Landon's death doesn't . . . affect your promotion, does it?"

My jaw drops. "*That's* what you're concerned about?" I snap.

"Don't talk to your mother that way." Dad's lips turn into a straight line, and he puts down his fork. "We're just concerned about you."

Mom narrows her eyes. "You were out late Wednesday night."

"And?" I ask.

"Didn't you say there was a party for work? Was Landon there?" asks Mom. "Were you with him?"

"I was at the club with him. That's all."

Mom raises her eyebrows. "Oh my God. You weren't doing drugs with him, were you?"

"No!" I snap. "Of course not! Why would you jump to that conclusion?"

"Bea," Dad says. "We're just being vigilant. You can't blame us for worrying about you getting into trouble—"

"Seriously? You automatically assume I've gotten into trouble?"

"So where were you last night before you came home completely drunk?"

"I was with a friend!"

Mom shakes a fork at me so hard, the chorizo falls off. "You know, Tita Uba has been asking about you at Mass and why she hasn't seen you lately. You're coming with us tomorrow."

I roll my eyes. "She's not my real aunt, Mom. Have other people been asking about me?"

"People always ask," says Mom. "They're interested in what you're up to; I tell them you're a big lawyer, and I show them photos. Oh, Uba has a nephew who's single."

"Do they ask about what I used to be up to?"

"What does that mean?"

"Like, my past? Has anyone been asking questions about when I was younger?"

Mom clams up and stands. "You sound paranoid. That's a symptom of doing drugs, you know."

"Seriously? I'm not doing drugs, and I'm not going to church."

Tight lipped, she begins to collect plates from the table, including Dad's, though he's clearly not finished. But he doesn't even notice half his uneaten breakfast being carried away. He speaks slowly. "You would tell us if you needed help, right? Any help at all."

I want to scream *Yes, yes I do.* But instead, I steady my face and keep my palms flat on my thighs to keep them from shaking. "I would tell you."

Mom is calm, which is always ten times more terrifying than when she's yelling. "What's your friend's name?" she asks.

I pause.

"Someone from the firm?" Dad offers.

"No, not from the firm."

Mom sighs. "I hope this isn't a friend like Caleb was a friend." She says it under her breath, but just loud enough for me to hear.

"Why would you say that?" I ask, hurt.

"Because you are coming in late, drinking, and then asking strange questions about the past?"

I push my chair back; the legs scrape harshly against the hardwood floor. "Never mind," I snap. "I should have known I can't count on my own parents to understand. You offer your help, but you're just waiting for the chance to judge me when I admit I need it. That's always how it's been, and I don't know why it would be any different now." I know this isn't true, but I say it anyway in my bitterness at their suspicions. It's even worse because they're absolutely correct.

"We've always helped you," Mom snaps. "And since you want to bring up the past, maybe we should remind you that we always stood by you, no matter what. We always helped you, even when everyone talked about us."

"Oh really? You were always with me? That's a relief to hear all these years later, because it felt like I was pretty fucking alone when you dropped me off at a rehab center that took away my phone and any way to contact the outside world after the accident!"

"It was for your own good!"

"I'm not seventeen anymore."

I go into my room and slam the door. Exactly like a seventeen-year-old would do. That didn't go as planned at all. I am alone in this. Like in everything else, I am going to have to figure this out on my own.

The first time I remember needing my mom's help, she didn't give it. I've come to understand as an adult that things seen through the eyes of children are so much bigger than we remember. When the fifth graders at recess made fun of the way I said certain words, I told Mom. I wanted her to hold me, tell me it was okay, tell me to be proud, call the parents and tell them what little shits they had for kids. She didn't do any of those things; she stayed standing, eyes on her spoon, stirring like it was the last pan of sauce left in the world, and told me she would stop speaking Tagalog in the house. "From now on, it's English only."

That was easy enough; Dad was happy to not have to deal with Mom's cringing at his accent over the Tagalog words he said "too white."

"Sounds like you're squeezing the vowels through a sphincter," Mom said about his pronunciation. "*O*-puhn your *mow*-the." She would spread her lips wide and flatten her tongue against her bottom row of teeth to demonstrate the kind of flexible palate one needed. The kind Americans didn't possess, clearly.

But I was young and moldable, and I picked up the words quickly and easily, mashing them together in Taglish. In first grade, a phone call home from my teacher prompted a talk from Mom and Dad that the mashing up of my two native languages wasn't welcome in school. Nobody could quite tell what I was saying.

Taglish was reserved for home after that. And after the teasing in fifth grade, Taglish was banned altogether. "My daughter will be American," Mom said; she fed me Happy Meals and dressed me in Old Navy sweatshirts to ensure the American stuck.

In retrospect, I wonder what that sacrifice was like, to take away language from her only child, the language that connected us both to a common homeland, all in service of ensuring I would be accepted in her adopted country. And how much did it sting when the sacrifice was for nothing?

I had been using Jill's Ritalin for weeks. During what should have been a pretty simple calculus exam, the equations danced in front of me, and I felt queasy. Allegra reached over from the desk next to mine. "Are you okay?"

I shook my head.

Jill noticed us and whispered, "How much did you take, Bea?"

"Shut up!" I hissed back. My chest fluttered, and I felt as though my heart was beating so loud the entire class could hear. *Am I having a heart attack?*

"Ladies?" The teacher eyed us suspiciously. "Is there a problem?"

I raised my hand. "I need to go to the bathroom. I'm not feeling well." Gripping the hall pass, I ran past the restrooms and straight through the double doors at the end of the hallway and out to the parking lot. I ran out past the corner and held myself, back against the wall, breathing in the cold, fresh air of October. The hall pass clattered out of my hands, and I pulled my sleeves into my palms and dabbed at the sweat cooling on my face.

I closed my eyes and willed my heart to slow, but it was thumping against my ribs like it might burst through. I sank down to the cool ground and laid my palms on the jagged asphalt.

The test—how could I finish it? I could barely stand up without feeling like I was going to pass out. *Never again,* I thought. *I'm not taking those stupid pills anymore. Stupid Jill . . .*

"Hoo, what do we have here?"

I squinted one eye open and looked up at three backlit figures standing above me. A tilt of my head to bring my sight out of the direct sun revealed them to be two guys and a girl. A trio I didn't know, but the fake leather jackets and studs in their baggy jeans, along with their presence wandering the school grounds during a class period, told me enough. I closed my eyes again and ignored them.

"Get kicked out of the library for not returning your books or something?" The girl spoke. A strong scent of marijuana drifted toward me.

"Leave me alone. I'm sick. And that smell is making it worse."

"What's wrong with you?" I hear her sneer. Let them laugh; I was busy trying not to die. There was a long silence.

A shuffling of feet, then a guy's voice. "Whatever."

I heard the footsteps recede, and when it was quiet again, I opened my eyes and breathed a sigh of relief to find myself alone. My head fell back against the brick wall. How long should I wait before I told someone I was having a heart attack? I'd have to tell them it was caused by using Ritalin that wasn't prescribed to me, so then I'd probably have to tell on Allegra and Jill. My parents would kill me. Would I go to jail? With a criminal record, I would never get into college. My stomach turned, and now I was about to vomit too. I gasped for air. "I'm having a fucking anxiety attack."

"No, you're not." One of the boys was back. The one with the dark hair and darker eyes. He was lean, with bad posture that made his middle look hollowed out. I rolled my eyes at the teenage angst of it all.

I groaned. "What do you want? Can you let me die in peace?"

He laughed. His voice was rich. "Now I'm confused. Are you dying or having an anxiety attack?"

"It can't be both?"

"Should I get the nurse, then? Or call the cops?"

"No!"

The boy raised his eyebrows.

"Look, I took some Ritalin to help me study, and this has never happened before but I feel like I'm having a heart attack. Or an anxiety attack. Also I might throw up."

"Why didn't you say so? What do you normally take for that? Zannies, tranks, moggies?"

"Are those words?"

"Never mind. Here." He unzipped his bag and produced an orange pill bottle. It would become my favorite color, that translucent pumpkin hue, the color of reprieve; later the color of forgetting. When he shook the bottle, it produced only a thin rattle. He held it up. "Only a few left. Want them for the road? Looks like you need it more than I do."

I took it. "What are they?"

"Xanax. It's for anxiety anyway, and you say that's what you have, right?"

I nodded. "Thanks." I slid a little blue oval into my hand. A wave of nausea hit me, and I didn't think; the pill went easily down. I turned the bottle over and read the prescription label. "Who's Rhonda Crown?"

"My mom. She's got a cabinet full of these. She can't even keep track of all the pills she takes."

Allegra burst around the corner. I shoved the pill bottle back into his hand before she could see. "Bea! I've been looking all over for you! I thought you died! What happened?" She pulled me to my feet and only stopped to give my new acquaintance a skeptical side-eye. "You okay, Bea?" she asked me, her eyes never leaving his face.

The boy only pushed his hands into his pockets and smirked. "We're cool."

"Yeah, it's cool," I agreed. "I'm feeling better now, I think."

"Good. Come on." Allegra grabbed my arm and marched me back inside, where the halls were bustling in between periods. "I'm so sorry I started you with Jill's shit. No more, okay? No more for either of us. Are you really okay?"

"Yeah," I said.

"Jesus, you really did scare me." She paused. "Also, what were you and Caleb Crown talking about?"

I shook my head. "Nothing. He was helping me calm down."

She glanced behind us. "He's trouble, you know. He's, like, a druggie."

I laughed. "So are we."

"Ugh, not like him. Just, don't mess with him." She crossed her arms and bit her lip.

After school, I was crossing the parking lot when I heard my name being called; I turned to face the boy from earlier. His floppy black hair crossed over his eyes, so he had to constantly tilt his face and peer out from under his long bangs. With the sun in his face, I could see his eyes were a golden brown.

"Forget something?" He tossed the bottle to me.

I caught it, surprising even myself. I rattled the little blue pills inside. "I don't want these." I tossed it back, and he snatched it midair.

"That's fine. So what, you smoke?"

I set my teeth and shook my head. "No."

"Suit yourself." Then he was gone. As he walked away, I kicked myself. I thought he would press harder, to be honest—try and convince me so I could at least feel good about initially resisting when I finally gave in. Because no, I didn't smoke, but for some inexplicable reason, I wanted to keep talking to this boy. Maybe because he broke rules and I never had before; by proximity I could rebel without actually having to. But as I watched his leather jacket disappear through the cars, I was afraid I had lost my chance to change my life's course.

So I drove home—to homework and church and going to bed early to do it all again.

Chapter 13

The memorial is downtown, and I decide to order an Uber to avoid dealing with parking on a Saturday. When I arrive at the Rainier Club, a doorman escorts me into the grand brick building. The social club is nestled in between shinier and flashier new construction, but as soon as I enter, it feels like I'm in an exclusive space. I'm directed to a room with tall coffered ceilings and arched windows interspersed with walls painted a deep marigold yellow. A bar is set up near the oversize fireplace, and the room is full of people chatting and laughing; it seems less like a somber gathering and more like a party. Just like Landon would have wanted, I guess.

A staff member offers to take my trench coat, but I kindly shake my head. I need it as a comfortable cover for the little black dress and tights I'm wearing.

I wander a bit and see some familiar faces. I'm not there long before Greg finds me. "What are you drinking?"

"I'm not."

Greg raises an eyebrow. "I convinced the firm to budget in the open bar, so please order something."

"I'm not really a drinker," I say. "Despite what you saw on Wednesday." I feel my face turn warm—no alcohol necessary. "Besides, is an open bar appropriate? It's not a wedding reception."

"People are sad, Bea. Booze helps sadness."

I look at Greg's outfit, gray pants and a blue cashmere sweater; looking around, I notice more color than not. My black dress seems dramatic all of a sudden. I wrap my brown trench a little tighter around me. Greg notices. "Why did you dress hotter for a memorial than you ever have for work?"

"What do you mean? I thought people were going to be dressing in black . . ."

"It's not the funeral. And there's dressing in black, and there's dressing in a short black dress with those high heels. Don't make that face. You've got a nerdy uptight librarian thing happening." He shrugs. "Not everyone's bag, but I'm into it."

"Wow. This is so respectful of the dead." Through the crowd, I recognize a face. "Hey, are there Saul Group attorneys here?" I ask.

"I'm sure. Most of the big Seattle firms are represented. Landon was well liked."

"Uh-huh. I have to go say hi to someone."

I approach the woman I recognize. "Hi, Amy!"

"Bea!" Despite the formal surroundings, Amy is dressed casually in comparison. She has on dark-blue jeans and an untucked white button-up, paired with black high heels and a very Parisian red lip against an otherwise bare face. Her blond hair is pulled back into a ponytail. I didn't remember her being so pretty.

She gives me a hug. "I'm happy to see you after all these years, but sad it has to be under these circumstances." She motions toward an empty high-top near the fireplace; I follow. "I was surprised to get your message the other day. Are you really thinking of leaving BCC?"

"Well, I'm not so sure now."

"Of course. I can't imagine what it's like over there at BCC right now or how your team is coping." She raises her hand in the air suddenly, as if she's remembered something. "And Granite! Jesus, are they raising hell? The talk around Saul Group is that Landon single-handedly poached them from us; they must be really regretting their decision to jump ship about now."

I bite my tongue so hard I can taste a tinge of coppery blood fill my mouth. "Well, it wasn't single-handedly Landon. We all worked hard on that pitch."

"Oh sure, that's not what I meant." She sips her red wine. "I really was happy to hear from you. We did hang out in law school sometimes, so I actually don't know why it's taken us so long to connect. I meant to reply to you when I got your message, but I'd just finished a hellish trial. And then when I saw the news about Landon . . . You probably don't want to talk about this, but I can't believe it."

"It's really sad," I say. "Did you know him?"

"Kind of. He and Saul had this weird mentor-mentee rivalry happening, so I met him a couple times professionally. You were on his team—what do you think of him? What do you think happened? The rumors are pretty wild . . . People are saying he was killed."

"Did you say Saul was Landon's mentor?"

"Yeah, I'm not sure how exactly, only that they've known each other forever. Or . . . knew each other."

We fall quiet, and I gaze into the small tea light candle that's been set out on the table. Amy sees me, and she holds her palm open over the tiny flame. A spark of a memory unlocks. "My friends and I used to play that game," I say. "See how long you could hold your hand open over a lighter."

Amy withdraws her hand, wincing with a smile. "My sister and I were always playing with candles," she said. "We would be in the basement with those long candles you would set out at Thanksgiving, just lighting them and playing with the wax. I think all kids are fascinated with fire."

I laugh. "Oh no, this was when I was like seventeen! This was after we'd lit up our joints, of course."

She claps her hands. "Amazing." She frowns and points. "Do you know that guy?" I follow and see Greg smiling and approaching, each hand holding a martini.

"Sadly, yes."

"Hello," Greg says. "Gregory Farrell." He hands me one of the martinis. "Are you a friend of Bea's? I'm her colleague at BCC. Bea, why are you gatekeeping your cute friends?"

"Law school friends. University of Oregon Law."

Greg does an air fist pump. "Go Ducks. Love your football team."

"That's right. Don't usually get that reaction in Washington Husky territory." Amy smiles.

"Eh, I'm a Loyola man," Greg says. I take a long sip of my drink. "We don't get to have cool football mascots. But had to go for the legacy. If you'd told me I would grow up to be a lawyer like my dad, I would have laughed at you. But you know how it goes. All the guidance counselors begin to get in your head about the stability of a law degree, then your college advisers give you the sales pitch, and all your parents' friends are promising letters of rec and jobs out of the gate too. It's hard to say no, right?"

Hard to say no to the cheat codes that get you ahead.

Our trio continues to chat about movies, traffic, and Greg's CrossFit routine until Amy says she has to go. "Anyway, Bea," she says. "When we're not at a memorial, we should catch up."

"I would like that," I say.

Greg leans down to me. "If I were Marnell, I would not have left the Saul Group as long as she was working there."

"Ew, Greg. And Granite left because of Landon. That's what Amy said."

He puffs his chest out, and his chin juts forward. "Uh, not just Landon!" Several heads turn our way. Greg coughs. "God rest him . . ." He continues at a lower volume. "I mean, despite all Landon's bullshit, you're a damn good attorney, Bea. You know everything there is to know and can school anyone, even the partners. I know this because you constantly talk about the law and have all the answers to everything. But you never talk about yourself? Why is that?"

Greg looks at me strangely now while twirling the toothpick in his martini, spearing his olives. He's not grinning or even judging, that I can tell. Could it be genuine interest in what I have to say? I shake my head, which feels fuzzy. It must be the extra Xanax with this martini.

"I don't talk about myself because . . ." I breathe, feeling my heart beating hard. "Remember? I'm just not that interesting."

Greg shakes his head. "I don't believe that for one second. Maybe before I might have. But the way you walked into Solo and laid into Landon?

Jesus, I would have never thought you would be the one to do something like that. And then when you did?" He let out a laugh. "I don't think Landon is used to women standing up to him. I mean, *was* used to . . . shit."

"This feels weird. Us here, kind of talking shit at his memorial." I pause.

"Yeah. Makes you want to appreciate things, right? You never know . . ."

"Do you know if that detective found out anything about the, ah, circumstances?"

He shakes his head. "Not unless you know anything else."

My heart drops. "What does that mean?"

"Look, I saw you and that girl leave with Landon."

"We gave him a ride because he was wasted."

"Don't get defensive with me—only letting you know," Greg says, measured. "If you need to talk to anyone about anything, I'm here for you, yeah? Like I said back at Solo, I can take care of you." He winks. My stomach turns.

Despite my initial revulsion, I want to crumble. I want to tell him yes and confess everything, to tell him I'm not sure what happened but I can't shake the awful feeling that something *did* happen. After all, Greg is a lawyer, a good one, and he probably knows really good criminal lawyers who could clear up this whole misunderstanding. But there's one thing that holds me back from spilling it all to Greg. I don't trust him one goddamn bit.

Somehow we stay at the memorial all afternoon, and I don't leave Greg's side. I don't even want to; he's being witty and kind. He gets me another martini. Time moves like liquid.

At some point, speeches begin, and there are real tears and real emotions. I actually find some of the stories about my deceased boss amusing, maybe even endearing.

After all, I remember, he was a real person.

Who is gone.

Because of me.

It's dark by the time everyone is dispersing. "Can I walk you to your car?" Greg asks.

"I took an Uber here," I say. "But thanks."

"I'll give you a ride home," offers Greg. My feet hurt from my heels, and my rideshare app tells me it's going to be a ten-minute wait and surge pricing on a Saturday evening.

"Okay," I agree.

We drive in silence.

I stare out the window and pretend not to notice Greg's glances toward me, like he's trying to start a conversation. Finally he speaks. "I know I was giving you shit about it earlier, but that dress really looks nice on you."

I smooth my palms over my thighs, stretching the dress hem down. "Oh. Thanks." I continue looking out the window. Is Greg trying to flirt with me while driving me home from Landon's memorial? We pass by a restaurant, and Greg mentions it's good, then proceeds to talk about his favorite spots in town. "Where's your favorite place to eat?" he asks. I answer, and I relax a bit, because this is a Greg that also seems relaxed and, dare I say it, normal. He's not puffing out his chest with bravado or trying to speak over everyone else in the room. He's asking me questions and then actually listening. We're having a real conversation. I look over and laugh at a joke he tells, and he smiles back.

When we get to my house, I open the car door and step out onto my driveway while he runs around the car. "Hey, I was going to open that for you," he says.

"Sorry." Not sorry. I pull my jacket close and step back toward my house, creating distance between us. "Well, that was something. Thank you for the ride. Anyway, I guess I'll see you on Monday?" I don't really mean it to be a question, but my voice ends in a high note. It's the opening Greg needs. He reaches out and grabs my arm, pulling me toward him.

"Why wait until Monday? Tonight doesn't have to end yet."

I resist and pull back. "I'm kind of tired."

"Want to invite me in for a nightcap?" Greg thinks I'm playing a sexy game of tug-of-war and yanks me hard against him; I fall against his chest. I instantly push away and hold my palms up toward him.

"Stop," I say. Any trace of the warmth of our earlier car conversation disappears, and my defenses spike. "Look, I'm not into you like that. I'm sorry."

In the dim light of the streetlamps and the edge of where my porch light's perimeter extends, I watch Greg's eyes flash with confusion. "But I drove you home."

"Yeah, from our boss's memorial service, Greg. What were you actually thinking would happen?"

In an instant, he changes. "Well, they were right about you, then. You're a cold bitch."

I want to hit him. I want to scream at him and tell him, *I don't owe you anything. I do not have time for your toxic male fragility at the moment.*

Instead, I say nothing. I walk away and ignore him. And it turns out this is the worst thing I, a woman, can do to him.

"Who do you think you are?" he yells. "Get back here."

I don't turn, but instead close my eyes and brace for a blow, or a grasp, or anything else this slightly intoxicated angry male might choose to do in this moment. I feel a firm grip on my shoulder . . .

Then I hear the front door to my house open and a familiar voice call out, "What do you think you're doing?"

When I open my eyes, Mom is standing on our porch in all her glory—fuzzy robe, matching slippers, hair up in a scrunchie, arms crossed—and there's no mistaking her face: she's pissed. In another world, I might be mortified, but right now, I've never been happier to see her. The fuzzy robe is a bonus. "He was just leaving, Mom," I say. Glancing over my shoulder, I see Greg as confused as ever.

"You live with your mom?" he says.

I look back at Mom, and her eyes are wide, eyebrows raised. She takes one step, then two, down the porch steps. *Oh,* I think, *you've done it now.*

Greg clearly doesn't know what's about to happen. He stands defiantly as the small, barely five-foot older woman approaches him, his hand still on me. She walks straight up to him until her nose is almost touching his chest. Then she puffs up her own chest, standing tall, and looks up into his face. I don't have to see her eyes to know the look. Greg sees it for himself and, wisely, takes a step back, still holding on to my shoulder.

"Okay, Mr. Fancy-Ass Lawyer Guy," Mom says. Her voice is eerily calm.

Greg looks to me and mouths, *What the fuck?* I shrug. *You did this,* I think. *There's nothing I can do for you now.*

"Get your hands off my daughter," Mom says. When Greg doesn't move, Mom asks, "Sorry, is my English not good? Get your fucking hands off my daughter right now."

Greg releases me and spits on the ground at our feet. "Screw this."

Mom stands in the driveway with her arms crossed and watches until his car disappears around the corner.

"Are you hungry?" she asks. "I saved a plate of dinner for you."

"No, thanks."

Inside, the TV is paused on a Netflix K drama, and a blanket is on the couch. "I don't know why you have to always associate yourself with the worst kind of people, Bea."

I balk. "What?"

"Ever since you were a kid, you've found the troublemakers. What's wrong with you?"

"Good night, Mom."

She follows me, determined to continue. "You always have so much potential, and you don't know what to do other than waste it! What would have happened if I didn't come outside now?"

"I was handling it," I lie.

"I don't know if I can handle you making the same mistakes at this age—you're a grown woman! After tonight and the way you came home Wednesday—"

"How did I come home on Wednesday?" I ask.

The argument has woken Dad, and he groggily comes into the hallway. "What's going on?"

"Tell her," says Mom. "Tell her how we won't stand for her dragging us all down again."

Dad holds his hands up. "Hold on. Let's not get carried away."

"What was I like Wednesday night?" I ask again.

Mom holds her hands to her head and rolls her eyes to the heavens. "Oh Lord, she doesn't even remember!"

Dad scratches his chest. "Uh, you couldn't really use your key to unlock the door, so you kind of pounded on it until we woke up and let you in. It was really late. You seemed pretty, well, drunk."

"Is that all?" I confirm.

"Isn't that enough?" Dad furrows his brow. "And can we all talk about this tomorrow? Please?"

Mom begins muttering to herself in Tagalog and goes back into the bedroom. Dad walks out to the living room and turns off the TV and lights. "Give your mom a break, huh, Buzz? She has a reason to be worried about these new people you seem to be hanging out with lately."

I take off my heels and stretch my feet out flat on the cool wood floor. "I don't hang out with Greg. Wait, 'these new people'? Who else does she mean?"

Dad yawns. "The girl who dropped you off Wednesday night. She didn't even wait around to see if you were okay, according to the Ring doorbell. Practically dragged you out of her car and left you on the porch."

I feel myself tremble. "Dad," I say. "I have to see that video."

Chapter 14

The video is pixelated and grayscale, and the time stamp says 3:00 a.m. But it's her—there's no mistaking it. A car pulls into the driveway, and I can see my head slumped over in the passenger seat. A figure comes around and opens the front passenger door, then quickly squats to catch me as I nearly fall out of my seat. I look like I laugh and then hold on to the figure as I stand. It's strange looking at this video of me doing things I can't remember.

The figure turns toward the door, and I see a woman who looks a lot like Kelli. Whose car is that? Was she driving? She helps me stumble to the doorstep, and I sit down on the porch and fumble in my bag for my keys. I wave her away.

Turning up the volume, I hear nothing but our giggling and gibberish. "Are you okay?" she asks.

"I'm fine!" I reply. Then she waves goodbye and walks out of view. The car backs away, and the lights disappear. I continue looking through my bag until the camera times out.

Weird. I don't seem upset in any way in the video. And nobody is acting like we just witnessed a death.

As I lie on my made bed now, the video replays over and over in my mind, and the more I think of it, the more I know I'm missing something. Kelli isn't telling me the whole story. Why would I attack Landon?

I lie back and stare at the ceiling, rubbing my arm on the space still burning where Greg put his hands on me, not far off from where Landon also laid his claim to my skin. Their entitlement was almost as frightening as the looks in their eyes. But with Greg it was different; I didn't see it coming with him. I worked with him every day and never saw it.

I don't know what I would have done if Mom hadn't come out when she did. A frightening thought crosses my mind, though. What if Landon, intoxicated, tried something with me? What if, like Greg, he didn't want to listen to a no? Would I have fought to stop him? And if I wasn't in my right mind, would I have been happy to sit and watch him overdose?

I shower to wash Greg's cologne out of my nostrils.

Back at my computer, a message pops up.

It's from Simon, some work thing. "Why are you still awake, nerd?" I mutter out loud. As soon as I say the words, an instant message comes through. Also from Simon. It reads, hey nerd, why are you working this late?

I can't help but laugh out loud. Damn, I forgot my online indicator was on and showing green.

I was thinking the same about you, I write back.

Look at us overachievers.

I'm not responding to your email right now.

Plz dont. I'm signing off. But if you read it and have thoughts you can text @ the number on my sig line.

I scroll down to his name and number. Simon Woodward. I read the message again and wonder if I'm misinterpreting, or if he was inviting me to text him about nonwork things too? I put the number into my phone and then simply thumbs-up his message. Then I sign off. He's cute, sure, but I'm not in the mood right now. Not after Greg. Not after Landon.

I lie back, and my mind drifts to a time when I might have wanted to pursue something with Simon. Or anyone, for that matter. I haven't had a crush in years, a decade or more. And that crush? It ruined my life and the lives of everyone around me.

◆ ◆ ◆

After an especially bad night out, Mom came to get me from the city jail. She arrived at almost four in the morning in jeans, a pressed blouse, and a jacket, her hair and makeup done. She had made sure to make herself presentable before bailing out her delinquent child. Her seventeen-year-old daughter had been lying on a concrete bench after being in the vicinity of some kids accused of attempting to rob a gas station.

"What's wrong with you?" she demanded when we arrived home.

"It was a mistake. I wasn't doing anything!"

"Those hoodlums are troublemakers, and they're turning you into a criminal, just like them!"

I laughed right in her face to show her I didn't care. "Hoodlums? Are we in the fifties?"

"Say something to your daughter," she screamed at Dad.

Dad sat sullen at the kitchen table. "You smell like pot" was all he had to add.

I spread my arms wide. "They're my friends. They understand me, unlike you."

"They're a bad influence. Especially that punk boy."

"Caleb? He's not a punk boy. He listens to me more than either of you ever has. My friends care more about me than my own family."

"Is that why, when they got caught stealing, they ran and left you at a 7-Eleven to get picked up by the cops?"

"Whatever," I mumbled, fleeing to my room. I immediately stuck my hands underneath my bed and gasped. I stomped back into the living room, looking for a fight. "Where is it?" I demanded. "Give it back!"

"This is the reason you're getting into all this trouble, isn't it?" Dad had revealed the small bag of joints sitting on the table in front of him. "How long has this been going on? Did Caleb give this to you?"

"How dare you go through my room," I hissed. "You don't understand—"

"I should take you right back to the police," Mom threatened.

The fights went on and on, always the same.

My parents prayed for my deliverance while also paying court fees and the therapist's bills, only to receive a report confirming I was merely a "well-adjusted teenager with a rebellious streak." I would read it aloud to Caleb, sitting on his bed and getting high. I wasn't being dramatic—Caleb did understand me more than anyone. Even more than Allegra at that time, who had taken to being my second mother, always scolding me when Caleb came around.

He was a place to escape. I remember him lying on his back on his bedroom floor, one hand behind his head of messy black hair and the other holding a hand-rolled joint. He was always telling a joke or singing a song—anything to make me smile, he said. "I like you best when you're happy," he told me.

We never touched each other. I didn't know that I wanted him to touch me anyway. For a time, Caleb was the most important person in my life. Why would we mess up such a good thing with sex? The rumors and the hype couldn't be real, I thought, even as I stared at his golden-brown eyes through the wisps of smoke. Sex couldn't be as good as what we had now, the openness and the trust of "just friends."

Looking back now, I know it was love. But what could I do? I was only a girl, and the threshold of womanhood was imminent, a precipice I couldn't bring myself to face.

I was seventeen years old and terrified to death of the rest of my life.

Chapter 15

Monday

My phone buzzes, and I'm surprised to see it's Amy. Nice chatting over the wknd. Let's definitely get together for lunch.

I reply, today work? Happy to meet you at yours.

While the BCC office projects a modern law firm—light and airy, all glass doors and cream upholstery—Saul Group represents the old guard. The lobby is impressively massive, with dark wood and bronze lighting fixtures. The receptionist sits behind an impossibly tall oak desk; I almost expect her to ask for my bank account number and inquire if I'd like to make a deposit or withdrawal. Instead, I ask for Amy Carren, and she asks me to sit and wait on the worn leather couch. There are no windows in this cavern of jurisprudence.

"Bea, I'm so glad you're here!" We share a hug.

"Thanks for being available on such short notice. So what are you thinking for lunch?"

We choose a salad place in the building and catch up over chopped kale. After the usual updates about ourselves and mutual friends, we take a few bites in an awkward stillness, the sounds of the workday lunch around us. "Speaking of your team, you know what's funny?" Amy says, her voice and demeanor hesitant. "That Greg guy messaged me on Saturday night."

I almost choke on a tomato. "What? Greg? I didn't know you guys exchanged numbers. What did it say?"

"You'll die." She begins to laugh and holds up two fingers. "Two words. 'You up?'"

"Stop. Did you reply?"

"Not joking. And hell no! I was asleep and saw it in the morning anyway. I would bet you money he was out on some date and got cockblocked and so he was fishing for anything he could get at that point."

"I bet it was something like that," I say.

She laughs. "I'm so done with drama, you get me? I'm too old for these boys and their ego Olympics."

"Agreed. So remember when I was asking about opportunities at Saul Group?" I ask.

"Oh?" she says, surprised. "Are you still considering making a move?"

"Maybe not in the near future, but I always like to know what's out there. Any way I can take a quick tour upstairs?" It's a feeble attempt, and I'm already formulating another move to keep Amy with me.

To my surprise, she agrees heartily. "Sure thing, I love showing off our offices. The vibe is so old money—it makes me sick in the best way."

Amy isn't joking. She walks me through the oak-paneled halls and points out notable attorneys who hide behind heavy doors with their names on plaques.

Busts of old white men pop up in corners to frighten unsuspecting passersby. I keep track of all the offices we pass, and none of the plaques say "Franklin Saul," but his office wouldn't be down with the plebes anyway; surely it's on an exclusive floor that Amy doesn't have access to, let alone the ability to show visitors.

We pass associates and staff, all of whom wave politely or nod. "Which department is Kelli in?" I ask.

Amy shakes her head. "I'm not sure I know a Kelli here. What's her last name?"

"Stewart."

"Sorry, this place is so big, and new people join all the time. Here's the best room in the joint now."

She opens the door to a conference room, and I peek in, then gasp. It's the first room I've seen with proper windows, and what a view it has. "This is our premier conference room. This is where we used to have meetings with Granite." The floor-to-ceiling windows overlook the glistening gray waters of Puget Sound. I watch the water taxi cutting through the waves on its way to West Seattle, and the ferries docked on the piers. Even BCC can't boast a view like this. It's a shame only the richest people in Seattle, and those who work for them, ever see it.

Against one wall, an array of framed articles is displayed. I wander over and look. A feature on Saul from the *Seattle Times*, a puff piece on the firm for its tenth anniversary, and then at the bottom of the collage, a piece with the headline LAWSUIT FILED BY VALENCIA SURVIVORS DISMISSED.

The photo accompanying the headline shows a young Franklin Saul with the caption "Seattle attorney Franklin Saul and his team were behind the defense's skillful argument in getting the case dismissed." What catches my eye isn't the youthful Saul in the photo, no doubt pontificating about something brilliant to the judge, but one of the figures in the rows of courtroom seats behind him. I snap a photo of the article.

Amy joins me. "Amazing, right?" She holds her hands up toward the dizzying view.

"Almost unbelievable," I say. "Hey, can I ask you something? Is this . . . ?" I point to the face in the picture.

Amy gasps. "Oh, look at that. Wow, all the times I've looked at this article, and I never even knew Landon Laurie was in this photo. Kind of eerie now, don't you think?"

"So he used to work for Saul Group?"

"At the time it wouldn't have been Saul Group," Amy says. "I think Saul was a solo practitioner at that time, and Landon must have been an intern."

The door opens again, and a woman walks in, talking on her phone before spotting us. "Sorry, the room is reserved for a one-thirty meeting for Mr. Saul."

"No worries, Karolina, we're only looking," says Amy. "Leaving now."

"Mr. Saul is coming in right now?" I glance at my phone, noting the time.

"Well, not while you're here." Karolina rolls her eyes.

Amy ushers me into the hall, and we're closely followed by an irritated Karolina. I watch her go down the hall, where she meets an older man slowly sauntering through. He looks almost ancient.

"Is that Saul?" I ask Amy.

She nods. "In the flesh."

At an invisible signal from Saul, Karolina takes something from her jacket pocket and gives it to him. Is it—an orange pill bottle? Saul nods slightly and then tucks the bottle into the inside of his own jacket.

I follow Amy back to her office, humbled by the rest of the office standards.

"What's Saul like?" I ask. "And was that his assistant or something?"

"I don't know him very well, but he's pretty much a legal genius. He may look feeble, but he's formidable. Any attorney in the city would do anything to avoid going up against him. And that was Karolina. She's his personal assistant," Amy scoffs. "But more like a girlfriend." She lowers her voice and cringes. "Rumor is they stay late and do it right here in the office."

My eyes go wide. "Seriously?" I press my lips together to keep from bursting into laughter. "But did I see her just hand him some pills?"

"Yeah, I think he has a heart condition. All I know is one time I was at a meeting where he had some kind of heart issue, a palpitation or something, and Karolina had to give him this medication to stop it. He's never without it now. Apparently, without the medication, his heart could just stop at any moment. It's really scary."

"No kidding." I pause for a beat. I remember when Dad started complaining of chest pains when I was in college; it took Mom and me months to get him to go to a cardiologist. The doctor prescribed him medication and told him to limit his stress. Another reason for me to clean up my act—I felt as though my behavior was literally killing my parents, and now I had the diagnosis to prove it. "My dad takes heart meds too," I say. "What does Saul take?"

Amy looks at me. "Uh, no idea. Beta-blockers, I guess?"

I nod. "Right. But maybe if he weren't engaging in such exciting extracurricular activities, he wouldn't need the pills?"

Amy only raises her eyebrows and grins. We talk a little more about people in common, and we make plans to not let it be so long before we meet up again.

As I return to the office, I step out of the elevator to see Detective Branson sitting in the lobby. I walk past her without looking and without a word, and wait until I'm safely in my office.

My chest is tight, and I can barely breathe. What is she here for?

Chapter 16

I text Kelli. The detective is sitting in BCC's lobby.

She responds quickly, Really? Why do you think she's there?

No idea. What should I do?

Nothing!

I type back several responses, all different stages of freaking out, but delete each one. Finally, I see the typing bubbles appear, and a new message from Kelli arrives.

Actually, you can do something. Come over for dinner. We can talk then.

To be honest, the last thing I want to do is hang out with Kelli, but in a weird way, she might be the only person I can really be honest with right now. An evening without lying might be nice for a change. I give her invitation a thumbs-up.

In my inbox, I see a couple of new emails from Simon. He did say to message him anytime . . . I text Simon, any chance we can work at your office today?

He responds in seconds with a nearby address.

When I leave through the lobby again, the detective is gone.

I approach Simon's address, but the building I'm in front of looks more like a plain brick apartment building than a fancy tech company's office; only the modest plaque on the door informs me I'm at the right place to find Granite Holdings. Simon is waiting for me inside.

"This place is amazing," I say.

He smiles. "Welcome. This was built in the 1930s as a boardinghouse. It was due to be demolished, but Granite bought it and renovated it. Fun, right?"

Fun is the understatement of the day. In complete contrast to the humble facade outside, the inside is a fusion of traditional and ultramodern design. Exposed-brick wall surrounds us up until what would have been the second floor; then modern white walls continue up to a steel-beam ceiling featuring large Sputnik-style lighting fixtures. A floating staircase leads to a workspace, I assume, since I can hear a quiet buzz of workplace activity coming from above. Around us, a few employees sit at tables on brightly colored pouf stools, typing away at laptops or heads down over iPads. If the decor at BCC reflects law firm gravitas, the Granite interior design is Seattle tech to a tee.

"Where's the Ping-Pong tables?" I ask, joking.

Simon points up. "Fifth floor next to the beer taps."

I blink. "You're serious."

Simon motions up the stairs, and we climb to the second floor. Indeed, there's an open space with tables and workstations populated by the Granite staff. Around the perimeter are offices with the dreaded glass doors. "They kept most of the original boarding rooms and made them into offices," Simon explains. "Some of them even have random piping left running through, for aesthetics. The best is the corner office on the third floor. It was one of the few rooms in the building that had a private bathroom. Most people living here had to use a communal bathroom in the common space. When they were demoing, that room had a cast-iron clawfoot tub in the bathroom. It weighed over four hundred pounds, so they were trying to figure out how to get it out without damaging anything. Then one of the execs saw it and decided she liked it, asked them to leave it. She uses it as a place to put all her plants now."

We stop at a desk in the middle of the open floor. "This is my humble abode," Simon says. He scratches his neck and looks down. "I don't have a fancy office like you or anything." He shuffles some papers and folders to make room for my things. He finds a chair for me and pulls it over.

"This is fine." I sit and begin taking my laptop and files out.

My phone buzzes, and it's a text from Olivia. Where are you? Detective Branson is here and has more questions for people.

I respond: Working at Granite this afternoon. Easier to interface with Granite analysts this way.

I put my phone face down. "More than fine," I say. "I didn't want to be in my fancy office, remember? It's suffocating. Thank you for being okay working here."

Simon and I get into our reviews and are in the thick of our analysis. He's easy to work with, and for the first time in days, I forget about the turmoil in my life. We work, but also talk and joke; I don't look at my phone or worry about texts or other work emails, and I don't have to worry about any of my coworkers or law enforcement appearing unannounced.

The afternoon and evening fly by; I don't even notice his coworkers slowly disappearing or the light fading into night outside. My reverie of work and Simon finally breaks when we're interrupted.

"What do we have here?"

"Hi, Mr. Marnell," says Simon. "I think you know Bea Ku from BCC?"

I freeze. I haven't seen Marnell since I ran into him, literally, and I don't know what he knows about Landon and all that's happened since. "Hi again," I say. "How are you?"

"Good," he says. "They have you on due diligence for the acquisition project, is that right?"

I nod. "Yes, and we've made excellent progress today. We can email you what we have so far."

"Please do. I remember what Landon said about you, Ms. Ku—'One of the brightest.' We are all thinking of him and BCC, of course. Horrible times."

I can only smile awkwardly. Bless this man for being normal and not mentioning me running into him like a linebacker, and then actually complimenting me to boot. But I put on the appropriate face. Marnell nods solemnly and excuses himself. "Don't stay too late," he calls to us.

"I feel awful," says Simon. "I forgot about that whole thing. I haven't even asked how you are. You worked really closely with him, right?"

I nod. "I'm fine, thanks."

"The whole thing is so bizarre." Simon taps a pen on the table. "Look, it's been a long day. Let's email our report for the day and get out of here. Up for a happy hour?"

◆ ◆ ◆

"I kind of thought you'd take me up to the fifth-floor office kegerator," I joke.

Simon laughs. "Those are cool when HR is giving new people tours or when I'm trying to impress visitors. But who wants to stay at work and drink when you've been there all day?"

We're at a cantina down the block; I'm thankful not to be questioned when I opt for a dark back booth instead of a prime high-top by the windows or even a spot at the bar. Now that we're back in public, in the open, I'm back on defense—a paranoid head on a swivel and my eyes snapping to the front each time I hear the door open.

The waitress sets down our margaritas and nacho platter between us.

"So do you like being a lawyer?" Simon asks, piling sour cream, cheese, and pulled pork onto a chip.

"I used to," I say. "I liked law school. But that's a different thing. Practicing law is like signing up to have impostor syndrome every day of your life."

"I thought they debunked that."

"So I have impostor syndrome about having impostor syndrome?" I take a long drink and lick the salt around the glass rim.

Simon laughs. "But your family must be proud of you. Your family, friends . . . boyfriend?"

I grin at the obvious fishing attempt. "My parents are proud, sure. I don't have a boyfriend."

"Did you break up because you worked too much or something?"

"I haven't been in a relationship in a long time, and I haven't been in a serious one, like, ever. I don't even have friends really . . ." Is it weird of me to want to tell him the truth? "I live with my parents."

He stops mid chew. "Huh," he mumbles.

"But it's because I was kind of a nightmare when I was younger and they had to take care of me a lot. So now I help take care of them."

"Do they have health problems, or . . . ?"

"Nothing like that. It's just they wouldn't know how to live without me."

"That's all good, then," he says. "As long as it's not the other way round, right?"

I marvel at this guy across from me. His complete lack of pretense disarms me. "No, no. It's all good."

"Let me know if this is totally inappropriate," he says. "Could I take you out sometime?"

I'm caught off guard. "Really?" I sputter. "I mean, sure."

"What about Saturday afternoon? I think the weather will be nice. We can check out the waterfront downtown."

I nod. "Saturday is perfect."

"Great, is there any food you like or places—"

"Shit, no, I'm sorry. Saturday actually won't work. I have this baby shower thing my family is hosting. Would Thursday work?"

"Thursday, then. Date night, Thursday." He chuckles awkwardly. "Nice of your family to host. The baby shower."

I laugh. "I guess. It's for an old high school friend."

"So you do have friends."

"I guess you're right. But Allegra is more like a friend because we've been through too much together. Our families are friends, and I can't get rid of her at this point."

He smirks. "She knows where the bodies are buried."

I swallow wrong and cough as my own spit goes down the wrong tube. I choke and emit a very unladylike dry heave. Feeling my cheeks redden even more than they already had from the Asian glow, I hold up a chip to block Simon from my view.

"Are you okay? Need water or . . . Excuse me," he says. "Are you trying to hide behind a nacho?"

This makes me laugh even harder. "Yes," I admit. "Is it working?"

"Not at all. Who are you?" I lower the chip and see Simon shaking his head. "Do your coworkers know you're this weird?"

"They have no idea." I compose myself. "I would say nobody has ever taken the time to talk to me like you are now. But maybe that's not true. Maybe people have tried, but I've never let them in before."

"Why are you letting me in now?"

"I don't know," I say truthfully. The honesty feels good. He looks at me, and his green eyes are deep forest pools that I find myself reflected in, but lost within at the same time. "I don't want to hide from you."

It's a silly thing to say, but he keeps his gaze steady and looks at me as if I've said the most profound thing in human history. The table between us, littered with chips and napkins, feels both small and, also, like a great distance I want to cross. Though maybe it's best; I'm terrified of what might happen next if we were close enough to touch.

After the bill is paid and it's long past an acceptable time for a happy hour to end, Simon and I walk out of the cantina. I call an Uber, and he waits until I'm safely in my ride. I'm not even one block away before he texts me, that was a fun night.

Chapter 17

Tuesday

Allegra doesn't live far from us, but it feels a world apart. A mile or so south, toward downtown Seattle, we leave our neighborhood—filled with split-levels and ramblers and winding roads without sidewalks—and find ourselves in tree-lined blocks with sidewalks and little fluorescent-green traffic signs that say **DRIVE LIKE YOUR KIDS LIVE HERE.**

After Allegra started college at the University of Washington, her parents moved permanently to the Philippines, basically gifting her their house to live in. Maybe most young adults would have been annoyed to have to stay in their childhood home, but I think Allegra didn't mind. Certainly now, in the current market, looking back, she realizes she didn't know how fortunate she was.

Mom and I pull up to her tan Craftsman home with a wildflower garden in the front—"For the pollinators," she once explained to me. Mom pushes the Ring doorbell and sticks her face in front of the camera and waves. "We're heeere!"

I hold my box of centerpiece-making supplies and dread going inside. I hate visiting Allegra's house. I can't remember the last time I've even been here. And now, with everything happening, this seems like a waste of my time. Though I don't actually know what I should be doing instead.

"Welcome!" Allegra answers the door. "Come in, come in!"

In the entranceway, there are a few pairs of men's shoes and a men's jacket hanging from the coatrack. Caleb is everywhere and nowhere in this house.

She ushers us in and herds us to the dining room, where a group of women is already gathered. *Great,* I think. I'm irritated I wasn't informed there would be more than Mom, me, and Allegra.

I set down my box of supplies. Allegra looks in. "Oh, you found the little tea light holders. I'm so glad. And all these little river rocks!" She hugs me. "Thank you for doing this," she says.

"Sure." I stiffen in her embrace, but remember Mom's words. "This is a special time for you, and I'm happy to help celebrate."

Allegra places her palm on her chest, and her eyes widen. "Where is Bea, and what have you done with her?" she jokes.

I give a thin smile and look around at the group of faces. A couple of women I recognize from church, but I don't know the rest.

"Just us ladies," Allegra says, winking.

"Ah, got it."

"Now take this—it's our weapon of choice today." Allegra hands me a glue gun. I take a seat next to Mom.

"Bea," she says. "You remember Tita Lindy and Tita Rosie from church."

"Of course. Hi, Aunties, nice to see you." Despite the honorific, these women are not related to me.

"Bea was promoted!" Mom says proudly as I wince.

"Congratulations!" one of the aunties says. "Where do you work?"

"A law firm," I say. "Bellingham, Charles & Chan."

Her lips pull to the side. "That name seems familiar," she says. "I think I hired you guys for something?"

Mom nods and turns to me. "Lindy is a businesswoman." As if that explains it, as if this means Lindy must have a whole stable of lawyers at her disposal.

There's a swift clap, and our attention is pulled to Allegra at the end of the dining table. "Thank you all for being here," she says, cradling her stomach. "Caleb and I are so excited for the shower, and we can't tell you how much we appreciate all your help to make it happen. Especially Tita Miriam and Bea for hosting!"

Golf claps ring out. Allegra makes some more remarks while I speak through my teeth to Mom. "Why are we hosting when their house is ten times nicer than ours?"

"Shh!" Mom hushes me.

Allegra now turns it over to a woman who identifies herself as Anne from work. Anne from work gives a tutorial on how to make "living terrariums" for the baby shower favors we are constructing. She finishes hers in minutes while walking us through it step by step, and the finished product is adorable. It involves filling the round tea light holders with pebbles, then using a glue gun to attach a little clay prepainted red-and-white mushroom to the glass. She's even brought us real baby succulents to plant next to the little mushroom. I'm doubtful mine will turn out as cute and already feel bad for the attendee who gets stuck with a Bea Ku–original terrarium. Anne from work informs us we need to make at least fifty, which seems excessive.

Then we're turned loose.

Within ten minutes, I've burned three of my fingertips with the hot glue. However, I get into a groove, and soon I've even tuned out the loud gossip around me.

"I've got it!" Lindy exclaims. "I know why I know that firm name! It's been on the news—the lawyer who they found overdosed on drugs!"

The other end of the table has heard her, and Anne joins in. "Oh my God, you work there? I hope they're still investigating. This is the problem with white-collar professionals in America: they pretend they are better than us all, but they are the worst—because they know they can get away with it!"

Allegra frowns. "I don't know that was actually what happened, Anne."

Anne folds her arms. "So what happened then?" She turns to me. Everyone turns to me.

"I, uh, don't know." I look down again and focus on gluing the dumb tiny mushroom. "I just work there. I didn't really know him or anything . . ."

Landon and Kelli doing lines while I pass out on the couch. Only to wake up a bit later . . . "You attacked him, Bea."

"Shit!" I pull back my hand and drop the glue gun. I go to the sink and run the cold water over my bright-red palm, where a burning drop of glue dripped on me. I look up in the window above the sink at my own reflection; in the old cylinder glass, my face is distorted and wavy. I clench my hands tight.

"Are you all right?" Allegra asks. "Come on, let's find you a Band-Aid."

In her bathroom, I sit on the edge of the bathtub while she fishes through the medicine cabinet. "I'm sorry about them."

"Why would they ask me if I saw anything? Like, how would I know he had a coke problem?"

She pulls out a Band-Aid and tears it open. "Hand." I hold out my palm, and she sticks on the bandage. "I know he was your boss. It seemed like you two might have had a . . . complicated relationship. But that doesn't mean it's not tragic what happened, and people should be more respectful." She leans against the vanity.

"Thanks," I say. "Funny, I've been thinking about us in high school again lately."

Allegra frowns. "Why?"

"This whole Landon thing. I guess I'm just realizing how life is short, and thinking back, wishing I could redo some things. Well, a lot of things. Remember how dumb we were? We got into some shit, huh?"

"I guess so. Yeah, God, we were idiots."

"Be honest. By *we* you mean—" I point a finger at myself. "Me."

"Maybe. I was no angel, though. Do you remember the time we got caught by security at JCPenney?"

I laugh, even though I know I shouldn't. "Which time? The time we both pretended to cry so hard and the guard was so uncomfortable he told us to go away? Or the time I hid those earrings in my underwear and dared the same guard to search me?"

"What was wrong with us?" She shakes her head and groans. "Some stupid shoplifting was one thing. But, Jesus, I was so angry at Caleb for some of the things he dragged you into." She stops.

The name hangs heavy between us. "I made my own decisions," I say.

She stands in front of me and places her hands on my shoulders. "You're not who you were all those years ago, Bea. And you're not your mistakes. Then or now." She looks at my hand. "Are you okay to continue making teeny-tiny terrariums in honor of my unborn child?"

"I think I'll make it."

Before she opens the door, Allegra pauses and gazes at our reflection in the mirror. "I've read all the articles on Landon, you know. Because you worked with him. And they never said it was cocaine."

I stop cold. "What?"

"They haven't said it was cocaine. Nothing official to the public, anyway, as far as I can tell."

"Oh. I don't even know why I said that."

She smiles. "Oh well. Come on."

◆ ◆ ◆

Mom watches me from the passenger seat on the way home. The night is quiet, black-blue with silver clouds overhead.

"Are you okay?" Mom asks.

"Why wouldn't I be?"

"Your boss's death isn't triggering anything for you, is it? You know, after all—"

"After all, it wouldn't be the first time someone close to me has had something terrible happen to them?"

"Not what I meant."

"I'm fine, Mom." I come to a stop at a red light; we're the only car in the intersection. "I'm leading Granite, I like this cute boy . . . I'm not on Landon's team anymore. It's all the things I wanted, really. So yeah. Never been better."

Mom is silent until the light turns green. "Who's this cute boy?"

"Nobody," I say.

She smirks. "Mm-hmm."

At home, I head to my room, but pause and turn back again in the doorway. I look at Mom, who's unpacking some leftovers and loading up our fridge. "Do you think they're happy?" I ask.

Mom squishes her eyebrows together, her wrinkles and valleys illuminated by the refrigerator's cold glow. "Huh? Allegra and Caleb? Why wouldn't they be?"

"Then why didn't you think I could be happy with him?" My voice nearly gives out.

Her face softens. "Oh, Bea." She closes the fridge and leans a tired arm on the kitchen island. "He was a different person when you were . . . hanging out with him. Afterward, he changed."

"After I almost killed him."

"No, I won't have that talk in here." She sighs. "Allegra was there when you couldn't be. Not because you didn't want to be—because it was better for you both to not be in each other's lives. Do you remember that?"

Of course I remember.

I remember the physical therapy rehab in the hospital for weeks, even though I was long since sober, the drug-and-alcohol substance abuse program I was court ordered to complete after being released from the hospital. In the end, I never returned to high school. I took online GED courses because it was easier with my injuries. But I often wondered if it was because my parents were too ashamed to put me back into private school, even if they could afford it, which they couldn't.

There were so many legal things I didn't understand at the time, like all the lawyers who told me no contact with Caleb Crown was nonnegotiable.

"I remember. Night, Mom." Before I go, I think I see the tears welling up in her eyes. But I don't stay to comfort her. And I don't want her comfort now.

I remember being in law school and finally living a new life, one that felt a million miles away from the one I'd lived in high school. By choice and by necessity, I didn't keep in touch with anyone from then. Even if Allegra made the odd attempt to reach out, which I ignored, there was nothing for me back there.

And then one day it arrived, sealed in an ecru-white envelope, the fancy kind where I could see and feel the fibers in the paper. I opened it and dropped it before I finished reading. It was a wedding invitation. For Allegra and Caleb.

I couldn't fathom it. She hated him, so how could they get married? And he . . . The betrayal knocked me down like a car crash, and I retreated inward for months. I barely graduated law school.

Sometimes I wonder if I was jealous. Maybe a little. I like to think it was less that and more of the fact that I had forgotten that life was going on without me, that the two people I counted on most in the world had found their way to one another in spite of my absence. In fact, they'd thrived in my absence. When they'd told me I was their friend or they loved me, they had been lying the whole time.

Chapter 18

I could still hear the police sirens, even though they were long gone and we were in a deathly quiet hospital room, only the murmurs and hushed tones of nurses and the beeping of my oxygen monitor to be heard. But the wailing of the sirens was deafening in my ears; the scent of burning still clung inside my nose, the sight of the broken glass and his crumpled body buried among it all still vivid.

"Bea, you might have killed him."

"What?" I looked up. Mom was perched on the hospital bed, while Dad stood against the wall. I scratched my head, careful to work around the IV stuck into my veins.

Mom breathed a heavy sigh and shook her head. Tears were about to let loose from her eyes. "They're saying you might have killed him."

I shook my head again, trying to knock the memories free. Why was it so fuzzy? Why couldn't I remember? "Who?" I asked.

Dad came over and sat down next to Mom, placed a hand gently on my left leg. "It's okay," he said. "It's the pain meds. They're making it difficult." He eyed Mom, and she folded her arms across her chest with a sniff. He continued. "Caleb," he said. "He's not doing well, Bea. They put him into a medically induced coma, but we have to be honest with you—they said it doesn't look good."

Caleb.

That's when it all came back to me. My chest deflated, and I felt my entire body begin to tremble. Then I opened my mouth and let out a sob. I'd killed my best friend? I shook my head. "No, no, no." I hunched my back, rocking as I pushed my balled fists into my eyelids. "No, it's not true. It's not true!"

I felt a harsh grip on my arm. "Bea, pull it together," Mom said, frantic as I was. "Listen, if that boy dies, they say you could be facing homicide charges! Murder, Bea!"

"Seriously?" Dad snapped, eyeing Mom. "Isn't she going through enough right now?" He turned to me. "Bea, you just have to tell them what happened, and it will all be fine."

Mom's jaw was set, and she looked up at the ceiling. "You're filling her head with false hope," she said. "It won't be fine. Look at us." She held out her palms. "What will everyone say?"

Dad stood up and walked out of the room.

"Mom," I said between my tears. "I can't remember what happened."

She sighed. "Maybe it's better that way, huh?"

But that was a lie. I could remember, up to a point.

◆ ◆ ◆

It was a cool summer night, one of those days when the languid heat of the afternoon was blown away by an evening chill. Now that the stars were out, I wrapped my arms around me as we walked outside, leaving the humid pack of bodies from the house party inside. Caleb rubbed my shoulders. "Cold?" he asked. "Let me warm you up." His hand drifted toward me, as if to hold me, but at the last minute he put me into a headlock and gave me a noogie.

"Ugh, you're an idiot!" I fought him off with a smile. He laughed in that drunk and wild way I always loved.

We were on our way to the third, maybe fourth party that night: me, Caleb, and Jill.

Allegra followed us out and stopped me, hands on her hips. "Don't you think you should wait a bit? You're beyond wasted." She took a long drag on her hand-rolled cigarette as her eyes followed Caleb, who was stumbling down the driveway to where our ride waited.

"We're fine, A." I rolled my eyes. "I know you never believe it, but I'm a big girl. Besides, Caleb is good looking out."

"Not if he's as wasted as you." Her eyes shot daggers at Caleb's shadow figure stumbling down the lawn.

"Jill is fine to drive," I said.

Allegra stubbed a cigarette out on the porch railing, leaving a black ashy burn on the wood. "Ugh, I don't even know why you're leaving with him yet again, and leaving me."

"I'm tired, Allegra. I just want to go and sleep."

"In his bed," she said.

I raised my eyebrows. "You know it's not like that. You can come with if you want."

"No way, I'm not going to be your third wheel. Besides, I'm still having fun here. Just be careful. And fucking don't let Caleb drive."

I gave a salute. "Aye, aye."

Jill leaned into the driver's side and pushed hard on the horn as I walked to the car. A raucous and anonymous whoop from the house answered in return; I nervously glanced around the otherwise sleepy neighborhood. "Jill, shut up," I chided.

"Sweet ride, Caleb," said Jill. "Where did you get this exactly?"

Caleb shrugged. "Mom's boyfriend works at the dealership, and he just brought it home. Said he got a hookup."

Jill rolled her eyes. "Yeah, I'm sure he did." Her phone rang, and she held up her middle finger toward us while she answered. "Hey, babe." She spoke into the phone, and I tuned out as she chatted, closing my eyes for a second and longing to be home.

"Sorry, y'all, I gotta hang here. Boyfriend's on the way." As a consolation of sorts, Jill reached into her bag and pulled out a small Altoids mint container. She popped it open and held it out, and I considered the array of colorful shapes on offer. In the end, though,

I chose my old standbys—I took two Xanax and swallowed them in one movement.

"Well now what are we supposed to do?" Caleb asked. Jill held up the car keys, shaking them, and Caleb snatched them away.

"Oh no," I said. "I promised Allegra your ass wasn't driving."

Caleb looked at me, incredulous. "Like you're okay to drive?"

"I am."

"Are you?" Jill asked.

"Yeah, I'm fine, Jesus. Just buckle up."

Jill waved as we pulled down the driveway. And I was fine, at the start. Of course we took a back road to avoid cops and traffic. The one-lane highway was dark and winding. Caleb was in the passenger seat and explaining all of the car's features, he had to yell over the music that was blaring from the speakers.

In the dark, my phone on the dash lit up with a call.

Allegra.

I hit "Reject Call."

After a little bit, my phone lit up again. This time it said "Mom." I ignored the call and turned the phone over, looking up at the stars instead.

We had gotten into a fight before I'd left home earlier that night, per usual. I didn't know what time it was anymore, but she was calling to see when I was coming home, no doubt. She always called and I never answered. It was too little, too late as far as I was concerned. If only she had been so attentive to my needs years ago, when I was struggling and asking for her help and support.

Instead I'd found support in Caleb and my pills.

◆ ◆ ◆

You're moving too fast, she would say. *You're living too fast and too hard, and it will catch up with you.*

The pressure you put on me was too hard, too much, I told her. Why would I want to live in that world when it was so much easier to inhabit the place I shared with Caleb? While Mom had thought she was doing what was best for me, to harden me into a strong thing, a hard thing, Caleb had cut through and found me inside. That small and frightened girl I was keeping inside. He'd helped me climb out and find the joy that existed when you could just let it all go.

It's a dream world, Bea. These drugs aren't real. They only help you escape.

Maybe so, but then why would I ever want to go back to the real world?

Wake up, Bea. Caleb is using you, just like the drugs are using you. Tell us what you need—we can help you!

Please, just leave me alone.

Wake up, Bea! We're going too fast.

What—

"Bea, wake up!"

The scene stretched out before me like in a movie. Caleb's new car was twisted and crumpled like a ball of aluminum foil in the ditch of the dark road. Another overturned car that had come out of nowhere was stopped in the middle of a curve. I somehow climbed out of the wreck and collapsed on the cold blacktop as I struggled to stay awake. When I looked back, Caleb's body was still stuck in the car. I think I screamed for help. Then the sirens.

What had I done?

I had killed him.

Then I hadn't.

In the end, Caleb woke up.

The official police report from the night describes a car accident caused by the reckless driving of an individual under the influence of drugs and alcohol, with serious injuries sustained by both the underage male driver and an underage female passenger. The passengers of the other car involved sustained only minor injuries and underwent a brief hospitalization.

The report states that when the ambulance arrived at the emergency room with the unconscious passenger and the barely conscious driver, the driver was adamant that the triage nurses know all the medications and substances the female was on, in case that affected her treatment. The report states that although the driver was also clearly under the influence and also seriously injured himself, he was adamant that the female passenger receive help first. The female passenger remained unresponsive but was able to be stabilized; only then, nurses said, did the driver succumb to his own injuries and eventually have to be placed in a medically induced coma.

The driver would ultimately confess to driving a stolen vehicle, as the car involved was identified as one stolen earlier that night from a local dealership. However, there was no evidence to actually connect him to the theft. The report states the name of the driver as one Caleb Crown, the name of the passenger as Bea Milner.

That's what the official report states, but it's all wrong.

Caleb lied to save me.

Then I abandoned him.

Chapter 19

Wednesday

The laminate countertop of Kelli's small kitchen is covered in small bowls filled with garlic, fresh oregano, and diced mushrooms, along with several bottles of spices. I'm on double duty, chopping up asparagus stalks while watching a pot of fettuccini boil on the stovetop. On the other burner, Kelli sautés pink salmon fillets. Her blond hair is in a messy bun, and she's wearing some oversize gray sweatpants and a matching cropped sweatshirt. She looks charmingly disheveled here at her home; she wields the sauté pan with surprising zeal.

Landon has been dead for one week.

I'm spending the anniversary with the only other person I saw him with last.

"I kind of thought you meant spaghetti and canned sauce when you said pasta was on the menu," I say.

"Hold your tongue," she says, making a face. "I would not invite you over for anything less than my world-famous homemade fettuccine Alfredo. Well, Seattle famous, anyway."

"Maybe Saul Group famous?" I offer.

She shakes her head. "Believe it or not, I try not to associate with lawyers outside of working hours. I have very specific rules when it comes to both lawyers and vampires."

"They can't cross your threshold without your express invitation?"

"How did you know?"

"You're not the only one acquainted with bloodsuckers." I smile. The pot of fettuccine pasta comes to a boil, and I bring down the heat until it's a simmer. "So you don't date lawyers, then?"

"No, I don't really date. It's too much work. I can't afford to be distracted by anything if I want to have a career, you know? Maybe one day, but right now I have goals that I can't take my eyes off of, even for some dick."

I laugh so hard I snort. "Amen, sister."

"So when I do have time, I like to cook." She gently presses the salmon with her fingertip. "These are done." She removes them from the pan and allows them to rest on a wooden cutting board. "Asparagus, please."

I let the bright-green stalks fall into the pan, and she adds salt, pepper, and more spices and finally dumps a big leafy bunch of herbs on top. The herbs sizzle and wilt in the heat while Kelli adds the mushrooms to the pan and gives it all a stir. She points to the pasta. "That's finished. Drain it."

I turn the knob on the gas stovetop to "OFF" and grab oven mitts to pour the pot of steaming pasta into the colander over the sink. Then I watch while Kelli whisks together garlic, Parmesan, heavy cream, and more butter than I think anyone should legally be allowed to use in one recipe.

"I know it seems like an instant heart attack," she laughs. "But trust me, homemade with grass-fed organic butter and real cream from real cows—it not only tastes amazing, but it's so much better for you than you think. This is the real food our bodies crave."

"You do not have to convince me that my body craves butter and cheese."

"Dinner is served!" Kelli has arranged the seemingly simple dinner like a restaurant dish. A twirled bundle of fettuccini topped with asparagus and mushrooms sits next to the perfectly seared salmon fillets. A drizzle of her Alfredo sauce is splashed across like brushstrokes.

I carry the dishes over to a small table. After I set them down, Kelli comes over holding two empty glasses and a bottle of red wine.

"Oh." I hesitate. "I'm not sure . . ."

"I'll keep you honest." She winks.

"Seriously, though," I push back.

She leans forward, holding the glass out. "Really? Come on, Bea. It's just wine. Look—it's not opened. Why don't you open it and pour it yourself if you're worried?"

Sure. With a sheepish smile, I accept the offer. I open the bottle—the cork comes out with a satisfying pop—and pour us both glasses. We sit and toast. "Cheers," she says. "To new friends."

I take a bite and have to admit, it's heavenly. Indulgent. "This is delicious. Is this a family recipe?"

"No. I don't really have family recipes. I grew up more on those canned sauces you referenced earlier than nana's Alfredo sauce. What about you?"

"My mom is a fantastic cook," I say. "She raised me on Filipino cooking. Her and Dad and I ate dinner together every single night. Imagine my shock when I went to a friend's house for dinner the first time and the family ran to the kitchen, picked up their plates, and went back to their respective rooms. Dad back to his office, the kids into their rooms with their TVs or Nintendos, and Mom was left eating alone in the dining room. I asked my friend if we should go sit with her mom, and she looked at me like I had grown a second head, and turned on VH1's *Behind the Music*."

Kelli is quiet. "That sounds like my house."

"Well, it made me appreciate my family dinners. Until I didn't, right?"

"We never appreciate what we have in the moment. Or maybe we're too young to even know better." Kelli smiles. "But the plus is that you must be a great cook yourself, right?"

"Hardly," I admit. "The problem with having a mom who makes you food all the time is that you don't have to ever learn for yourself. But I should really learn some of her recipes. My friend is having a baby shower this weekend, and Mom is going to make a huge plate of her pancit. I'm pretty excited for that. There will be so much food, it's going to be embarrassing. Actually, the mom-to-be's parents can't make it for the shower, because they live in the Philippines most of the year. But they ordered lechon for the party! That's a whole roast pig! It's getting delivered to our house and everything."

Kelli's eyebrows rise. "I've never even seen a whole roast pig!"

"Well, you should come to this shower."

"Really?" she asks.

I nod. "Sure, why not? As I mentioned, there's more than enough food to go around. And you know Filipinos—we love treating everyone. It's this Saturday at noon. I'll just tell my parents to add you to the head count." I pause, embarrassed at what I'm about to confess. "And yes, I still live with my parents, so there's that."

Instead of the usual reactions—blatant amusement or false admiration *(Wow, you're such a good daughter . . .)*—Kelli's face falls for a moment. A flash of something before she catches herself. Is it jealousy? "My parents died when I was pretty young," Kelli says. "I think it's really special what you have."

"I'm sorry."

"No need. It was a long time ago, and therapy works, right? Well, as a kid I didn't really want to talk to anyone about it. But that changed when I discovered art therapy." She gestures behind her to the painting that has previously escaped my notice. "That's one of mine from that time, in fact."

"Really?" I ask. It's oils, I think, and the brushstrokes are vivid reds and oranges that rise up and around one another in an abstract whirlwind. It's both energizing and ominous. There's no artist's signature. "That's amazing! You did that, as a child? A cook and an artist. I'm impressed. Do you still paint?" I ask.

"I don't. When I was younger, I needed an outlet to express my feelings, and the art did that for me. I guess as I got older, I didn't need art so much anymore. That piece is the only thing I've kept from that time."

"It's beautiful," I say again. "Reminds me of a huge bouquet of poppies. Or a sunset. All the bright colors."

"Poppies. I like that interpretation. It was messed up, though—sometimes when I was a teenager, my girlfriends would tell me I was lucky I didn't have a mom. How fucked is that?"

"That's horrible."

"So that's my long way of saying I think it's really special you are close with your parents."

I immediately feel silly. "Of course. We are close, right. Maybe we haven't always had the best relationship, Mom and I especially. We always seem to be caught in this battle of tragedies, to prove who is the most miserable. What is it about mothers and daughters?"

Kelli sips from her wine and spears a chunk of salmon. "I think it's Freudian." She grimaces and twists her mouth. "What were you like as a teenager?"

I pause, an asparagus spear hanging from my fork. "The usual rebellious phase." I chomp into the tender veggie and feel the sinewy fibers separate between my teeth. I'm watching my wine swirl hypnotically in my glass when I see Kelli's reflection, upside down but sharp, in the bloodred liquid.

"How long have you lived here?" I ask, remembering something.

"A couple years now."

"Huh." I tilt my head. "Funny, I swore you lived north for some reason, by me. I think you told me that when we were trying to get an Uber that night . . ." My voice trails off. *That night.*

"So," Kelli says. "Strategy."

"Yes."

"The strategy is to do nothing."

"Is that smart? The detective—"

"Doesn't know shit. This is just another case of a rich white guy thinking he's invincible, and turns out he wasn't. If you don't say anything, I won't." She drinks.

I put down my glass and fork. "Someone died, Kelli. How can we just sit back and watch? We can just tell them I didn't mean for it—"

"How do you think that will go? Seriously, Bea, think. You don't know if the man had family, people with resources who will make sure you—and I—will pay. I'm thinking of me too. Sure, you were the one who insisted we not help, but . . . they were my drugs. I don't want any part of this, so trust me on this. We just stay quiet."

My breath seeps thinly out my nose.

"Bea? Can you do that?"

"Yeah," I say. "We stay quiet. We do nothing."

Kelli stands and claps her hands. "Man, the wine is just going straight through me! I'll be back."

I no longer have an appetite. I lean back in my chair and look again at Kelli's painting until the chaotic strokes of color make me uneasy. I stand up and wander back into the living room, where I see the mail pile I went through on my first visit.

Next to the pile, I spot a familiar image. My heart jumps.

When I first passed by the Lake City Crown Cannabis location a couple of years back, I had no idea the "Crown" meant Caleb Crown. But I should have known instantly; even the logo was the graffiti-style crown with three points that Caleb was fond of drawing all over his notebooks, and even on his Chucks, with permanent marker.

And now lying on a side table in Kelli's apartment is a vinyl sticker with the Crown logo. As I trace the logo's thick black lines, my heart begins to echo in my ears. Is there any reason that Kelli could be connected to Caleb? I try to calm myself; it's a silly jump for me to make. Kelli probably just buys her gummies from one of his shops.

My phone vibrates. I return to the table and see it's a text from Mom making sure I'm doing okay. When Kelli returns, I tell her, "I'll help you clean up—then I should probably get going. I think Mom is wondering why I'm out so late on a school night."

"That's really sweet," says Kelli. "I bet she's anxious, what with all the lawyers dying around here." She laughs, but my mouth drops open. "Oh sorry, is that too soon? It's a joke, but maybe I've gotten too comfortable with you, Bea."

"Ha, yeah." We load the dishwasher, and I turn to the various pots and pans on the stove, but Kelli stops me. "Don't even think about it. I rarely have guests, and I'm not going to let them do any more cleanup. Get on home."

I thank her for the dinner and for inviting me to her apartment. As I'm walking out the door, I feel her hand on my shoulder. "Hey," she says. "You know this whole Landon thing will blow over."

"I know."

"You seem really nervous about it."

"I am." I lower my voice. "Why wouldn't I be freaking out on a constant basis?"

"Because I'm telling you not to. Maybe look at it this way: Landon's absence gives you a little space to do what you've been wanting to do, right?"

I suddenly feel cold in her gaze. It hits me that this is bizarre, spending time with this girl. Though I would be lying if I tried to tell myself I wasn't drawn to her for some reason. If nothing else, we share this secret, this one awful and horrifying secret. "I should go. Thanks again for the dinner."

Kelli smiles. "We have to do it again soon."

I wrap my jacket tightly around me as I walk to my car from her building. I sit in the car and scroll through my phone while I wait for the interior to warm up. Before I drive away, I look back up toward her apartment. I swear I see her figure in the window, but when I wave my lit phone up to say goodbye, the figure doesn't wave back.

Chapter 20

Thursday

Simon's made us reservations at a little wine bar in Columbia City, in South Seattle. It's a homey spot along Rainier Avenue, and we have to take care not to jostle into anyone as we traverse the Friday-night crowd along the popular Main Street. We pass one restaurant, and I can smell the strong curried air wafting out; while we walk past another, I can practically taste the fresh Jamaican spices. I'm holding onto Simon's arm, and my fingers caress the smooth suede of his tan bomber jacket sleeve.

It feels like a perfect fall evening.

The wine bar is cozy and chic; we order a cheese plate and two glasses of Oregon pinot noir. We slide into a booth next to the window to best make use of people watching while we sit.

"Have you ever played the story game?" Simon asks.

"I don't think so?"

He gestures to the steady stream of people passing by us. "It's easy. Pick someone and make up a story about them. For instance, this couple with the dachshund . . ." I follow his gaze and see them, an older couple: the man is wearing a beret and stylish sport coat, the other man a trench coat. "I think they are a retired restaurateur couple from Manhattan, where for the last decade, they owned and ran a vegan café for dogs. It was named Herman's, after their dog, of course. Eventually, they sold all their secret recipes to Martha Stewart and came out here to retire on their fortune."

I laugh. "Amazing," I say. "Did you just now make that all up?"

"To be fair," he says, "I have the retired dog café story as an old standby. Okay, your turn."

I look out the window. "Um, I don't know," I say.

"Well, what about her?" Simon gestures to a woman smoking against a parking sign on the sidewalk.

"Ah, I don't know," I say again.

"Come on," he says. "No wrong answers."

"Okay. Well, she's wearing a server's apron, so I guess she's on break from waiting tables around here . . ."

Simon laughs. "It's supposed to be you making up a story, not making observations!"

"Okay, fine!" I look at the woman slumped against the sign. She's maybe my age. She flicks her ashes onto the street and looks up; when I look up, too, I see the same golden leaves she's looking at, the same gray skies, and suddenly I feel the same weight as her too. "She's a writer," I say. "She won a writing contest in high school, and her English teacher told her she was going to be the next great American novelist. So she took out loans and went to Sarah Lawrence, because that's what you're supposed to do. Then she took out even more loans and got her master's in fine arts. She had to move home to Seattle, even though real writers live in New York City. Or at least Nashville. But she couldn't afford anything, and so now here she is, waiting tables for tips. Her finished manuscript is in her desk drawer, but she's too scared to show anyone. She thinks, *What if it's too late?*"

I finish, and Simon doesn't say anything, just looks at me while we listen to the jazzy beats of the overhead speakers. "Jesus," he finally says.

"Here you go!" A waitress places our drinks and cheese plate between us.

Simon picks up a piece of cheese. "Saved by the cheese." He grins.

"It's Bea," I point out, grinning.

"So it is." He opens his mouth and places the creamy wedge on his tongue. I shift in my seat and clutch my fingers around the wineglass stem as his teeth bite down.

"Do me," I say.

He blinks. "Sorry?"

"The story game," I laugh. "Do me."

"I wouldn't know where to begin," he says. "Why don't you take this turn?"

"Sure." I pick up a grape from the spread. It pops between my teeth. "This woman"—I flourish a hand toward myself; the corners of Simon's mouth rise—"this woman is a lawyer. She's an okay lawyer, if we're honest."

"Oh, don't start," he says.

I continue. "She's worked her whole life to get to where she is today, but she's not sure where exactly that is. Until high school or so, she was a strict rule follower, with her whole life mapped out before her. Then one day, she made a choice. She tried this pill, to get ahead, and then that one little pill opened the door, and she met a boy, who she might have been in love with, but she would never admit it. And even though everyone told her to stay away from him, she thought that's what everyone was obligated to say. She kept seeing him, and she kept losing more and more of who she was. Until there was a horrible accident, where her and the boy could have died. In fact, the boy went into a coma."

I pause to drink. Simon is listening, rapt and silent. I can't tell if the expression on his face is sympathy or horror.

"They told the girl she was responsible and there would be a price to pay if he didn't wake up. Well, he did. Not only did he wake up, but he took responsibility for the whole thing. He sacrificed himself so the girl didn't have to. Even though it really was all my fault." I stop, because if I say another word, I might choke on the tears I'm holding at bay.

"You were a kid," he says.

"I was a kid who ruined a lot of lives," I say. "Caleb went to jail. For me. My parents had to take out loans to pay for the defense attorney when the passengers in the other car wanted to bring suit for their injuries, since the car I was driving was stolen and didn't have insurance."

"It was stolen?" Simon looks shocked.

"Yeah, I heard later that the real culprit was one of Caleb's mom's boyfriends, who worked as a mechanic at a dealership. But it didn't matter when the car was totaled, and Caleb certainly didn't have the money. My parents ended up paying the dealership back."

"Wow," says Simon. "Bea, I had no idea."

He moves closer and places an arm around me. "But look at what you've made of yourself. You're not your past mistakes."

"That's what I keep hearing," I say. "But what if I keep making the same mistakes?"

"You keep driving under the influence and getting into wrecks?" I know he's joking, but if he knew how close he was to the truth . . . "Was he okay? The guy?"

"Caleb? He was fine," I say. I look outside again, escaping his stare. Rain has begun to patter down, making tearstained drops on the sidewalk. I think of Caleb, who could have told the truth and said it was me driving that night. But instead he said it was him. I want to tell Simon that I never spoke to Caleb after that night. Well, not more than a few words.

I never even thanked him.

But I left for undergrad so quickly after graduation anyway, and then never even returned home until after law school. And he could have reached out to me if he'd wanted. He could have asked Allegra to talk to me, even . . .

Simon leans forward. "You're a good person, Bea. I hope you know that."

Shit. "Am I?" I ask, giving a slight laugh.

"I can tell you are. I wouldn't be here with you if I didn't believe it."

Oh, Simon, I think. This good man in front of me believes I'm a good person. My breath catches, and I want to confess to him. I want to tell him he doesn't know the half of it. If he only knew I'm an actual killer. Suddenly I realize I don't even know what I did to Landon. Who knows what I could be capable of if I lose control again? What if I'm with Simon the next time?

I'm a danger to him, I realize. I'm a danger to everyone around me.

I push my wineglass away.

What am I going to do now?

"You know, I'm sorry—I think I'm done with the wine," I say.

"Is it not good?" He sniffs his glass.

"It's not that. I have a headache."

"Ah, sorry to hear that. You know, I'm done too."

"That's not necessary," I say, feeling bad now for no reason.

"It's not a problem."

I nod. "Okay. Are you going to give me your story now? Or what?"

"Jesus, no," he says. "And not because I'm boring and there's no story to tell. But I think maybe we're done with past sad stories for now. How about future happy stories?"

"Like what?"

He dips a finger into the honey poured onto the plate and holds it out to me, inches from my mouth. In a primal move I can't stop, my tongue emerges, and I lick it off; I taste the sweetness combined with the salt of his skin.

I smile. "I think I like this story."

◆ ◆ ◆

In his bed, we grasp each other and taste more salt, more sweetness, until I'm demanding release. I've forgotten the pressure of someone else's hands on my naked hips, forgotten the pleasure of sinking into his mattress with all of him driving deeper into me. I grasp his hair and pull. I move his hand across my throat, and he only questions me for a second before he gently presses down. He's holding my throat and looking into my eyes when he comes. I close my eyes at the last second.

After, we both catch our breath and laugh as we lie against each other. "Was I pressing too hard?" he asks.

Sweet thing, I think. "No," I say. "You could've gone harder, actually . . ." If I weren't already red, I know I'd be blushing.

"Well now I guess I'm not surprised you were a bad girl in your time," he says. "After all, you know what they say—it's always the quiet ones." I push him playfully, and he grabs my face to kiss me again.

Later, when he's snoring, I gather my clothes, dress, then quietly let myself out. At home again, I undress once more. Before I throw my clothes into my laundry hamper, I press them to my nose and inhale—there's Simon's cologne, woodsy and sharp, like a Pacific Northwest beach. But after yesterday and tonight, I know I can't run from it anymore: I have to visit Crown Cannabis.

Chapter 21

Friday

During my lunch break, I search for the closest location of Crown Cannabis and realize it's close by. When I approach the sleek and trendy-looking shop, I realize how much Caleb has come up in the world.

I've never gone inside one of the stores until today. "ID?" a security person asks as I step in the door. I hand them my license, and they wave me in. I follow a green velvet rope to the counter, where a girl with a nose ring greets me cheerfully. "What are you looking for today?"

"Actually, I'm looking for Caleb." I point up and around. "Uh, Caleb Crown."

"Oh, he doesn't come into this store often," she says. "He mostly works from the Lake City location."

"Would he be there today?" I ask.

"Probably. Want me to call and check?"

"Sure. Tell him Bea wants to talk to him."

She nods and goes into the back. While I wait, I peruse the offerings and am impressed by the sheer variety of cannabis-infused . . . things that exist. None of this was around when I was growing up, and it's probably for the better. The last thing seventeen-year-old Bea needed was weed gummies that tasted like raspberries. Or CBD potato chips. "Clever," I muse out loud at the chips. "Killing two birds with one stone here."

Caleb was always smart, so it's no wonder he capitalized on something he knew well when there was an opportunity. A twinge of sadness hits me. I wonder if he would have made all this if I'd never left town.

"Bea?" The girl has come back. She hands me a Crown Cannabis business card with an address and number scribbled on the back. "He said to meet him there at six this evening, and this is his cell if you need it."

I tuck the card safely into my back pocket. I notice a pile of stickers on the counter—they're the Crown logo and exactly like the one Kelli had in her apartment. A handwritten sign next to them says **FREE!** I take one and put it in my pocket.

I go home to eat something before I make the trek out to the address on the card. When I look up the address, it takes me to some club by South Lake Union, which Google describes as a "trendy music venue for hip concertgoers."

My old worn black leather moto jacket is possibly the coolest article of clothing I own and was a triumphant thrift store find back in my law school days. I never wear it anymore, but think if there was ever a night for an excuse to break it out, it's a night when I have to pretend I'm a hip concertgoer. After slipping my arms into the soft buttery sleeves and zipping it up over my plain white tee, I can almost pass for a nonsquare. Now for the pants. I can never remember—are skinny jeans in or out? Ultimately, I give up and go for boot cut. Exhausted by the time I get to my hair and makeup, I throw my hair into a ponytail and make do with a swipe of mascara across each eye. *Imagine doing this each morning,* I think. There's a reason I don't.

The rain has ceased, but the chill lies across the city, and the clouds sigh heavy over the buildings. I dig my hands into my jacket. When I arrive at the "trendy music venue," I have to laugh. It isn't until I'm standing in front of the address that I realize what he's done. "Caleb, you bastard," I say under my breath. Despite the name change, it will always be the Dancing Goat—i.e., the shady establishment that let

Caleb, me, and our friends illegally drink. Before I open the door, I notice a new neon sign, a green glowing crown.

Inside, it's just as musty and dark as my own dim memories recall, and I'm fairly certain this is the same AC/DC CD still in rotation.

For a Friday evening, it's pretty empty in here, and I don't have to look hard to find him. Caleb is sitting at the bar, as if he's been waiting all these years for me to simply come back. He's staring at his phone and hasn't noticed me quite yet, so I take in how the years have been to my former best friend.

The soft glow of the phone screen illuminates his face. Even though we are the same age, I wonder that after all the years between us now, he seems so much older than the teenage boy I remember. Yet he's exactly the same. Only his formerly black hair is lighter and grayer now around the edges. He puts down his phone and stares ahead with a look that takes me right back to when we were teenagers, smoking on the roof of his parents' house and staring up at the stars.

"You've got that look again," I would say. "The one where you're somewhere else."

"Yeah, Bea, 'cause I'm high." He'd laugh.

"No," I'd say. "You're imagining another life away from here." His silence would let me know I was right. "Just promise me I'm there with you," I'd say.

"I promise."

He promised every time.

Seeing him now makes my heart wrench in two, and I regret all the years wasted between us. I feel shameful at my absence. I wasn't a good friend.

I can't do this.

I turn my head and hope he won't notice me before I can slip out; I'll tell him I couldn't make it after all.

"Bea, is that you?" Caleb smiles and calls across the bar and over the jarring, lush tones of "Thunderstruck." "Don't leave," he says. "Stay awhile."

"Hi, Caleb."

He motions for the bartender to pour me a drink. The bartender gives a salute. "Sure thing, boss."

"*Boss*?" I ask. "Do you own this place?"

"A new acquisition to the Crown portfolio, yeah. Just bought it a few months ago. After the cannabis stores, a bar seemed like a natural addition. And we can advertise our own products here too," he says, gesturing to another neon Crown logo sign over the bar.

"It's smart," I admit. Condensation drips down my pint glass and pools on the lacquered bar. I wipe it away. "Do you have coasters?" I ask.

"Nah," Caleb answers. "We're not that kind of establishment."

I sip my cold IPA and nod. "Some things never change. Are you going to change the name?"

"Although Dancing Goat will always have a place in my heart, I'm thinking of Crown Club. For consistency in the brand, you know?"

I turn up my nose. "Crown Club sounds like an airline mileage program."

He laughs, and I join him. It's been a long time since I've heard Caleb laugh. It sounds like a first crush. "Did you tell Allegra you were meeting me?"

"I didn't say anything," he says. "And not for any shady reasons. I honestly thought you wouldn't show up; why would you after all these years? But I'm so proud of you. I knew you'd be successful. And now a fancy lawyer! There was a time when I thought about you, and wondered if I'd even recognize you if I passed you on the street . . ."

My head lifts, and I meet his eyes. "I would recognize you, Caleb."

"Because I'm the same."

"No, you're not. You're a businessman!" I look around. "Well, besides this place. You should be really proud of yourself. Anyhow, that's not why I'd recognize you. How could I forget . . ." I look around, and the memories flood back. For anyone who knew anything, this place was the place to find your high of choice. It may have looked like a dive bar, but it was more like a drive-through pharmacy. "I didn't remember the address. I might not have come if I recognized it. Do the cops still come in here to shake people down?"

"No," Caleb says. "I actually enforce the whole minors-aren't-allowed rule."

"Boo," I say, smiling. "That would have really cramped our style."

"So, what, Bea? You avoid me like the plague for years, and all of a sudden, we're catching up over beers?"

I sigh. "I've found myself back *there* a lot these days."

He takes his drink and motions for me to follow. We go through a **STAFF ONLY** door and up a narrow set of stairs that lead to a rooftop ledge. The black waters of Lake Union sparkle in front of us; lit houseboats docked at the marinas bob in the night.

"Wow. This was here the whole time?" I ask.

Caleb smirks. "Right? Though it's probably a good thing we didn't have rooftop access."

"Fair. Somebody would have dared somebody to jump."

He pulls an electronic vaping pen from his jeans pocket.

"Is that a cannabis pen?" I ask.

He shakes his head. "Just nicotine. Would you believe I don't really smoke weed anymore?" He takes a pull and offers it to me. I take it and inhale, letting the warmth fill my mouth and then move down into my chest. Then I begin coughing.

"What the—" I stick out my tongue, then grab my drink and take a swig. "Yuck! What was that flavor?"

Caleb blinks. "Bubble gum. Why?"

"I . . . never mind. Please take it back." I shove the pen at him. "So you don't do anything, like, on the side here?"

"Not sure I get what you're implying."

"All *this*." I gesture to the air, drawing an invisible circle around the city and her lights. "And all the Crown Cannabis stores. It's all, like . . ."

"Clean?" Caleb sighs. "Yeah, Bea. I know it's hard to believe."

"That's not what I meant."

"Why are you asking me this?"

"I don't know." The truth is I didn't have a plan, coming here. "I'm sorry. This isn't how I wanted this conversation to go."

He takes a long drag on the pen. "Remember the time we skipped class and I convinced you to drive up to the Olympic National Forest with me?"

"Of course I remember. We were so high on Xanax and, Jesus, Molly, too, was it? We got so lost."

Caleb chuckles, a deep belly laugh that I can't resist joining in with. "So fucking lost," he says. "One minute we thought we were out there communing with nature, and the next minute, we're off the trail and our high asses are panic-gathering roots and trying to remember how to start a fire from the one episode of *Survivor* we watched." For a moment, it feels like we're back on his parents' rooftop.

"God, I thought for sure it was over for us that time. I honestly thought we were bear food." I laugh. "Good thing those hikers found us. The real hikers with real maps and not drugs."

"We would have found our way back to civilization . . . eventually." Caleb looks at me and rests his hand against his own chest, over his heart. "We did some stupid shit." The music below reverberates beneath our feet, and I wonder how many people are getting high down there right now. I feel guilty for thinking Caleb was connected to Kelli; how easy is it to get drugs from anyone now? Too easy if you know where to look.

For some reason, this makes me think about our last night together. It must be the drinks, or maybe being with him again, but my heart feels heavier than it has in a long time.

In the cool air, separated from Caleb by the darkness, I have to ask. "Why did you do it? Why did you take the blame for . . . ? I never even got to thank you . . ." My voice trembles.

Caleb looks away. "I did it because of the two of us, you were the one who was going to be someone, remember?"

I nod, tears streaming down my face. "Thank—"

"Water under the bridge, Bea."

I know now, in this moment. It's a sharp sting to realize this.

A voice calls from the staircase, "Caleb? Question for you when you get a moment!"

Caleb yells back, "Be down in a sec!" He purses his lips and casts his golden eyes up to me. "Coming?"

"I might take a moment up here," I say. "It's beautiful."

"You know the way out. See you around?"

"You just might."

Life is funny; who can ever know the paths and intertwining of others' lives? Maybe in another timeline, we could have been together, Caleb and I. Or maybe it was always going to be this way. But seeing him tonight makes me wonder—if he can own his past and accept responsibility for his mistakes and still come out the other side, maybe I can too.

Tomorrow morning, I'm going to Detective Branson's office and telling her everything. I'm going to tell her what really happened in Landon Laurie's home that night.

Chapter 22

Saturday

"Detective Branson isn't in the office right now. Would you like to leave a message?" The officer at the front desk of the Seattle Police Department headquarters awaits my response. I think about writing my confession on a Post-it Note and calling it a day, but decide against it.

"I'll wait."

The officer waves me to a seat before disappearing behind large metal double doors with crash bars; an **EMPLOYEES ONLY** sign hangs on one. I wonder if she's even in the office, considering it's Saturday morning. Do detectives get the weekends off?

I pass the time and scroll on my phone, trying to not think about what I'm doing—what I'm physically about to do—in this police station.

This morning, I hugged Mom and Dad before leaving.

"Where are you going again?" Mom asked.

"To the office," I lied.

"You're working too much these days," Dad said.

"I'm just trying to take care of all my shit," I said.

Mom clicked her tongue. "Language, Bea!"

"I mean, I'm getting some things in order."

"Well, don't get back too late. We have Allegra's shower today, you know."

"I know, Mom." I bit the inside of my cheek. Even trying to have a poignant goodbye before being hauled off to jail, I couldn't escape Allegra. "Look, I love you guys."

Dad put his coffee down, and Mom looked over the top edges of her glasses. "We love you too, Buzz," Dad said. "Everything okay?"

I put on a brave face. "Everything is going to be okay."

Mom went back to her phone. I gave Dad a hug and felt him hold on for a second longer than normal. As I pulled away, he said, his chin stuck out, "Take care of yourself, Buzz."

I embraced Mom as she sat at the breakfast nook, and she patted my arm across her chest, eyes firmly glued to the crossword puzzle on her screen.

Then I was gone.

Now I sit in the police station and wonder if I'm making the right choice. I open my messages, and my finger hovers over the thread with Kelli. I've been meaning to text her ever since I decided to go to the detective, but I can't bring myself to. Is it because I think she'll try to talk me out of it? Mostly.

But it's more about the fact that I can't tell anyone what I'm about to do. As soon as I do, as soon as I say that I'm partly responsible, I don't know if I'll ever be able to see them again.

An hour goes by, but it feels as if I've been stuck here in this waiting room of purgatory for much longer. To be fair, if I had told the officer I was confessing to manslaughter, he might have found a way to speed things up, or at least get someone's attention.

As people buzz around me and I see police go in and out of those double doors, I begin to feel forgotten. I return to the front desk. "Excuse me. Any idea when Detective Branson will be back?"

He looks at me as if he's never seen me before in his life. "What's this about?"

"An ongoing case she has." I don't know what else to tell him. "Landon Laurie?"

A spark of recognition from the name enters his eyes. "Uh, one moment." He comes out from around the desk and goes back through those doors, but this time as he walks through, I follow and hold the door open. I can see him walk down the hall and stop at a door on the left, near the end. I see him peek in, and then, apparently not finding what he's looking for, he turns to come back. "She's not there," he says, seeing me in the doorway.

"That's what you said," I remind him. "When will she be? Here, I mean?"

"Sorry, no idea. Can you leave your name and number?"

I don't know how much longer I can wait. In a moment of pure anticlimax, I take the small slip of paper he gives me and rifle through my bag for a pen. At that moment, the front doors burst open, and a distressed individual comes in, yelling to speak to an officer. The poor guy in front of me is the only one wearing a uniform, so the individual quickly spies him and makes him the object of their ire. Or enthusiasm—I can't understand a word they are saying.

The officer is forced to attend to them, leaving me alone. I look around. Nobody is paying attention to anything but the upset individual now. I look down at my name and number written on the notepaper, then up at the officer, who has his hands full. It's going to take another lifetime for him to actually collect this.

Maybe I can get to Detective Branson's office and leave her this note myself.

With one last glance around to make sure nobody is watching, I quickly back against the double doors, push them open, and slip through.

Once on the other side, I try not to look around or appear like I'm out of place. But for police officers, nobody seems very observant. I easily make it to the door I saw the officer stand in front of, and sure enough, the plaque on the door reads **DET. BRANSON**.

I try the doorknob. Unlocked. I let myself in.

Unlike in my own office, there are no glass walls here. I turn on the light as the door clicks shut behind me. The detective's office is clean and well organized; the daunting towers of files are on her desk in neat piles. I take a deep breath, trying to calm the blood rushing through my veins. I wish she was here so I could just get this over with.

Feeling dizzy all of a sudden, I lower myself down into her desk chair, placing the note with my name and number on the desk in front of me. I smooth it out until it lies flat, running my fingers over the curves of my name again and again. As I repeat this motion, my head clears, and I feel like I can stand again.

And as I do, I look over at one of the piles and see the name written on it: *Landon Laurie*.

My hands reach out, almost of their own will, and I slide it out of the pile. There's an extra notation on this file. It reads "Autopsy Report."

My breath leaves me once again. A quick glance at the door, and I decide I have to know. I open the file.

I step back and gag; there are photos of Landon, his bare chest exposed and his pale, lifeless face on a metal table. Dead. I've never seen a dead body before, even in photos. It seems wrong and disrespectful to look.

I read the notes. It's hard to decipher the medical terms—I skim through as best I can. I get to a section labeled "Toxicology" and read quickly, "Toxicology is positive for alcohol, cocaine, and fentanyl in postmortem peripheral blood."

Finally, I see a box that says "Cause of Death." Underneath, it reads, "Fatal overdose of fentanyl."

Was Landon doing fentanyl that night? I try to recall if he offered us any—surely I would have remembered *that*.

But then I think, *He wasn't the one who brought the drugs at all.*

Kelli was keeping up with Landon, line for line. If Kelli's drugs contained fentanyl, she would have also overdosed, no doubt. And if she somehow avoided that, there would have been no way she would have been sober enough to get me home. If I was that bad off and didn't even partake of her drugs, she would have been twice as intoxicated as me.

Unless she wasn't.

I take a photo of the report with my phone and, hands shaking, put the folder back in its place. I leave the station, not bothering to turn around when the front desk officer asks me what I was doing back there.

I don't know what it all means, but one thing is clear. Kelli is hiding something. Why else would she be trying to mislead me about what happened that night?

And what does this mean about Landon's death?

Chapter 23

Allegra arrives thirty minutes before the shower is set to begin. She's carrying shopping bags full of paper plates and streamers, and Mom scolds her. "Why are you carrying all that? Where's hubby to help out, anyway?"

She tilts her head to the driveway. "He's on the phone with the lechon people!"

I help bring in the bags of supplies. "Dad's outside in the backyard, setting up the tables. Want to see where the pig is going to go?" I lead her to the back, where a big white tent has been erected, folding tables lining the sides. Dad is on a ladder, securing hanging porch lights.

"It's beautiful!" exclaims Allegra.

"Now we just need a pregnant lady—oh, hi there, Allegra!" He winks.

"He's been up since eight fighting this thing." I wink at Dad, who puffs out his chest.

He climbs down the ladder and pushes a button on a cord; the hanging bulbs light up, soft glowing orbs floating around us. "Mr. Milner, you're the best!" Allegra gives him a hug.

"There he is!" Dad exclaims, and we turn to where Allegra's husband and baby-daddy-to-be is standing.

"Looks great!" he says.

"Isn't it perfect, Caleb?" Allegra puts her arm around him.

He kisses her on the temple. "Almost as perfect as you."

If I hadn't spoken to Caleb yesterday, this might have been the first time I saw him in years. Even after our meeting, there's an ache at seeing them together. With his business, he was always busy, and Allegra was sensitive to us needing our distance. We were experts at avoiding one another.

Mom begins delegating.

We continue to unfold chairs and set them up around the round tables in the middle of the tent. The day is cloudy and cool, but there's no rain in the forecast. Mom gives me a large round button that says "Call Me Daddy."

"Uh, what's this?" I ask.

"Allegra is wearing hers," Mom says. Sure enough, I glance over, and Allegra points to a big button pinned to the strap of her butter-yellow maxi dress. "Call Me Mommy," it says. I cringe.

"Go give it to Caleb," Mom orders.

"There's nothing I want to do less," I mumble.

I find Caleb in the front tapping his foot, looking down the street in each direction. "If these pig people are late, your mom is going to kill me," he says.

I hand him the button. "Here, I'm supposed to give you this."

He takes the button. "Thanks?"

I shrug.

A white Jeep turns into the street. "Think that's them?" Caleb asks.

The Jeep turns into the driveway, and a familiar figure waves from inside. *It can't be* . . . I think. Kelli gets out of the car. "Hi, Bea!" She gives me a hug. "And hello . . ." She spies Caleb's informative button. "Dad-to-be! I'm Bea's friend. She said I could come." She looks around at the empty driveway. "Am I early? You said noon . . ."

Caleb shakes his head. "On time," he chuckles to himself. "Amateur."

I shakily lead Kelli inside. "Um, I totally forgot I invited you."

She frowns.

"I didn't mean it like that," I backtrack. "It's just . . . we're still prepping."

"No worries," she says. "How can I help?"

Mom comes in and sees the new arrival. "Welcome," she says.

"Kelli's a friend from work," I say.

"Your house is so nice," says Kelli. "I know I'm early, but please put me to work!"

"I like this attitude," says Mom. "Let me show you where the napkins are . . ." She pulls Kelli away.

I can't believe I forgot I invited her. And now she's here. I think about the autopsy report. I have to confront her, I know, but when?

"Bea?" I snap back and see Allegra. "Help me get these terrarium thingies set out, will you?"

We almost finish distributing the tiny mushroom scenes and hanging out the banners and streamers by the time the first real guests begin to arrive. Then a stream of partygoers appears, and I have no more time to ponder Kelli or Landon. In fact, whenever I remember to check on her, she's holding her own and mingling like everything is completely normal.

The arrival of the lechon causes a stir, and the crowd follows the deliverymen outside to where they place the shiny, crispy delicacy in the center of the tent. Caleb immediately tells everyone to get it while it's hot.

Games begin, and I decide it can't wait any longer. I find Kelli in the middle of a baby bingo game. "Can I talk to you?"

She moans. "But I just need one more diaper to get bingo!"

"Now, Kelli." With a whine, she puts down her card, and I motion for us to go outside. I click my car open. "In," I say.

Chapter 24

The car door shuts, and we are alone now, just she and I. She tosses loose blond strands over her shoulder as she turns to me, blue eyes wide. "So?"

I look past her, out the window toward the house, focusing on the familiar red front door. "Kelli," I say. "Landon overdosed from fentanyl in his system." I pause.

"What do you mean?"

"You said that Landon and I had some kind of altercation and I assaulted him, that then he began to overdose and we just . . . let him. You made me think we were the reason he died, because I didn't let you call for help. But that's not true. He had a huge amount of fentanyl in his system."

She shakes her head. "Where would the fentanyl have come from?"

"It was your drugs, Kelli. You tell me."

"And you saw me do them too. Why didn't I die?"

"I don't know." I hold my palm to my forehead. She's right. Unless she didn't actually do anything. Maybe she was just pretending to partake.

"Landon did fentanyl at the club and before we even got to his place for all we know," Kelli says. She could be right, but I can't imagine that somehow. Landon probably had a reputable source of whatever he was using. And he wouldn't be so stupid as to do fentanyl, would he?

"How can you be so sure what was in your drugs?" I ask her.

"Are you telling me I'm a liar?" Her voice is trembling and slowly growing louder.

I lean back in my seat, my hands flat on my thighs and my fingers following the hem of my dress. "I didn't call you a liar." I bite my lip.

"So what are you calling me?" She stares at me, her jaw set.

I shake my head. "Nothing, Kelli—" My breath catches.

Her finger juts out at me. "You don't think I know what you're doing? You're trying to make me second-guess what I saw now, aren't you?"

The immediate defensiveness takes me aback, and I can only shake my head. "No, I—"

"I know what I saw," she continues. "And you were blacked out—you've already told me so. Why are you trying to change the story now?"

"Kelli," I snap. "I saw the autopsy report!"

She stops. Her head tilts, and this time she is the one leaning back in her chair. "Did you go to that detective?" she asks.

"No," I say. "Well, kind of. I was going to."

"Bea! Are you serious? Did you turn us in?"

I shake my head. "Us? No! I went there to turn me in!" I ignore her wide eyes, her mouth dropping open. "If I killed Landon, then I need to take responsibility! Or at least that's what I thought. But when I got there, Branson wasn't even there. But the autopsy report was clear. Landon died from a fentanyl overdose."

Kelli stares at me.

"The drugs," I say. "There was fentanyl in the drugs."

She shrugs.

I shake my head. "Did you know that? Did you know you and he were actually doing fentanyl and not coke? Because that's wild, Kelli."

"We were doing coke," she says matter-of-factly. "Well, Landon was, anyway."

I scoff at her sudden nonchalance. "Why are you acting like this? Aren't you freaked out that you could have overdosed too?" I pause. "Wait, what do you mean Landon was doing it? You weren't?"

A smile unfurls from her lips, pink and shiny from whatever lip gloss she's put on for the party. Her mouth opens, and she laughs, all teeth. "It was so easy to fool him," she says. "Both of you, actually."

A chill runs through me, and I feel sharp pricks on my thighs; I look down and see my fingernails digging into my skin. I turn to face her. "What the hell are you talking about?" I ask. "You gave him fentanyl and told him it was cocaine, then pretended to do it so he wouldn't be suspicious?"

She sighs. "No, Bea, Jesus. I gave him cocaine and he did cocaine. But to be fair, the cocaine he did was cut with a dose of fentanyl guaranteed to cause overdose. And yeah, you're right about pretending to do it."

"Wait, how do you know that?"

She squints her eyes as if I've asked a stupid question. "Because they were my drugs and I always know exactly what's in my drugs. Like a responsible person."

I nearly choke. "But why?"

"I needed you to think you were responsible. I'm sorry about that. But look at how smart you are—you've gone and figured it all out on your own. Honestly, though, going to the police is kinda messed up."

"Kelli!" I shriek.

"Shh!" Kelli hushes me, glancing around. It's still just us in the car, though; nobody is near us.

"What's wrong with you?" I hiss. "You mean you watched him die and you didn't even get help?"

"So you've changed your mind all of a sudden?"

"What?"

"I thought you wanted Landon Laurie dead?"

"No!" I immediately snap. I try to think back to that night. What did we talk about? I joked about my boss being dead, sure . . . Did I agree to kill him? I feel sick again. Why can't I remember clearly? A pressure behind my eyes pushes through, and I can't think. "No, I didn't want this," I repeat.

"Stop fucking around!" I jump at the ferocity of her words. "You told me you wanted him dead, so now he's dead. It was a deal."

It's a deal. The phrase rings in my head, and my heart sinks like a body to the bottom of a lake. I remember now. I want to tell her it wasn't a deal, it was a stupid joke, a drunken mistake, it was not real. But I look into Kelli's eyes now and see they're cold and serious. It wasn't a joke to her.

"Oh, I see it," Kelli says, bringing her face close to mine. "You do remember now. You know I'm right. So now you know you can't call the police, Bea. You're an accomplice. This was premeditated."

"That's not what this was. At all. I don't know who you are, but you took advantage of me. You set me up." I want to cry, to scream, to lash out at her stupid smile and rip it off her face. Instead, I can only sob. I think about the happy celebration going on inside and can't bear the thought of going back to face people. "I can't do this."

Kelli smiles and drops her shoulders. "I'll take care of all of this. We can talk later."

I bristle. "We're not talking later. We are never talking again because you are going to be caught and put into jail or an institution!" I put my hand on the door handle, ready to escape.

"Well, you would know all about those places, huh, Bea Milner?"

My hand stops, and my blood runs cold. I don't dare turn around to face her. "Who the hell are you?" I ask.

"You know me. I'm Kelli. And you're Bea Milner Ku. I know everything about you, Bea. I know the history you kept secret from your friends, boyfriends, colleges, and current employer. What would BCC think if they found out they'd really hired a teen delinquent?"

My eyes close. How does she know? "That's sealed—"

"So now that we both know who each other is, let's be real. You're not telling anyone about this. You're going to go home and go to sleep, wake up and go to work tomorrow and do your boring job like you do every day. You'll do it because I'll be watching you and making sure you do it. And at some point, you know you owe me your end of the deal, right? I'll clean this up now."

"This was a mistake. I'm leaving."

"You can't," she says, still smiling.

"Watch me."

"No, Bea." She lowers her voice and says it like an order. "You're going to stay because this is how you get out of this mess. There's a reason we met that night."

"You know so much about why I do what I do, don't you?" I snap.

I stay silent but don't break eye contact.

She nods. "You had your chance to tell on me. But you didn't. I have a couple of guesses about that too. The main one being that you know as soon as you point to me, you're pointing right back at yourself. Motive, Bea. I don't have it, but that's all you've got, and I don't think it will take long for the police to figure that out. Especially if you're going and hanging out at the detective's office."

"And the second one?"

"Second: he deserved it. And I know somebody else who deserves it." She pulls out her phone and shows it to me. On the screen is the Saul Group website, opened to the "About Us" page. At the top is a photo of Franklin Saul. She taps a fingernail on the screen.

"Are you serious right now?" I whisper. "Do you know what you're asking? Why?"

"You're not the only one who's been wronged by powerful men."

"I'm not doing this. How can you ask me this?"

Kelli's face shuts like a drawbridge; her eyes are stone. "We had an agreement. We are going to help each other."

I look at her and wonder if I'm simply arguing with someone who's lost her mind. But she knows my full name, a name I haven't used since high school. Since . . .

A sudden rap on the window glass; I jump. Allegra's brown eyes are peering into the car. She waves. "We're about to do the cake, Bea," she yells. I nod. Then, with a warning shot to Kelli, I open the door.

"Why are you both hiding out here?" Allegra asks. "I've been looking all over."

"Kelli was just leaving," I say.

"Oh no!" Allegra whines. "You have to stay for cake!"

Kelli shakes her head from the driver's seat. "No, you've been too kind letting me crash already. I've got to go, but it was so nice meeting you! Congratulations again!"

Kelli climbs out of my car and gets into her own Jeep. She waves all the way down the drive.

Allegra holds my arm, and we walk back to the festivities. "She's so sweet. I'm happy you have a friend, Bea."

"Why are you talking to me like I'm a kindergartner?" I ask. "Besides, she's not my friend." *She's a psychopath.*

Allegra shrugs. "She seemed like a friend to me. I think you need to open up a bit more to people, you know? Nobody is out to get you."

I can only stare at her as she walks over to her place next to Caleb. There's a photo op of them in front of the cake shaped like a little woodland scene, complete with marzipan mushrooms and neatly piped vines and trees. Allegra holds Caleb and poses with the millennial arm at her hip while Caleb's arm reaches around her; they're a beautiful couple. They both look genuinely happy.

Mom finds me leaning against the kitchen counter. She hands me a large knife. "Bea, here, start cutting."

I stab the little frosted woodland clearing, maybe too willingly. The yellow sponge cake is filled with raspberry filling, and the juicy red drops ooze out over the plate. I slice and plate, while Mom distributes.

What do Landon and Franklin Saul have in common? I try to think about what Kelli could be getting out of both of them being dead, and I don't buy the line that she was doing me a favor at all. What if she was targeting Landon from the beginning, and I conveniently showed up at Solo that night?

Dad approaches me. "Hey, Bea?"

I hand him a plate of cake. "Did you get some yet?"

He waves it away. "There's someone at the door for you."

"Oh, is it Kelli again?" I roll my eyes. The nerve of her to come back . . .

"No, it's not her. I think it's someone from the police?"

I set down the knife and look out over the party to the front door. Sure enough, underneath the **OH BABY!** banner framing the front door stands Detective Branson. I take a deep breath and plate a slice of cake.

Chapter 25

My heart is racing as I approach the detective. She's in plain clothes, but still looks official in a white button-down shirt tucked into jeans, her hair in a low bun. I haven't spoken to her since our first meeting at BCC, and she somehow seems larger than life outside that setting and inside my home. She sees me approaching and manages a friendly smile. "Congratulations," she says.

"Oh no, it's not for me!" I laugh. Her face reddens, and I take a small victory in seeing her thrown off slightly. "We're hosting for family friends." I gesture to the dining room, where the couple can be seen enjoying their cake.

Detective Branson peers through, her eyes locking on Caleb and Allegra. "I see."

"Cake?" I hold up the slice of sponge cake, hoping she doesn't notice how it looks slightly blood spattered with the raspberry bursting out of it.

She shakes her head. "Maybe we can chat outside."

"Sure." We step outside to the porch, closing the door on the eager ears and eyes that follow us. "What can I do for you?" I ask.

"Maybe you can tell me?" She pulls something out of her pocket; it's a slip of paper with my name and number on it. *Shit.* I remember now leaving it on her desk when I was in a hurry to get out after spying the autopsy report. *How could I be so stupid?*

"Is that Caleb Crown in there?" she asks. "He's the family friend?"

I pause. "It is."

She nods nonchalantly, but I can see it in her eyes now, the recognition. Because everyone knows Crown Cannabis, the largest locally owned legal cannabis chain in the region. And I'm betting she knows Caleb Crown, the owner, who walks with a cane due to a horrific car accident he was in during his youth. And now she looks at me and also knows he and I are connected. And even though Caleb has been clean and legit, as far as I know, ever since the accident, a connection to me and Landon's death is the last thing Caleb, or Allegra, needs.

The detective looks out over the neighborhood, and I am sure she's filing all this away to make note of later. "So why did you come down to my office," she asks, "the morning before you were busy hosting this party?"

"I'm sorry to waste your time, Detective. It was nothing . . ." I try and think of something, anything. I think of Kelli trying to trap me in her twisted web of lies. Maybe the detective's timing isn't so bad after all. "Actually, I was going to give you more information on that Kelli Stewart girl."

Branson raises her eyebrows. "Actually, we've already looked into your friend from the club."

"You did?" I blink.

She pulls a small notebook from her pocket. "Yeah, we found her information and paid a visit to her apartment not too long after we spoke with you. We looked up the Uber ride records from that night, too, from Landon Laurie's condo building. She took a ride to and from there that night. Unfortunately, neither car had any kind of security camera on those nights. We were able to talk to her, and she corroborated she was with you at the club, and that you both went home with Mr. Laurie and left shortly after."

My stomach clenches, and I can only nod. "Right." The police spoke to Kelli. They spoke with her. *Why wouldn't she tell me?*

"She did admit," Detective Branson continues, "that you both had drugs on you and shared with Mr. Laurie."

I shake my head in disbelief. Kelli said I had drugs? "No, I didn't—" I murmur in shock.

"Did you partake of anything that night, Ms. Ku?"

"No, not at all."

"Do you have a habit of drugs at all? I know you lawyers, high-stress gigs and all; who can begrudge you a little fun now and then, huh? Work hard, play hard."

"No," I say firmly. "I don't do any of that. Kelli was wrong." If Kelli already told Branson I could have given Landon drugs, now it's my word against hers. Here I was about to offer Branson something about Kelli, but she's already ahead of me.

"So Kelli wouldn't have gotten anything from you or anyone you know?"

My muscles quiver and tense. "If you mean Caleb Crown, no."

The detective flips a page in her notebook. "Right."

"Any other questions?"

She tucks the notebook back in her pocket. "I don't think so. You know," she says. "It's good of you to stand up for your friend. But you should be aware that Mr. Crown has a rough past."

I feel the hairs on my neck bristling. "We've all been through our share, Detective. Not sure what your point is."

"I only mean that people close to Caleb seem to share his luck. When he was eighteen, he got his teenage girlfriend into a bad wreck; she was in the hospital for weeks. He admitted later he stole the vehicle and was driving under the influence of multiple substances. Safe to say, he ruined that poor girl's life."

My breath catches in my throat. The sharp points of my fingernails dig into the inside of my wrist. "When he was eighteen? That's a long time ago."

"And his business is hurting. Public record says they just filed for bankruptcy."

"What?" *Oh no,* I think. Does Allegra know?

"It's interesting, because Crown Cannabis from the outside looks like the most successful cannabis shop in the area, right? Makes you wonder how they're going to pay off all those bills." She straightens her jacket. "Anyway, food for thought. Have a good day, Ms. Ku."

I breathe out steadily and watch until her car disappears around the corner. I lean back and let my body collapse against the house; the plate of cake falls from my hands and dumps out onto the moss-covered wooden boards beneath me.

Kelli never told me she spoke with the police. What else hasn't she told me? A sting of betrayal stabs my lungs. It was so stupid of me to believe she was some kind of friend. I feel wet lines of tears against my cheeks.

"What's going on?" Caleb is standing next to me now.

With a jolt, I stand up straight and wipe my eyes. "Nothing," I stammer.

"Thanks for the party, Bea," he says, his eyes smiling and lines spreading out from his soft grin. "I know it probably wasn't top of your list of things to do, throw a baby shower for me and Allegra. But you know we appreciate it and have love for you and the family."

My insides twist. "Of course," I say. "But Allegra did agree to name the baby after me in exchange for all this fanfare, just so you know."

"Worse deals have been made."

Don't I know it.

I flick the button on his shirt. "You guys are gonna be great parents. For real." He looks at me, and I'm transported decades into the past, when it was often just me and Caleb, talking and joking and getting into trouble. He was always that person who could instantly put me at ease.

"So then who was the badge?" Caleb asks.

"The woman I was talking to?"

"Yeah. I know law enforcement when I see it," Caleb says with a slight smile. He leans down and begins cleaning up the dumped cake. "And I recognize that detective. She's often coming into the stores and trying to connect us to every little shoplifting or porch-pirate ring in Seattle. As if the police didn't have better things to do."

I sit and consider Branson's comment about Caleb. Why would she say that? Is she trying to turn me against him? She thinks I have a thing for him, I decide. Maybe I'm protecting him. *It makes you wonder,* she said. And the more I think about it, the more I kind of agree. He just bought that old bar, for example. Why would he do that if his business can't even pay its bills right now?

"So why is she here talking to you?"

"Just loose ends from my boss's death." I sigh. "You know Kelli, who I introduced you to earlier? You wouldn't happen to recognize her from anywhere, would you?"

"Like where?"

"Like your stores?"

"I don't exactly work the till these days. Why?"

I shift my feet. "Just wondering. I was at her place and she had one of those stickers you hand out at the stores."

"Lots of people come through those stores. Lots of people like free stickers." Caleb examines me. "Are you okay? I know you, Bea, as much as you'd like to pretend I don't anymore. We would like to see you more. I'm speaking for Allegra and myself. You and I don't have to relegate our interactions to awkward family events."

The words cut into me. "I just don't know that we have much in common anymore." I shrug. It's a cheap excuse, and he knows it.

"I think a shared history like ours is enough. We've been through a lot together."

"Maybe too much," I mumble.

He stiffens. "It was never too much to forgive."

I keep my face steady, or else I'll give away the fact that I feel like a giant stone is crushing my chest. I want to tell him that some things are too hard to forgive, but not for him or Allegra; I can't forgive myself. I can't say another word, or I might spill everything that's been dammed up this whole time.

Caleb watches me, anticipating something, anything. When I don't respond, he sighs. "With the baby coming, I hope you'll be around more, is all."

"You don't want me coming around your family," I say. "Knowing me, I'll just ruin it all again."

His eyes narrow. "Is that what you think?"

"Look, I can't do this." I bend down and snatch the plate from his hands.

He holds out his palms. "Fine. Never mind."

As I walk back inside, I can feel my face burning and my chest squeezed tight. This is why I stay away from Caleb; this is why we'll never be friends again. He knows me better than anybody else in the world.

◆ ◆ ◆

When the last guests have been thanked and the boxes of gifts loaded into Allegra and Caleb's car, I sit alone in the living room, surrounded by drooping balloons and ripped streamers. I can hear Mom finishing up the dishes; the running water and scrubbing echo through the small house.

What will happen, I wonder, when Franklin Saul dies? Will Detective Branson think it's connected or a coincidence he and Landon died so close together? Then I feel sick because I'm already thinking as if I've accepted Kelli's bargain.

And I can't.

Can I?

The detective is watching me now, even if she wasn't before. I left my own name in her office and led her straight to me.

My stomach drops even lower when I think about how I may have implicated Caleb. Turns out Mom and Dad were right when they told me I should stay away from him as a kid; little did they know it was me who was the danger.

Before I give up and go to bed, I stop in the kitchen doorway and lean against the frame, my arms holding themselves tight against my chest. Mom spots me. "Headed to sleep?"

"Yeah. It was a nice party, Mom. You did a great job hosting. I'm sure Allegra was thrilled."

She beams. "Thanks for your help."

I can't sleep. Even though I know I took my medication this morning, I take another dose of Xanax. As I lie there, waiting for it to kick in, I almost wish it was laced with something more, maybe even something deadly.

Chapter 26

Sunday

Mom comes into the living room, dressed in a nice lavender dress with long bell sleeves. She's carrying a pair of tall brown riding boots. "That's a cute outfit," I say.

"Thanks." She sets the boots by the door. "How are you feeling?"

"Fine."

Her eyes catch my own outfit, dark skinny jeans and a black turtleneck. "Where are you going? Please don't say another date."

I consider asking why I have to be going somewhere in order to look nice, but even I know when I'm making myself an easy target. "I'm going in to the office. I have to catch up on some work."

"Make sure you're back by dinner," she says.

I pack my laptop and leave the house before my parents do, taking the opportunity of free Sunday parking downtown to drive into the office. It's a sunny day, and when the elevator doors open onto the BCC floor, the blue sky seems to stretch forever through the lobby windows. The empty office is quiet but well lit, with winter sun pouring in from the rare clear day. I leave my office door open as I settle down and begin going through the emails I ignored on Friday. I flag several client inquiries and write out a couple of deliverables due.

It's not that Landon and Kelli aren't on my mind today—of course they are. But I'm alone now, me and the truth of it. I don't have to act right now or worry about being accosted by gossiping coworkers. I can focus on work, which I do.

In fact, the more I work, the better I feel. The more I dive into my memoranda and spreadsheets, the further I get from my real life. It's safe here in these cells, where I can control the values and formulas; I know the outcomes because I input the data. And the data support my conclusions and recommendations, and the clients love it. Before this impossible mess, I put everything I am into my job, and almost nothing beat the high of knowing I'm damn good at what I do.

People loathe the addict when it's pills or alcohol. But the workaholic? We love them—we reward them because society needs them to function. Corporate America is literally held up on the backs of the sick individuals like me who will sacrifice their happiness and lives for one hit of that "big win." My inbox is my dealer, trading in highs and lows like an IV into my eyeballs. I've traded one addiction for another.

That's why I'm so good.

◆ ◆ ◆

The day passes by, and the winter light grows pale before gently sinking into a deep indigo. When I finally stand to stretch and trigger the motion sensor for the overhead light, I'm surprised to see another light illuminated down the hall. *Jesus,* I think, rubbing my eyes. *I thought I was the only one here this whole time.* I crane my neck to see which office it's coming from, but the reflection is strange and playing tricks on me.

It looks like it's coming from Landon's office. A shiver goes across my scalp, and I gasp involuntarily. It can't be.

I cross my arms and slowly walk down the hall toward the eerie glow in the dark. It is coming from his office; I can see that clearly now. His door is closed, but the light is clearly on inside. I can't tell if there's someone inside or not. I step slowly toward it, my own echoing footsteps the only sound in the empty hall. Once I'm standing in front of the glass door, his name mocks me at eye level. I can see there's nobody inside. With a shaky hand, I grip the handle and slide the office door open.

"Bea?"

I jump and clutch my chest.

"I'm so sorry. I didn't mean to scare you."

I turn to see Olivia, who's pretending to look concerned, but I can tell she's really trying not to laugh at me. "Oh my God," I breathe.

"Are you okay?" she asks.

I shake my head and chuckle at myself. "Clearly not," I say. "You gave me a heart attack. What are you doing here?"

"Getting a head start on the week's work," she says. "I had no idea you were here too."

"No, I meant, why are you *here*?"

"Oh, you mean his office? Is it weird this makes me feel . . . closer to him?" She steps past me and sits at the desk. Landon's desk.

A little weird, I think. "Not at all," I say. "That makes sense."

"Can I ask you something?"

"Yeah."

"Do you miss him at all?"

Air fills my lungs, and I breathe out deeply. "I do."

Olivia smiles and gives a small laugh. She *laughs*. "Really? Because, Bea, you know people saw you and Landon at Solo, and there's talk about you arguing with him."

I'm beginning to get irritated. "So? People who saw us arguing also saw me walk away from him. It's not a secret there was no love between Landon and me that night."

Olivia continues, "I would get it . . . if you felt a little relieved he was gone. It was pretty obvious there was bad blood between you and Landon."

"There wasn't bad blood," I say. Oh God, if people think there was bad blood between us . . . Bad blood enough to make him disappear? "And even if there was, I wish to God every day he was here and alive." I'm not even lying.

Olivia nods. "No, you're right." She puts her hands over her face. "God, that was stupid to ask you. I'm sorry. I still can't believe he's gone sometimes. I feel like any moment he could walk in here with a sexist joke and demand a coffee from downstairs. I'm so sorry, again. And I'm sorry you're having to deal with all this boys' club bullshit. I'm sorry it took Landon literally dying for you to get your flowers."

I look around.

"It's okay," Olivia says. "It's just us."

"Right," I say. "And it's fine."

"It's not fine."

"I'm trying to do my best."

"It's called self-preservation. We are really alike, you know? We are both patient. We didn't come from the places they come from. We know sacrifice, so we know struggle. We're happy to wait in the corners and on the sidelines for our opportunities. Because unlike them, we are always watching. What is it they say? It's always the quiet ones you have to look out for." Olivia winks.

I let out an awkward laugh. "Weird, someone else said that to me the other day. I'll let you get back to your work."

She glances at her watch, giving it a quick tap. "You know what, I've been at it all day, and my brain is fried. I think I'm calling it." She shuts her laptop.

"Same. I didn't realize how late it was getting." I give a wave. "Have a good evening."

Back in my office, I begin shutting down and packing away my things. Mom will probably be annoyed that I'm as late as I am.

As I'm leaving, Olivia stops by my door, zipping up her coat. "By the way, there was a package up front with your name on it."

"What could that be?" We walk out together, and sure enough, a small cardboard box is sitting on the counter in the lobby. I use my car keys to quickly cut through the tape, and after I remove some packing paper, I lift up a heavy trophy. It's crystal carved into a quill pen standing upright. I look at the base, and my name is etched into it in cursive script. "It's my award," I say, holding it and feeling the heft of the glass.

"Oh, hey!" Olivia reaches out and touches the corner. "Nice! Congratulations on that again!"

I place the award back in the box and cover it up with paper.

"I remember when I got mine, forever ago," she says. "I think my plaque is stuffed away in my bedroom closet, to be honest."

"You got this same award?" I hold the box to my chest and somehow feel prouder knowing Olivia and I have it in common.

"I used to do a lot of pro bono work for juvenile youth—defending against bogus loitering charges, sealing or expunging records, even emancipation cases."

I wish I could tell her I know a thing or two about juvenile law and sealing records. "I had no idea."

"It was actually one of the most rewarding times of my life. Oh God, I can't believe I forgot this—there was a massive case where I was working on one side for Legal Aid on behalf of juvenile victims of this massive fire, and none other than Landon Laurie was working the other side. That's really where I first met him and got to know him. Before you ask, he was the exact same. A complete bulldog."

"A fire?" I ask.

"Yeah, it was a long time ago, when I was more of a crusader for any kind of cause." Olivia smiles sadly and drops her eyes. "Back when I was a believer."

"A believer in what? Justice?"

"Among other things."

"So why is it in your closet? Had to make room for more awards?" I joke.

She looks down. "Maybe something like that. To be honest, the fire case affected me, really got into my bones, you know? I couldn't look at the award for a long time. You should display that, though."

"What was the name of the fire case?" I ask.

"It was a lawsuit against this apartment building called Valencia Towers; it was such a tragedy." She looks at her watch again. "I really have to get going. But have a good night, Bea."

"Thanks, Olivia." I watch her get into the elevator and disappear behind the doors. When she's gone, I return to my office and unpack the trophy again just to look at it. I've never gotten an award before. I stand it up on my desk like a glass monolith.

I turn on my computer again and search Valencia Towers.

Chapter 27

The results are mostly news articles, the most recent from 2003. I click into it and read.

> A King County Superior Court judge has dismissed an amended complaint for a wrongful death lawsuit brought by the survivors of the Valencia Towers apartment complex against the management and real estate holding company, Brooks Partners.
>
> The Valencia Towers apartment complex, located in South Seattle, was completely destroyed by a fire on December 10, 2000. The blaze ravaged through the complex in the early hours of the winter morning, resulting in hundreds of fatalities and hundreds more tenants without homes.
>
> The lawsuit, originally filed by the surviving family members of the deceased tenants, alleged Brooks Partners knew of multiple electrical hazards in the apartment building but had done nothing to make repairs or comply with safety regulations. Documents describe the fact that the tenants were generally lower income, further alleging that the owners didn't care to spend money on the aging apartment complex.
>
> A complaint filed Friday in King County alleged

that Brooks Partners' negligence directly caused the multiple deaths the night of the fire.

The suit alleged, "Brooks Partners knew, or reasonably should have known, that both the tenants and the maintenance staff of the Valencia Towers were routinely filing complaints and work orders for repairs of wiring in the buildings, originally built in the 1940s."

The original lawsuit also alleged that "Brooks Partners is liable in this action because the company did not act to make any necessary repairs to Valencia. They should have reasonably known that it was only a matter of time before a tragedy such as the fire would occur."

Washington state law defines wrongful death as a death "caused by the wrongful act, neglect, or default of another person." To prove Brooks Partners' negligence or intentional actions caused the wrongful deaths of those lost in the fire, the defendants had to demonstrate that Brooks Partners owed a legal duty to the deceased tenants, they breached that duty, the breach resulted in the deaths of the tenants, and the victims' families have suffered as a result.

In his dismissal of the lawsuit, Judge Leroy commented, "My heart goes out to the victims of the fire and their families. However, their lawsuit at this time does not meet all the elements of a wrongful death suit." This is the second suit filed in this case. The original wrongful death suit was filed a year after the fire in 2001.

The lawsuits were filed by attorney-at-law Robert Ducheney, on behalf of the victims of the Valencia Tower fire.

Brooks Partners is represented by attorney Franklin Saul.

My cursor hovers over the last line. Franklin Saul. I copy and paste the article and link into a blank Word document. I go back to my search results and scroll down until I see an article from December 10, 2000, the day of the fire.

> Early this morning, fire crews responded to a large fire at the Valencia Towers apartment building in South Seattle. The fire is under control, and crews remain on scene to extinguish the fire, the Seattle Fire Department reported.
>
> Regis Palano, who lives down the street, awoke to screaming and fire engine sirens. "I've never seen a fire that big before," he said. "The flames lit up night like day."
>
> Multiple fatalities are being reported.

I save this one too and go back to reading. So this fire is connected to Saul. Then I come across an article that looks familiar. I read the headline: LAWSUIT FILED BY VALENCIA SURVIVORS DISMISSED. But I know where I've seen it before when I see the photo with the caption: "Seattle attorney Franklin Saul and his team were behind the defense's skillful argument in getting the case dismissed." It's the photo that shows Saul and, behind him, Landon Laurie, starting out in the legal field as a lowly intern.

That's how they're connected.

But why Kelli? And more importantly, why me?

When I return home, everyone else is asleep. I set my glass award on my dresser; I'll have to find a nicer place for it later. Then I open my laptop again.

The night passes, and I can't sleep, I can only read article after article on the fire. Soon, though, there are no more articles. There were only a couple more after the last article about the dismissal of the wrongful death case, and they were simply articles marking the five-year anniversary of the fire, with no new information.

But down the internet rabbit hole I go—I string together new search terms for the names of victims or survivors. I can't find them, aside from a few fundraiser pages ("Help us pay for Daniel's skin grafting surgeries. #ValenciaSurvivor") and a Facebook event page for a church bake sale to help raise a rental deposit for a displaced family of five ("Give the Moraleses a Home for Christmas").

It makes me physically ill that during times of crisis, Americans are forced to go online and beg for help from strangers. But then I wonder how much a settlement from Brooks Partners would have helped Daniel and the Morales family.

A settlement that Franklin Saul made sure never happened.

That's it. It has to be.

I call Kelli. To my surprise, she answers. My voice quivers. "I know about the fire."

"Oh." No snarky line, no pretense or threat; she knows I know, and this is her laid bare.

I close my laptop and lie back in my bed, tears already falling down my cheeks and onto the pillow underneath my head. "You were in the fire," I say. "You lost someone?"

She sighs. "I lost them all."

◆ ◆ ◆

"I was too young to remember the actual fire. I would be told later that my mom was able to hand me off to the firefighters right before the ceilings collapsed. Sometimes I dream that I can remember that apartment—I see the Christmas lights around a picture window overlooking the water, a tree with presents underneath. But much later, I saw a diagram of all the apartments, and my family's was an inner courtyard apartment. The only view we had was of the neighbors across the way. I guess I made up these memories because my actual memories from childhood are hospitals and foster homes.

"I do remember when the lawyers came to get our statements, though. The nurse was telling them I was too little, that I'd lost my parents and sister. I don't think she knew I could hear her. That's how I found out. Anyway, the lawyers didn't care. They asked me questions I didn't understand, and I cried until a doctor came and had security kick them out. I didn't know it at the time, but after the first few foster homes, and once the lawsuit was dismissed for good, I finally figured it out: me and my story, we were nothing but dollar signs to these people. Even the lawyers that brought the suit on behalf of us survivors, they only did it for the payday at the other end. Once the judge said *Enough,* they said, *So sorry,* and we never heard from them again. All their promises were nothing."

"But you were so young," I say. "And grieving."

"I didn't know how to grieve. Nobody showed me how. Besides, I was too busy surviving in the system. Did you know I have a burn scar all along my right torso? Imagine being a child and having to deal with that pain and the pain of knowing your family burned to death while you lived."

"I can't imagine—"

"No, you can't. So I had to show them what it feels like, so they could experience all the pain that I did."

She's killing them, I think. *She's after every person that had to do with the fire or the dismissed lawsuits after the fact.*

"So Franklin Saul has to die because he defended the management company? This is part of your revenge?"

She scoffs. "Haven't you been listening? It's not revenge. I'm not so petty, despite what you might think of me. The lawsuit shouldn't have been dismissed; the survivors should have been allowed a fair trial to show the facts against Brooks Partners. We never had a chance. And then three years go by, and the lawyers tell us the statute of limitations is up, and that means our window to sue is closed. But how can that be? They murdered our families! There's no statute of limitations for murder. It's not how it works, they say. Best to move on. Move on? And just forget?

"I grow up, but I don't forget. I go to law school, and I read all the textbooks and ace all the exams. I get the clerkships and the jobs, and then I become an attorney, and I think, *Finally, I can get justice for my loved ones, because nobody else will.* I looked at everything, all the pathways to appeal, all the different ways to assign liability to hold someone, anyone, responsible. I even looked at getting the case reopened. But you know what?"

I do know. "You can't find a way," I say. "In all your studying, in all the case law and anyone you talk to about how to make Brooks Partners pay legally, there's no way."

"Because our system is broken. That was my real mistake, spending too long trusting in a legal system that was never designed to help me. It's not revenge, Bea. It's justice."

"And now you need my help with this justice? Why now, and why me?"

"Maybe the right place, right time—you ever think about that? Haven't you ever needed saving? We can save each other."

"Not like this."

"Yes, like this, and you don't have another option. I hope you're working on a way to fulfill your part of the bargain."

I take a deep breath. "I never asked you for anything. The only murderer here is you, Kelli. You should be thanking me I'm not turning you in for killing Landon. But I will if you ever come near me again."

"No."

"No?"

She begins to whisper into the phone, quickly and with an urgency that makes me recoil. "I'm not a murderer, Bea. I saved you. You told me Landon was toxic, he was a predator. Think about it! Isn't your life better with him gone? That's why we agreed to do what we did. I fulfilled my end of the bargain. Now it's your turn. We made a deal—"

"Fuck your deal." I hang up.

I find the Brooks Partners website and see they're still in business and, in fact, are one of the biggest real estate holding companies in the Northwest. I wonder if they're in need of new counsel. I click through their website and stop at an article highlighted in their "Recent News" section. It's an obituary for the former president and CEO, who passed away unexpectedly a few months ago, it seems. Though that's not what catches my eye. It says he died in a fire in his home.

Jesus, how many have there been? I wonder. *And how many until it's enough?*

I sit in the quiet for a long time, expecting her to call back, to send a threatening text, but she doesn't.

I wish Landon were still alive. Then it would all be different. I would still be trying to get that promotion, sure, but that existence was better than this, surely. But he would still be manipulating me, bullying me and others, using people as he pleased. What would be different? Everything and nothing.

Why do the narcissists and abusers never get held accountable? But then I wonder—how would they ever be held accountable by a system they built to uphold them?

And while the Valencia victims were silenced forever, the rich men responsible only got richer. And the powerful continued to hoard all the power until the powerless had no choice left but to respond.

My skin is buzzing and my insides are twisted, and a tiny pinpoint of doubt appears in my core. I'm ashamed because I think Kelli might be right. How else would the bad guys ever be punished?

Chapter 28

Monday

My pill bottles stare at me from their shelf. I can't remember if I took them yesterday or not. But my insides are a yawning pit I have no desire to fill. What could possibly make me whole? The thought of swallowing anything, even water and medicine, makes me queasy. I leave the bottles closed and shut the cabinet.

The day moves slowly, if not productively. If nothing else, I'm able to escape into the work and forget my troubles for a few hours. When I look at the time and see the workday is almost over, I'm hit with panic.

I can't go back to everything. So I work for a couple more hours. I lose track of time and then realize it's almost eight. Mom will be annoyed I missed dinner. I quickly pack up and leave.

But when I pull into the driveway, I'm greeted by a car I wasn't expecting. It's Kelli's unmistakable Jeep.

I unlock the door and push it open. Mom is seated on the couch, and Kelli is right next to her, drinking tea. I can smell the freshly grated ginger. "Hi, honey," Mom greets me. "Kelli stopped by! I told her you'd be home soon from the office."

Kelli grins. "We've been gabbing away here waiting on you, Bea." She sips from her mug. "Your mom has been telling me the funniest stories from when you were a kid. Mmm, and this tea is delicious. What's it called again?"

"Salabat, and please, call me Miriam," Mom says. "Bea, are you hungry? I completely forgot to make you a plate of leftovers—"

"I'm not hungry at all, actually." I drop my bag and coat on the dining table. "Kelli, can I talk to you in my room?"

She stands and smooths out her high-waisted slacks. "Thanks, Miriam. That tea is amazing. I can tell why it's Bea's favorite after a stressful day."

I don't even wait until the bedroom door closes behind us; I push Kelli into my room and shove her as hard as I can. She trips and falls onto the bed.

"Oh my gosh, Bea!" She laughs. "I wouldn't have guessed you were into the rough stuff. Though you do have that whole repressed thing going on." She fluffs the pillow next to her.

"Shut up," I hiss. "Why are you here?"

"It doesn't matter," she says. Now, up close to her, I can see her eyes are red and her skin is dullish. She looks like she's not sleeping; for the first time, I can see her veneer cracking. She wipes her eyes, and her mascara smears across her eyelids. "What is your plan, huh? This needs to happen soon. Especially if this detective is making house calls."

"Listen," I say. "I can't believe I'm telling you this, but Saul has a heart problem. He takes this medication for his heart regularly, and he carries it with him everywhere, or at least his assistant carries it. I've seen it. All you have to do is swap out the pills with something else."

"So he'll have a heart attack?" she says. "It's not a bad plan. Switching pills . . . this is like some mid-'90s thriller shit, Bea. Good thinking."

"Thanks, love getting accolades for my murder methods." But if I'm honest, I like this plan because it's not even really murder this way . . . I'm just taking away medicine, not causing death. It's the heart attack that would actually kill him. But then I snap back to reality. *What the fuck, Bea? Why are you trying to justify this?* But maybe I can keep Kelli thinking we are in this together just a little longer, long enough for me to figure something out.

This has to end. I can't keep living and thinking this way.

"Okay," I continue. "So I get placebos. Then how am I supposed to switch them?"

Kelli's face twists. "Placebos?" she hisses. "That's ridiculous. We can't just sit around and wait for him to drop dead because his heart medication routine became ineffective. Think. We need to swap his pills with pills laced with something else, something sure to cause death."

I think of Landon. "Fentanyl," I say. "So you have these pills?"

She shakes her head. "This isn't my job. It's yours. I already did my part, remember? I'll get you the name of the medication somehow. But it's on you to figure out how to get the stuff and how to swap it out." Somewhere outside, a car turns on. Kelli's eyes widen, and her face turns in the direction of the sound. She digs into her pocket. "Here, this is my Saul Group–office key card."

"Don't you need this?" I ask.

"I have another one. Just take this in case you get an opportunity. But first thing is getting those pills—make it soon, lawyer girl."

"'Lawyer girl'? You're 'lawyer girl' too," I mumble, but she's already opened my door and is halfway out.

I hear Mom and Dad tell her good night and to get home safe.

"I like her," says Mom. "She loved the salabat."

I lie in bed, unable to sleep. I should be thinking of pills, deadly drugs and how to obtain them. But I already know how. I just don't want to admit it. Caleb says he is legit now, but the more I think about it, the more I wonder about him. Maybe Branson is right—there has to be a reason he's buying properties while on paper he has no money left. He could be the only one left to help me.

Chapter 29

Tuesday

"Surprised to see you again so soon." Caleb stands behind the bar of the Dancing Goat, or Crown Club, or whatever it's called now. "What can I do for you, Bea?"

"I need a favor."

Caleb sighs and walks toward the stairs. I follow. We go up to the roof; it's frigid, and the sky is a cloudy net above us.

"The favor."

I pause. "Just promise you won't ask questions."

"Sure, promise."

I take a deep breath. "I need fentanyl."

His eyes widen. "No," he says.

"No, but listen—"

"I won't." He looks up at the clouds.

After a couple of seconds of silence, I try to explain. "They have to be in pill form. Specific pills. I'll send you a picture of what they have to look like. It's not for me—"

"I have a question."

"You promised no questions."

"Just one."

I shrug. "Go ahead."

"Would we be talking right now if you didn't need this favor?"

I tell him the truth. "I don't think so."

Caleb continues. "I'm not doing this, Bea. I'm not getting you what you asked for. Even if I could, I wouldn't. I don't know what you're into, but you need to think carefully about what you're asking for. These are dangerous games. I'm a business owner. I'm a husband, and I'm about to be a father. But I'm also a guy who has a past, and I can't be messing around with that stuff anymore. If your detective friend shows up again, I could lose it all."

I clench my fists in my jacket pockets. "But you must know someone, at least," I push. "Just give me a contact."

"I said no," he snaps.

I shake my head. "So does Allegra know you're bankrupt?"

He steps back and raises his hand to his temple, dazed. "What did you just say to me?"

"How are you keeping the businesses afloat when you have no money? You have to have another income stream . . ."

"Is that what you think?"

"I think people have a hard time changing."

"You changed."

I draw a sharp dagger of air into my lungs. "I fooled myself into thinking I could, I think. But that detective—"

"So you trust her more than your childhood friend now?"

"There has to be a reason she's watching you, no?"

"Are you kidding me?" He shakes his head.

"You never had a problem being my supplier before," I say.

His head hangs down onto his chest, then rises slightly as he tells me, "Get out."

My chest squeezes. I shake my head. "Wait—I'm in trouble, Caleb—"

"I can't help you. Please leave now." His voice almost trembles.

"Shit!" I scoff, and my breath turns into a cloud of white in the air, like I just took a hit from a vape pen. "Oh my God, I'm so sorry." My voice is hoarse and small. I've gone too far.

He holds the back of his neck and closes his eyes. "Maybe let's just go back to being strangers again."

My heart sinks into the depths of the lake in front of us. It was wrong of me to come here, so very wrong of me to ask him this.

Without another word, I hurry to my car and sit in the driver's seat with my phone in my hands. A rich thickness in my throat begins to rise up, and I cradle my head in my arms against the steering wheel. I cry in the darkness, tears for opportunities lost and futures ruined, my finger hovering over his name. I finally type out the message: what are you up to? I hit send fast before I can change my mind.

Simon responds quickly. Nothing, want to come over?

◆ ◆ ◆

I don't know how late it is when I arrive at his door, but he opens it and invites me in without asking why I'm there. Hell, we both know exactly why I'm there. Simon looks at me as I take my jacket off and hang it up, then take my boots off and line them up neatly next to his shoes near the door, trying to ignore his watchful and hungry eyes. I take my phone out of my bag and put both on a side table, and when I have nothing left to pretend to be busy with, I tilt my face to his.

"What is it?" I ask.

"Have you been crying?"

I kiss him hard to push away the lingering memories of Caleb that are still gathered in my mind. He takes my hand and leads me to the bed, where on the soft worn cotton-jersey sheets, he peels off my jeans. I lay my head back and stare upside down out his window at the night sky, my fingers holding his hair, feeling his whispers between my legs.

When he comes up and kisses me, I can taste myself on his tongue. My worries drift away, and I let myself melt into him; in the dark we're safe from ourselves and consequences for now. It's a familiar plunge, and I fall headlong. It's a long way down; worrying about hitting rock bottom can wait until the morning.

Chapter 30

Wednesday

My alarm wakes me with a jolt. I sit up and look around in the dim room. Where am I? A warm body stirs next to me. Oh, right. I go into the bathroom and splash water on my face. My stomach feels off, normal for me these days. *Shit,* I think. I have to remember to take my meds when I get home. I go to set a reminder on my calendar and then see the date.

It's been two weeks since Landon Laurie died.

I didn't kill him. But I may as well have.

A text from Kelli waits on my phone. I snuck into saul's office and youll never guess what i found!

It's accompanied by a photo of an empty pill bottle in a trash bin. I take note of the drug name.

The other texts are from Mom last night asking when I'm coming home. I sigh and swish some toothpaste around in my mouth and return to bed.

"Do I want to know where you were before you showed up crying at my door?" Simon lies with his leg hanging off the bed, half-covered by his duvet. I lean on my elbow next to him, holding my face and looking up at the ceiling. "Or why you smell like cigarettes and old cover bands?"

"Old cover bands? Oof," I laugh, thinking about whether Caleb would like that description or not. I think he just might.

Simon turns, ponders me like a cornered animal, though I'm not sure if the animal is me or him. "What are you thinking?" he finally asks.

"Oh no, the dreaded 'What are you thinking?' Isn't it a bit early in our relationship for that?"

"So we're in a relationship?"

I gently push his face and turn away. "I just have some shit going on that's weighing on me."

"No. Okay, at least we're being honest now." He takes a breath. "I'm a good listener."

He deserves something, but I can't tell him the truth, obviously. So I give him something close enough for now, part of the truth.

"I went to see an old friend. To ask a favor. But then it turned out I had no right to ask him anything at all. Remember the friend from my story? It was him."

His eyes widen. "Oh. Okay. The one who—"

"Yeah, that one."

"And?"

"I think I might have really messed things up this time."

Simon sighs. "I'm sorry. Were you, like, trying to get back together with him or something?"

"What? No! Not at all. It's not like that. He's married to a childhood friend of mine."

"Oh. I guess I just figured . . . Gotcha. A childhood friend? Like, not a friend anymore?"

I consider it. "I don't know. I don't really have friends like that."

Simon laughs. "You know how to sell yourself."

"It's true!" I laugh into the pillow and try to cover my face with a blanket.

He gently moves the blanket so we are looking at each other face to face. I don't look away.

He shifts back, blinking. "I never know how to read you. What do you want?"

"I think I want you?"

"I think I want you," he repeats, but without the question mark. "I'm sorry it's all fucked up with your friend. Can I ask what the favor was?"

"It was so stupid. I'm embarrassed."

He rolls toward me. "Tell me. Maybe I can help."

I squint and cover my face with a pillow. "I need pills." I say it into the feather down. Then lower it and say it again: "I need pills."

Simon shakes his head. "Okay. What kind?"

"Fentanyl . . ." I wait for him to admonish me.

He sits up. "Wait, is this for you?"

I shake my head. "It's for . . . a friend." I turn over and sit up too, bringing my knees into my chest. "I kind of owe her something." I stare straight ahead, feeling his unwavering gaze on me.

"I can get a lot of things, but I don't know . . . I'll have to ask around." He pauses. "Are you in some sort of trouble?"

My breath catches in my throat. I don't say anything. And it tells him everything.

"What's going on?" he asks. "I might not be able to get you what you need, but I can still help you."

"I don't think you can." My mouth trembles. "Things just got out of control . . ."

He embraces me, and I find my cheek against his shoulder. He's warm and safe. He kisses my head and whispers into my hair. "We can figure it out. You just have to trust me."

I wince. My track record of trusting people isn't so good in recent days. I pull back, but take his hand. "I wish I could tell you everything. But the fact is I'm scared. I think I really messed up, Simon."

"Give me the short version," he says.

I smile. At this point, what have I got to lose? "The short version? Um, I accidentally agreed to murder my friend's boss after she kind of killed mine."

He blinks. "Are you serious right now?"

"Deadly serious."

"On the news it said Landon died from an overdose. But you're saying you and your friend caused that? How? Did you . . . plan it?" He draws back from me like I've burned him.

I shake my head. "No, no, we didn't. At least, I didn't plan it. I thought it was an accident, and then I found out that it might not have been at all, and both Landon and I were targeted."

Simon's eyes are wide. He holds out his hands. "Wait, you need to back up and explain all this from the beginning."

So I do. I don't leave out anything. When I finish, I'm a bit in shock that he is still here and listening.

His chest expands with his breath, and his fingers shake slightly intertwined in my own. "Okay," he says. "You know if I got you, uh, what you asked for, that would be making me an accessory to murder?"

My hands fly to my face. "Oh my God! I didn't even think about that," I cry. But of course it's so obvious. It's my job to know? My stomach drops as I realize what I could have done to Caleb, to his new family. "Simon, I'm so sorry. See? This is why I can't be close to anyone! I don't think—I just ruin everything and everyone in my path!"

"Shh, shh." Simon puts his hands on my shoulders. "You're not ruining me. It's okay. Let's think."

I fight the urge to flee from him. Something stronger than fear wills me to stay.

He continues. "What specifically do you need?"

"The plan was to get pills that looked like heart medication, but were actually laced . . ."

". . . with fentanyl." He frowns. "That's a whole different kind of ballgame, Bea. Custom made-to-order fake meds? Even if I could, there's no way I would know where to start obtaining something like that. Again, that is, if I agreed to help you kill someone . . . which I'm not." He looks straight into my eyes. "Do you think you can actually kill someone?"

"I don't think I have a choice," I say, feeling the tears building up behind my eyes. "She has me trapped. If she reveals . . . what she knows, I could lose everything. Worse, my parents would lose everything too."

He nods. "Then there has to be another way. A different approach. What would you do if this was a case?"

I scoff. "It's not a case."

"But think of it as one. You can't commit murder, Bea. It's not who you are."

My mouth cracks a smile, because I want to actually laugh from the ridiculousness of the conversation. "You don't know anything about me."

"I do. You told me about your past and that accident. But a teenage mistake and a plan to kill are very different things. Now, focus on solving this like it's another case on your desk."

I snap, agitated. "It's not a case! This isn't a spreadsheet of assets and companies, Simon! It's not a portfolio for Granite!" I gasp. "Wait . . . Granite has a pharma portfolio . . . and you have a friend in a pharma start-up."

His eyes narrow. "What about it?"

"Maybe I can do this." I straighten my back. "But I'll do it my way. If I trust you, can you trust me?"

Simon nods. "I trust you."

"So if I ask you again to get me some pills, do you think you could?"

He asks, "What's the plan?"

◆ ◆ ◆

After leaving Simon's, I can't stop thinking about the Valencia fires. I remember Kelli saying she had done the research, looked into all the angles for appeals or even reopening the case, but maybe she missed something. Maybe her rage blinded her to something helpful; maybe without knowing it, she didn't want to find a legal solution—she just wanted to lash out and hurt those who hurt her.

I go back to the research notes in my phone and pull up the attorney that handled the suit brought against Brooks. Robert Ducheney. A quick search on him tells me he's still practicing law in Seattle and has an office not too far away.

The Law Office of Robert Ducheney is a suite in a larger coworking space downtown, near South Lake Union. I follow the directory in the lobby to the third floor and knock on a door next to a digital sign with Robert's name displayed.

"Come in!"

Pushing the door open slightly, I see a single man about my age behind a desk with binders of paper and notes all over the place. Glancing around, I don't see any other staff other than the slightly disheveled man in front of me. He doesn't look up at the new visitor. "Do you have an appointment?"

"No, I was hoping to talk to Robert Ducheney?"

He stops and pulls off his glasses. "You're lucky. I'm only in the office twice a week these days. Are you looking for an attorney?"

"Kind of. Are you Robert?"

"I am. Have a seat."

Sinking into the plush gray chair across from him, I note the office is bare bones, without even the mandatory law degree framed and hung on the wall. He notices my looks and reads my thoughts. "I'm renting this place two days a week, like I said. For contract writing, I don't need an on-site staff or fancy offices—all just more overhead. My clients run lean, like me, so I don't have to charge you for lemon water and fresh flowers out in the lobby."

I smile. "Like my firm does."

"Oh, you're an attorney?" He looks me up and down. "Sorry, how can I help you, again?"

"I just wanted to ask a couple questions on one of your old cases." Now that I say that, a glaring detail hits me: he's too young. He looks maybe a little younger than me. There's no way he was a lawyer during the time the Valencia case was happening. "You know what?" I say. "I think I have the wrong person. I was going to ask about something that happened almost two decades ago."

He leans back in his chair, arms folded. "Well now I'm curious."

"It was a big fire case."

"The Valencia Towers?"

"Yes, how do you know?"

"I'm Robert Jr. Valencia Towers was my dad's case."

"That's fantastic. So I do have the right place, kind of. Can I talk to your father?"

Robert Jr. clasps his hands on his desk, rubbing his knuckles. "Well, no, unfortunately. Dad passed away about ten years ago."

"I'm so sorry," I say.

"It's all right. Valencia was something of an albatross for Dad. He was so disappointed in that outcome. He really tried his best, but . . ." Robert holds his hands palms up and frowns. "What can you do? These corporations have too much money. They were never going to lose."

"This might sound out of pocket," I say. "But is there any way I can see any old files or notes your dad had? I'm doing a . . . pro bono research project. I've recently become really interested in the case and just have to know if there was anything your dad might have missed. If there's any way in the world the case could be revisited."

"You would have to start by changing the statute of limitations," Robert says. "But I don't see why you can't have a look. What was your name again? Do you mind if I google you or something? You look normal, but you never know, right?" He grins.

"Of course," I say. "There are some nutcases running around, and we don't even know it."

I give Robert my information. The case files aren't here at his rent-an-office, of course, but he has them all digitized and promises to send them to me when he gets back to his home office and can access his external hard drives. I thank him and tell him if I ever need a tech start-up agreement drafted, I'll give him a call. As I am about to leave, I have to ask him, "How did your dad pass, by the way?"

He whistles. "It was brutal, actually. It was a hit-and-run. He was just trying to cross the street in our own neighborhood, if you can believe it. They never caught the driver."

Chapter 31

Allegra is waiting for me on the porch when I get home. I knew she would come here at some point—I was just hoping I had a little more time. She doesn't even wait until I'm out of my car; as I open the door, she comes down the porch stairs and over to me. Her face is a hot scarlet. "Did you ask Caleb to get you drugs?"

I hold out my hand, palm facing her. "Wait, calm down—"

"Don't," she snaps. "Did you?"

"I did, but—"

Her face breaks. "How could you? Do you know what kind of trouble he could get into? Why would you ask him that? After years of making it a point to not talk to him, then you ask him for this? Of course you only come around when you need something. And I'm not even going to get into the fact that you are the last person who needs to be using—"

"It's not for me!" I whisper and look around. "Come inside, at least."

She slams the door as we walk in. It doesn't appear like my parents are home, thank God. "Where do you even get the balls to go to him for that?"

"I'm not using," I insist.

"Jesus, is this connected to your boss's overdose? Were you supplying him or something?"

"No!"

She folds her arms. "It's typical. You and your rich friends can play and get into trouble, and you'll never have to have a reckoning. But a man like Caleb, who is actually an upstanding citizen, will be judged until the day he dies. He's become a better person than any of us were, yet he will always just be the druggie kid."

"You know that's not true for me," I retort. "I had to reckon with the consequences."

"Of your own choices, Bea!" Allegra snaps.

"My own choices," I laugh dryly. "This is hilarious, Allegra."

"How so, exactly?"

"I remember when you were the one warning me about him. And as soon as I'm gone, you get with the exact guy you spent so much time telling me to stay away from? Were you jealous the whole time of me and him? I bet you were so happy when I left."

"You're dead wrong. And exactly—you left. Caleb and I didn't get along then, but we both had you in common. Then you were gone. You didn't even say goodbye."

"You knew I was leaving for college, Allegra. Everybody left."

"But not the day after. You never told us you were moving down to Eugene even before graduation."

"Why would I stay? I wasn't getting my diploma! I had to leave. Do you know how hard it was for me to be here? Even after the physical recovery, I had to be here with all the talk, the gossip. My life was ruined."

"Not just yours—"

"I know!" I yell. "I know about all the lives that were changed because of my actions that night, most of all Caleb's. It haunts me. That's why I can't be around you, either of you. I almost killed him, Allegra. He was so close . . . and then to have the state coming after me, the lawyers threatening me and the interrogations as I lay in my hospital bed? Then after I'm discharged and just trying to make sense of what happened, the legal shitstorm that wouldn't stop." I hold my head in my hands. "Until it did. Until Caleb woke up and took the blame for all of it. I know I was wrong to ask him for what I did. I guess I assumed he was still connected to that world somehow; maybe because sometimes, lately, I feel like I've still never grown past what happened."

Allegra sits next to me. Her hand rises and hovers just slightly above my knee; then she pulls it back. "We tried to reach out to you."

"I know you did."

"You say you had to leave, and maybe you did. And you say everyone else left anyway, and that's true too. Our friends all left for school or to travel or just to get out of their suffocating hometown. But you know who didn't leave? Me and Caleb. We stayed because we didn't have a choice. Don't you think I would have loved to get out of the state too? But staying here was the cheapest option, so the only option. Caleb and I stayed, and we lived in the aftermath of the damage you did, Bea. We tried to reach out so many times, but you never responded, and at some point, we finally gave up. Then we found comfort in each other, a way to move on, through each other. He is different now."

"He's not so perfect," I spit. "Did you know his business is bankrupt? Did you know he's buying bars and leveraging his business to get loans he can't pay back?"

Allegra falls silent. "I did know that." She shakes her head. "Are you trying to shock me? Turn me against him? Like my own husband doesn't tell me about our financial situation?"

The hurt hangs between us.

"He bought that bar because the owner promised us we could earn a fortune each month from the revenue it generated. We were hoping the bar would help us keep the cannabis businesses afloat. Obviously, we knew nothing about running a bar. And it's pretty clear now the owner was lying to get himself out of a sinking business." Allegra wipes her eyes and sniffs. "You don't think we know we're in trouble, Bea? We know! But what can we do?"

I lower my head. "I didn't know . . ."

Allegra continues. "I want you to know that we will always be there for you . . ."

"Thank you."

"But we can't see you for a while, Bea. Not where we are with this baby coming. We need to protect our own peace, the peace that Caleb has worked so hard for. Good luck finding a supplier, Bea. I wish you the best."

I stare straight ahead, knowing she is right. I watch her get up and leave, the door swinging shut behind her and closing off a friendship that maybe should have ended a long time ago.

From the hallway, Dad comes in. Shit.

"Dad?" I say. "I didn't know you were home."

"Just trying to work in the bedroom." He sighs. "Is what she said true? Were you trying to get pills from Caleb?"

My mouth hangs open. There's nothing I can say that will make me look good here; there's nothing good here to say. So I close my eyes and drop my head. I hear Dad expel a long breath.

"I'm sorry, Bea," he says. "You have to leave."

"What?" I stand and look at him in disbelief. "Like, for the night?"

"No." He sets his jaw firm. "Until you sort out whatever it is you've been going through."

"Dad, please, the pills weren't for me—"

"I don't think that makes it any better, and I don't want to know anything more."

"Where's Mom?"

"She is going to agree with this decision. We've talked before about what our plan is if you happened to slide back—"

"Slide back?" I repeat. "So you've been waiting for me to screw up? You had a plan figured out in the likely event I made a mistake?"

Dad raises his voice. "We've given you chance after chance! And now you're trying to pull Caleb and Allegra back into whatever this is? They're having a baby!" He swallows and pulls back. "Please get your things together and leave before your mom gets home. We can help you get in touch with your old counselors and maybe the rehab center you went to after the hospital stay, but we can't pay for it this time. You're a grown woman now."

Without another word, I go to my room and hastily throw some clothes and my computer into a backpack.

"Where will you go?" Dad asks as I slip my coat on and shakily find my car keys.

"Why the hell do you care?" I ask.

◆ ◆ ◆

Where I go is a grocery store parking lot.

It's only 6:00 p.m. or so, but the sun has long since set, and I find a lone spot in the farthest corner of the lot and away from the glowing circles of the streetlamps. In the darkness, my phone on the passenger seat keeps lighting up with texts from Mom and Dad. Maybe they're regretting their words and will ask me to come back home, but I can't bear to hear from them if it's not that. As long as I don't answer, the story in my head that they are reeling with guilt can still be true.

Chapter 32

When I finally uncurl from my upright fetal position, head tucked against my arms and propped over my steering wheel, I look at my phone. Four missed calls from Dad and Mom, but one from Simon.

I dial him back. "Hey."

"Hey," he says. "What are you doing?"

"Nothing."

"Want to come over? I have something for you."

◆ ◆ ◆

His place is bright and warm. When I walk in from the cold, he places a thumb on my bottom lip. "You look freezing. Were you on a nighttime walk or something?"

"Kind of."

He peels off my jacket and then takes it and hangs it in his coat closet. I sit down on his couch and wipe my hands across the natural tan leather, worn soft over time. An overgrown monstera plant towers next to and above me, while muted music plays from a turntable in the corner. A corkboard with photos and assorted concert tickets hangs next to his TV. "I guess I've never been here when it's not obscenely late at night, not in the living room, at least," I observe. "Your place is so homey."

"You should spend more time here, then," he says. "Maybe even while the sun is out."

"Let's not get carried away," I say, smirking.

He sits alongside me, facing me. He gives me a kiss. "How was your day?" he asks.

I burst into inappropriate laughter. "How was my day?" I repeat. "Well, it was kind of horrible."

"I'm sorry."

"It's okay." It's not.

"Have you eaten?"

I haven't even thought about food. On cue, my stomach grumbles. "Not exactly."

◆ ◆ ◆

Over a coffee table covered in Thai takeout, Simon holds out a small white bottle. I hold out my hand, palm facing up and ready to catch the item when he drops it. "That was fast." I push and twist open the child-safety top. The little red-and-white capsules tumble out. "These look pretty similar to the real thing." I examine them, in disbelief over how accurate they appear at first glance, before noticing the faded pigment and how the two sides of the capsule don't align perfectly.

Simon scoots over, extending chopsticks full of noodles. I bite. "Do you think this will work?" he asks.

"It has to."

I text Kelli, Got the pills.

Pic? she responds.

I take a picture of the bottle and the pills and send it.

My phone dings. Saul and Karolina are working late tonight, office is empty. Go there now. Floor 32, office A15.

I stare at the glowing rectangle in my hand. In my other hand, I hold Kelli's key card. Is this it? Is this my chance?

If I do this now, it will be finished, I think. *I'll be able to make things right with Mom and Dad, and even Allegra and Caleb.* What else is there?

"I have to go," I say.

"Now?"

"Yes, now." I stop to kiss him. My fingers pause on the doorknob. I look back. "This has been really nice," I tell him. "Thank you again."

◆ ◆ ◆

The rain is a gray mist, drops merely hovering in the dusky glow of streetlamps illuminating the city under the impending storm. I barely feel the cold.

Pushing through the heavy doors into the Saul Group building, I grip tightly onto my bag. The security guards look at me approaching and give a small wave. Nodding back, I wave the key card over the sensor and wait for the turnstile to activate.

Nothing.

Did Kelli screw me?

Another swipe and a pause. From the corner of my eye, I see one of the guards rising from his chair behind the big control center, a panel of screens and camera views. At the last moment, the sensor beeps green, and I hear a click from the turnstile. I shove it with my hip and pass through to the elevator banks, shrugging it off as the guard sits back down, turning his attention to his phone.

As I wait for the elevator, I check the time. Quarter till eight in the evening and almost thirty minutes since Kelli's text, despite me moving as fast as I could to get here. I hope Saul hasn't left.

The elevator doors open up to the elevator bank of the Saul Group, and I use the key card once more to open the heavy wooden doors I so recently passed through with Amy, though it seems like years ago now. The lobby is dark and quiet; the receptionists have long gone home. I slowly step into the middle of the hallway, and the motion sensor lights above me flicker on. But beyond that, no lights are visible along either corridor I look down.

To avoid more recorded security card swipes than necessary, I find the internal stairs and go up, my bootheels echoing in the narrow stone-and-steel shaft. I quietly open the door to the thirty-second floor.

It's quiet here too. Though as soon as I come through and shut the door, I can see lights on. I follow them, and sure enough, I hear voices—a man's and a woman's. I brace myself against the hallway walls and slink toward the light and sounds. The rest of the floor is dark.

As I get closer to the lit office, I can hear them better, and it quickly becomes clear they are not discussing work. I place my hands over my face and pause. *Why?* I think. I'm now directly outside the office, and it's Karolina's, according to the name plaque I'm standing next to, and she's inside with Saul.

I can hear them—rather, him—breathing hard and panting; Karolina is moaning as well.

Oh God, no, please.

On the other side of the door is another lit office. I glance up at the nameplate and see that under Karolina's name, it has a number: A14. That must mean the other office is A15. Saul's office. Now I just have to cross over . . .

I take a quick peek into Karolina's office. She is bent over her desk, with Saul behind her, his pants around his ankles and his hands firmly on her bare shoulders. I whip back around and try not to make a sound. Thank goodness he's facing toward the window.

After a deep breath, I tiptoe past the doorway. I stop and brace myself for a scream or a yell, but there's no pause or break in the action. With a sigh of relief, I slip into Saul's office. His jacket is hanging on a coatrack next to the door. I sit on the floor, right next to the coatrack, and with shaking hands go through the pockets. I can't believe it—the bottle of pills is here in the inside jacket pocket. I open the bottle and reach into my bag to grab Simon's pills. My hands fumble, and I'm nearly outsmarted by the childproof cap, but I manage to open it. I dump out the real pills into my bag and in their place pour Simon's pills into the little orange bottle.

With a twist, I close it and drop it back into the jacket pocket.

My heart is pounding louder than what's going on in the office next door. I gulp and wonder if he should be engaging in this kind of activity with a heart condition in the first place. With shaky legs, I stand. Before

I leave, I notice the family portrait of Saul hanging over his desk. He gives a million-dollar smile while standing hand in hand with his wife, I'm assuming, and two teenage daughters stand on either side of them.

Resisting the urge to break into a run, I head the opposite direction, knowing all offices like this are designed in a loop. I'm so distracted, I almost miss the stairwell entrance. Back on the thirty-first floor, I only let myself breathe once I push the down button for the elevator; overhead, numbers light up briefly as the elevator rises toward me. I let myself pause for just a moment, trying to calm down.

"Bea?"

Out of the dark hallway, Amy emerges. "What are you doing here?"

"Amy?" I grip the strap of my bag, pressing Saul's loose pills against my body. "You scared me!" I laugh faintly.

Amy looks around, into the darkness and back to me. "How did you get in here?"

"I was here to see a friend," I say.

"Who?"

"She works here . . ." I grasp for words. "But she wasn't here after all. I, Amy, I . . ." The elevator doors open. "I have to go."

"Bea?"

I slam my palm onto the button for the lobby. The doors shut. Amy's voice cuts through them. "Bea!"

◆ ◆ ◆

I can't go back to Simon's. I can't go home.

So I go to the only place I have left, the office.

The pills swirl around the toilet bowl and then vanish. When I emerge from the women's restroom at BCC, it's pitch black outside through the windows and silent as a mausoleum.

My phone lights up on my desk. It's Amy. I ignore it. The phone goes silent, only to light up again a few moments later. I don't even look to see who it is this time. It's most likely Amy, I'm guessing. But if it's Kelli, I can't talk to her right now. If it's anyone else, what could I say?

I set down all my stuff and then run to the bathroom again to throw up. I brush my teeth after.

Spinning in my office chair with legs crossed, I hang my head backward. I wonder how early the earliest BCC employees come in. If I set my alarm for 4:00 a.m., will I have time to get dressed and ready in the bathroom without anyone walking in on me?

A noise catches my attention, and I put my foot down to stop my chair; I sit up. It's the elevator. My stomach jolts. Is it the detective coming to find me? Is it Saul, who could tell the pills were fake? Lights flutter on, and I can see the figure of a woman walking down the hall, her hair pulled back.

"Kelli?" I breathe. She turns the corner. "Olivia?"

She glances up as she passes my office, then screams and jumps back. This makes me yell and jump out of my chair. Olivia holds her throat and begins to laugh. "Jesus Christ, Bea! What do you think you're doing? You could have killed me!"

"I'm sorry," I say, not seeing why it's so funny. "What are you doing here?" I ask.

"I forgot my laptop, of all things, and I wanted to get something out tonight. I could ask you the same!" Then she spots my duffel bag against the wall, my change of shoes next to it, and maybe most telling of all, my toothbrush on my desk.

She puts her hand to her ponytail. "Are you . . . staying here?"

"My parents and I had a fight . . ." I hold back tears.

"Oh, Bea, I'm sorry. Do you . . . do you want to stay with me tonight? You can't sleep here."

"No, I can't put you out."

"It's nothing. It's a quick drive to mine, and I have a guest room. You can just follow me in your car. Please, I won't let you say no."

As I leave the office building, I toss the unmarked white pill bottle into a trash can on the street. It clatters against the metal side before disappearing.

Chapter 33

Olivia unlocks her apartment door and helps me with my duffel bag. Her place is dark and quiet, a simple two-bedroom by the looks of it. "Do you want something to drink or eat?" she offers.

"No thanks," I say. "I just need to sit down for a moment. I'm still processing everything, I think." We go to the living room, dark and lit only by the city streetlights shining through the tall windows overlooking the quiet neighborhood below.

"The guest room is ready for you, if you want to go and change. I'll set out some spare pajamas for you to borrow."

"Thank you. That's so kind of you. I'm sorry I'm crashing in on you like this."

"Not at all. I don't know what's going on, Bea, but we are going to figure it out, and in the meantime, you're safe here. Come on." She leads me to a spare room, a cozy guest space with a full bed. "I'm going to shower, but afterward, the bathroom will be all yours," Olivia says. "Is there anything else you need?"

I shake my head. "No, thank you so much again."

She nods and leaves me to it.

On the comfortable bed and in the quiet, my body begins to come down from the adrenaline I've been running on for the last several hours. I close my eyes and feel myself drift.

I don't know how long I've been out when I hear my phone and computer ding simultaneously in my bag. I sit up and almost don't know where I am for a moment. Then I hear Olivia's footsteps go from her room down the hall to the bathroom. And I remember.

As she turns on the shower, I hear the old plumbing creak and water begin to flow through the old plaster wall I share with the bathroom. I roll over on the bed and check my phone. It's an email from Robert and a link to the Valencia files. I break out the laptop and eagerly click through to a directory of files, hundreds of documents, and none of them named anything remotely helpful. I open one and see it's a scan of the original filing Robert's dad made in the case. Another one is a transcript of the deposition of one of the building owners. As I scroll through a few others, my heart drops. This will take me forever to go through.

Still . . .

Scrolling through the files, I stop at one titled "Dependents—Legal Aid Assigns." I open it and begin to read. It's a compilation of all the minor children affected by the fire—in other words, any children left without a guardian as a result of the blaze. My eyes begin to water as I click through the pages: so many names, so many innocent faces. Some with injuries, all of them without hope. *These were real children,* I think, *not just names in files.* They deserved some justice.

And then I find Kelli. Her name in the file is Kelli Duncan, but those big blue eyes are the exact same. Where photos of the other children show understandably sad faces, hers is defiant—chin stuck out and eyes staring straight into the photographer's lens. She was determined from the start. I read her file.

There are not a lot of details. Both parents deceased; she told me as much.

Then there are photos of drawings. Well, more than drawings; it's her art therapy portfolio. I guess you could call them paintings, but it's more like raw emotions spilling onto a canvas. Like in the painting from her dining room, Kelli has expressed herself in bold, bright splashes of color. Some of the paintings are crossed out with big black *X*s. My heart hurts for the child who had to go through such a tragedy. Then

I get to her assigned Legal Aid representative for the duration of the proceedings.

Olivia Oxford.

The shower shuts off. It's quiet, and I can still hear her through the walls, hanging her towel on a squeaky rail, opening and shutting drawers as she goes through her nighttime routine.

How odd, I think.

A sudden memory wrenches forward in my mind. The night at Solo, when I was trying to find Olivia, I saw her talking to someone at the bar. Someone I didn't know. Until I met her. I've completely forgotten until just now that she was talking to Kelli.

Have they been in contact this whole time?

My stomach feels sick, and my lungs flutter against my rib cage.

A rap at the door startles me. "Bea? The bathroom is free if you want it now."

When I try to answer, no sound comes out. I try again and manage a hoarse "Okay!"

I open the bedroom door slowly.

"Bea?"

Olivia is framed in the doorway. She's wearing sweatpants and a T-shirt, and wet hair frames her bare face. "What's going on?" She takes a step toward me and looks past me at my computer, where I've left the screen up with Kelli's art. "Oh wow," she breathes. "I haven't seen that in a long time. Where did you get that?"

I shake my head. "After you mentioned it, I just got really interested in the Valencia case. I was doing some research, that's all."

She squints past me. "But how do you have those? Those should be confidential." Her eyes focus back on me. She frowns. "Are you okay? You look really nervous."

"I think the past few days have really started to get to me." I'm aware of my voice trembling, and move my hands behind me so she can't see they are doing the same.

"Why, exactly, were you sleeping at the office again?" she asks.

"My parents and I had a fight."

"About what?"

I pause. "That's a little personal."

She nods slowly. Her wet hair has dripped down onto her shoulders, her gray T-shirt dark from the dampness seeping through. "Were you really with Landon that night?" she asks. "I mean, were you doing drugs with him?"

I shake my head. "No, no—"

"Is that why you fought with your parents? Do you need help, Bea?" Her voice is flat and emotionless.

"Why are you asking about Landon?"

She sighs. "You don't have to pretend anymore. You don't have to hide from the truth, Bea."

It hits me. She *knows*. Because this whole time, Olivia and Kelli have been in on it together.

That's how Kelli found me. She didn't happen to run into me that day at the coffee stand. It was all orchestrated.

Of course Kelli wasn't working alone. And of course it was Olivia. Olivia would have known about my problems with Landon. If they were looking for someone to help them, I was perfect. But what if they were looking for something more? The thought washes over me like a wave, and I am left gasping for air.

They weren't looking for help; they never needed my help. They were looking for someone to frame. This was never going to end after Saul's death.

I was never going to get away with any of it. And now I'm here with Olivia—I let her lead me straight to her apartment. What can she be planning now?

I turn and get my bag with my keys and phone. "I have to go, Olivia."

She doesn't move. "I don't think that's a good idea."

"Just let me go, please." My voice is a whimper.

"It's okay." Olivia nods her head and grins, a strange fake smile. "This can all be over now, if you want it to be."

"I know! I know all about you and Kelli!" I shake my head. "Don't try to deny it, Olivia. I know about Landon!"

Olivia straightens, and her eyes darken. "Who's Kelli?"

"You know exactly who she is."

"Bea, I don't know what you're talking about, and you're beginning to scare me. I think you just need to stay in your room, and we can talk in the morning." She steps back and puts her hand on the door. She's going to shut me in here. I push past her and walk down the hall.

She moves fast after me. "Don't!" she yells.

Her hand grabs at my arm, but I evade her grasp, and instead my hand grips her wrist. I push her away. She jerks back, but in her attempt to steady herself, she reaches for my arm again, and we both fall against the hallway wall.

"Get off me!" I yell. I feel her weight pulling me, and we all but tumble into the bathroom.

She releases me. In the confusion, in the small space, I struggle to stand, and my elbow finds her cheek, connecting with a thump. She spins around. Her back leg extends to find footing. Instead it finds a slick spot on the tile.

She stumbles and slips and throws her arms toward me.

She goes down. Her head hits the bathroom counter, a sharp crack like the sound of a gravestone being split open. Her damp tendrils twist around her head like vines; a small stream of red seeps out from beneath her.

Slowly backing away, I shiver. "I'm sorry, Olivia."

I reach the front door and stop. *Enough,* I think. It's been enough. I pull out my phone and make two calls. The first is to 911. "There's been an accident. Please send an ambulance." I give the address and hang up. The second is to Detective Branson, so she knows where to find at least one of Landon's killers.

Chapter 34

I drive.

Mom and Dad are gone. The house is dark. I let myself in and turn on lights.

Maybe I should have waited at Olivia's for Detective Branson. But I have to say goodbye one more time to Mom and Dad. They should hear all this from me. They should hear it from their own daughter.

I hear footsteps on the porch, and thank God Mom and Dad are home. I go to the door and open it. But standing under the porch light isn't Mom or Dad. It's Amy.

"What are you doing here?" I ask.

"Coming to check on you!" she says. She looks past me, into the house. "Are you by yourself?"

I step aside, and she comes in. The door swings shut behind her. "How do you know where I live?"

"Believe it or not, I called Greg, and he gave me your address. You really freaked me out earlier, sneaking around at Saul Group's office mumbling about some friend? And then you weren't answering my calls, so I wanted to make sure you were okay."

"You really didn't have to. I'm fine." My voice shakes as I say it.

Amy furrows her brows. "Hey, it's all right. What's going on? Jesus, Bea, you're shaking. Here, sit down."

She leads me to the couch, and I have to brace against her to not collapse. I take a deep breath and let it go. "Amy, things are so fucked!"

"What is going on?" She puts her arms around me.

"I know who killed Landon," I say.

Her body stiffens against mine. She breathes in sharply. "What do you mean?"

"I haven't been truthful. I thought it was an accident. But then it turned out it wasn't, and this girl was planning it the whole time." The words flow out faster than I can think, let alone stop them. It's like a dam has burst inside me, and there's no going back now. "The worst part is she used me to help her, and then she used me again to help her plan another murder." The words sound crazy.

"Why are you telling me this?" Amy asks. "Aren't you worried I'll go to the police? Why didn't you go to the police?"

"I tried. I wanted to!"

"Did you, though?" Amy asks. She pauses. After a second she says, "Who is this girl anyway?"

"She was a victim in the Valencia fire. Her parents died in the fire, actually, so while this plaintiff's attorney was preparing his suit on behalf of the survivors, the minors were assigned Legal Aid representatives. I just got those old files tonight. And it turns out the girl was assigned to a lawyer I know who's at BCC now. Her name is Olivia Oxford."

"I know Olivia," says Amy. "So what does that mean, then?"

"They were working together! You ask why I'm telling you and if I'm worried you might tell the police. I'm not. And it's because I'm going to tell them. I'm going to bring everything I have to this detective and confess my part of it. But they have to be held responsible." I swallow. "And I do too."

"You figured all this out because you found Kelli's file?" Amy asks.

"Yes, this whole time I was trying to understand what connected all of us, me and her . . . I couldn't figure it out. But now it makes sense. Olivia would have known where I was, and they could have tracked my movements."

"It's hard to believe, Bea."

"I know. But it's true." I hold my forehead. "I have a headache," I say. "Do you want some ginger tea?"

"Sure."

In the kitchen, I pick up a knife and begin peeling and slicing up a ginger root I grab from Mom's supply on the counter. As I chop, I slow and then lay the knife down on the cutting board. "Amy?" I call out to the living room.

There's no response.

I grip my arms. "Amy?" I call again. My skin flashes hot; pinpricks sting the back of my neck as all my tiny hairs stand on end. "How did you know her name was Kelli?"

"What do you mean?" Amy leans against the kitchen doorway, playing with her hair.

"I never said her name was Kelli," I tell her. "Was Greg really the one who told you where I live?"

Amy smiles, then smirks. "Aw." She's chuckling slightly and looking down, as if I just caught her cheating at a board game. "You said you figured this all out when you saw Kelli's file. I wonder—if you'd kept looking through the files, how long would it have taken for you to find mine?"

I swallow hard. "Amy?"

"Kelli did have help. Just not Olivia."

The front door swings open, and in the light I see her. Kelli. "Hi, Bea!" She waves. With a grin, she turns to Amy and waves at her too. "Hey, Sis!"

I shake my head. "No, Kelli's sister died in the fire."

"I never said that," says Kelli. She enters the kitchen and comes over to me. Too close. "Oh, I love this ginger tea." She inhales deep. "I said I lost my sister. Which was true. We were separated into different foster homes, and she disappeared into the system for years. When we finally reconnected, Amy was almost finished with law school, and she became my guardian. We both kept the last names of the last families we were with."

Now that they are both in front of me, I can see the resemblance between the two women. Amy is slightly taller; it was her in the Ring video, I realize. "You were there," I say. "You were at Landon's that night. You took me home."

"I called an Uber to get a record of it," says Kelli. "So I got into mine, and it was Amy who picked you up."

"And tonight when I ran into you at the Saul Group building, you were there making sure I went through with swapping out the pills. How did you get involved with something like this?" I ask with disbelief.

Amy purses her lips. "When I took her in, I knew Kelli was angry. I was too. I don't think it was until we were reunited that we realized just how much was taken from us. Not only our parents, but our chance at growing up together, at having a sister. When we found each other, it was like a new chapter for us."

"Amy understood," Kelli says. "Like nobody else ever could."

"But how did it all start? When did you . . ." *Begin killing men,* I want to say.

"It was my idea." Kelli sticks out her chest. "If you can believe it, I met the Brooks CEO at a club one night. He was there with a bachelor party." She rolls her eyes. "I recognized him right away. I'd spent years watching video of his depositions, hearing his lies as he dodged responsibility. So I tried to talk to him, and he immediately thought I was interested in him. Out of curiosity, I let him take me back to his place. He was so drunk I wondered if I could get him to say something about the fire, maybe mistakenly admit some fault. He didn't. But then I was there and looking around at his big fancy disgusting penthouse. I wanted to burn it all down. So I did."

Listening to her confess, I feel a dread stretching across my skin.

"And it felt *good.*" Kelli closes her eyes and inhales through her nose. She looks at Amy. "I was a little scared Amy would be mad at me, though."

"I was. Mad," Amy says. "But what could I do? Turn her in? We just swore not to speak about it again." Her eyes fall.

"But then it happened again," I say.

Kelli says. "I swear I was just trying to get them to admit they chose money over helping us get justice and move on." Her eyes gleam cold, but I want to believe her.

Amy swallows. "That was the problem. The deaths kept happening. But what choice did I have but to help her clean it up?" Amy looks at me. "I can't lose her again. But I can't control her either. I don't agree with what she's done, but . . . I would be lying if I said I didn't feel a little better each time."

"You both lost so much," I say. "I'm so sorry that happened to you, and I'm sorry you didn't get the justice you deserved. But this has to stop. How much longer can this go on?"

"You're right," says Amy. "It's gone too far. This is the last one, she's promised."

If I can't appeal to Amy, maybe I can provoke her. "So you're just following her around and cleaning up her messes? She's using you just as much as she's used me, pretending to be my friend."

Amy scoffs. "What would you know about friendship anyway? Kelli is the only blood I have left in the world. I'm protecting that, if nothing else, at all costs."

"Why are you speaking about me like I'm not in the room?" Kelli picks up the knife I've left on the counter. She grips it tight; the steel glints. She picks up the ginger root and deftly continues chopping where I left off.

"And Robert Ducheney?" Kelli looks up. "Yeah, I know about him too," I add. "He was trying to help you! He was on your side! So why did you kill him?"

"So that's how you got those files," says Amy. "You know, I told her the same thing . . ."

Kelli scoffs. "Please, he was useless! We had one shot, and he blew it. It was all there for him, but he couldn't give us the due process we deserved." Her knife slices become harder; the blade carves through the thick root and falls onto the cutting board with deep cuts, over and over again. "Bea, get me a pot of water, will you?" She holds up the knife.

Amy rolls her eyes. "Kelli, come on."

"I'm telling you, Amy. You should taste this—ginger and honey boiled in water. Bea, your mom was sweet to share her recipe."

I stand still, unsure of what to do.

"At least point me in the right direction if you're not going to help," Kelli says.

"The cupboard to your right." I point.

She opens it and pulls out a small pot. She then opens some other drawers and finds a jar of honey. After filling the pot with water, she clicks on a stovetop burner and sets the pot on top.

Amy taps her foot. "Kelli, really?" But her sister ignores her.

"So what?" I say. "You're going to turn me in and say I alone killed Landon? And Saul too?"

"Maybe we would have at one point," Kelli says. "But then you got too nosy. We can't have you telling what you know. You should have just stuck to what you promised," says Kelli. "What happened to our deal? What happened to sisterhood?"

"Murder pacts are not my idea of women supporting women."

She picks up the knife and holds it toward me; I inhale and step back.

I turn to Amy. "Please. We know each other. Amy, we went to school together. You know this is wrong."

"I don't love the idea of killing people," Amy says. Her face is scrunched, the corners of her mouth turned down. "But how else can we move on?" she asks.

"So you're going to stab me?" I snap. "That doesn't seem like it will match your make-it-look-like-an-accident MO."

"Good point." Kelli pushes the knife against my skin. The blade is hot on my throat. Then she moves it down against my chest, tracing the line of my collarbone, and down my arm until the tip rests in the inside of my forearm, just a couple of inches up from my wrist. "Maybe I'll knock you out and then make a slit just here." She digs in the point, and I feel the pinch on my skin. I look down to see a tiny needle point of red seep from my body.

"One slice." She moves the knife down and away from me, still following the flow of my arm, to my wrist, to my hand. "Another slice!" The knife sings in the air as she makes a second quick motion, this time at my other wrist. "Nobody will question Bea slitting her wrists. She was always unstable, always a liability. It was just a matter of time."

I look at Amy, pleading with my eyes for her to do something.

"Maybe this is getting a little out of control," she says. "Kelli, you said we were just coming over to scare her."

The pot of water is boiling, steam billowing up toward the ceiling. Kelli clicks off the burner with a quick turn of her wrist. "Ugh, I'm not even in the mood for tea anymore." She slides the carefully chopped ginger off the counter and onto the floor.

Amy holds up her hands slowly. "Kelli, think about this . . ." With one quick motion, Kelli turns the knife around in her hand, and I see the butt of the hilt come toward me. I duck away. She hits the countertop behind me, and the sharp crack echoes. We all jump at another crash. The front door flies open.

"Seattle PD!" Detective Branson holds a gun pointed at us. "Put down the knife!"

Chapter 35

I hold my hands in the air, and the sisters follow suit. Kelli lets the knife clatter to the floor. Branson comes in and leans into the walkie on her shoulder. "Backup requested," she says. She walks into the kitchen, gun held steady. "Thanks for the message," she says to me.

"It wasn't Olivia," I say.

"I know."

Kelli scoffs. "You told on us?"

Amy is shaking. I see a tear fall down her cheek. "Kelli, shut up," she says. "Oh my God, it's all over." It sounds like relief.

Branson kicks away the knife. It slides across the kitchen and under the dining table.

Kelli points at me, her eyes wild. "Thank God you're here, Detective. Bea is planning to murder Franklin Saul. You'll find drug-laced pills in his office, pills that Bea planted there in order to kill him! She texted me her plan—I can show you the evidence!"

The detective looks at me, but I smile. "They were placebos, Kelli. Just sugar pills. In the end, I could never do what you do."

Kelli's face pinches, and her chest falls. "You lied to me?" she gasps.

Branson reaches for her handcuffs, lowering the gun just slightly.

Kelli moves. "It's not over!"

I yell, "No!"

Kelli seizes the pot from the stove. Detective Branson lets out an inhuman scream as boiling-hot water is thrown across her chest and torso.

Kelli dives for the knife.

I run.

I go into the hall and into my room, scrambling to close the door behind me. An arm reaches through, and Kelli blocks the frame. I push my whole body against the door, but she's wedged in, and it won't shut now. The knife slashes erratically at the air. I have to step back to dodge the blade. She pushes in the door, and now she's in the room. I try to get past her, but she kicks out and catches my legs. My face hits the carpet with a brain-numbing thud. She stands over me, wielding the blade. I reach toward her, my palms held out. "Kelli, stop this."

"Gotta be honest," she says. "I don't see you making a move to the Saul Group anytime soon. Mostly because you're going to be dead." She twirls the knife at me.

Collecting all my strength, I yell and jump forward, grabbing her in a bear hug. She falls against the wall. I use her as leverage to stand upright.

She regains her own stance quickly. "I'm so fucking done with you," she sneers.

My hand flails out for anything. I grab the glass award from my dresser and hold the feather quill like the hilt to a mace. The weight feels good in my grip.

She lunges with a scream, knife aimed at my face. "We had a deal!" she says.

I strike.

The corner of the base goes into her temple.

She stops; her mouth opens in surprise.

She crumples.

Award still in my grasp, bright crimson drops fall from the corner that went into her head, refracted into scarlet prisms in the glass. I stumble back out of the bedroom.

Amy stands in the kitchen. I look down at Detective Branson, unconscious. I want to help her, but Amy stands there frozen, her eyes on the bloody trophy in my hand. "What did you do?" she asks. "What did you do!"

I drop the award. Amy is on top of me.

"No, please!" I yell.

Her hand covers my mouth, and she leans into my face as she straddles me. "You hurt her! We were supposed to help each other. This is why you will never get what you want and why you'll only ever have what you deserve."

Behind Amy, I see Branson groan and stir. She rises to her knees.

Amy raises the award and brings it down hard; the sharp point of the quill pierces into flesh, and I scream. She drives it in further, resting her weight onto it. I hear the tearing of muscle and then a sharp crack as it hits bone. It glances off my clavicle and goes through my shoulder.

My scream gets Branson's attention, and she spots us on the floor. She raises her gun; she has a straight shot. "Stop!" Branson orders. "Get off of her, or I'll shoot!" But if Amy hears, she makes no attempt to obey the command.

Like I'm nothing more than a slab of meat on her cutting board, Amy pulls out the trophy. I scream again in agony. I can see the glass point has broken off, leaving a serrated crystal blade. Amy holds it up higher this time, directly over my face.

I hear the cocking of a gun. Branson is aiming. And then I smell it. Gas. Branson is standing right next to the stovetop. The one with the faulty knob, the one that's been leaking gas into the kitchen and living room this whole time.

"Wait!" I hold out my hand.

I don't have time to cover my face. Amy doesn't have time to react.

Branson pulls the trigger. The miniature explosion that ejects the bullet from the chamber causes a spark, just a tiny one that, anywhere else, would be inconsequential. But here and now, it's anything but.

I close my eyes.

The world flashes in a white-hot roar, then silence.

◆ ◆ ◆

A flash of roaring flames. The pop of burning beams. I sit up and gasp. Hot cinders fill my lungs, and I wheeze for fresh air. Next to me is Amy; the clothes on her back are torched, and I can see her bare skin. I think she might be dead.

Then she groans and turns over, and the ripped fabric from her shirt falls away, exposing her right torso. And I see it. A burn scar, mottled and twisted skin, darker than the rest of her fair complexion and contracted in places like pinched valleys; this stretches from the top of her hip to the middle of her rib. Valencia.

She looks around her, shocked and disoriented.

I stand and hold my hand out. "Get up!" She looks at me like I'm a stranger. I grab her wrists and yank her upright. "We have to get out!" I yell.

"Where are we?" she asks.

She looks at the flames that sear around us, licking at the ceiling. The curtains and the couch nearby us are already engulfed. The heat is unbearable, and I'm slick with sweat. There's only one path to safety, the open front door just steps away. "Come on," I say, gesturing to it.

"No!" She pushes me away. "I have to get Kelli!"

We look back to the bedroom and down the hall. It's a tunnel of swirling blaze. Amy runs toward it. I follow her, but grasp her forearm just before she enters. "It's too dangerous!" I shake my head and mouth, *I'm sorry.* She cries out, a soundless moan of anguish.

Then I look down and see Detective Branson, who took the brunt of the blast. I swallow hard and cover my mouth, holding back vomit.

"I have to find her!" Amy yanks her arm away.

"Amy!" I scream. "She's dead."

She shakes her head. "I can't leave her again. She's my sister!"

She turns and looks at me, then at the door. She holds her arms over her face and walks into the fire. I watch until her form is gone, swallowed by the shining darkness.

I turn and run.

I cough and gasp for oxygen. I've waited too long.

The world fades.

The cold night air hits me. Sirens blast, and the fierce brightness of the flames is replaced with red-and-blue strobes.

I collapse.

As I'm swarmed by people in blue uniforms, I point to the house and try to tell them about Kelli and Amy. But no sounds come out of my singed throat.

Oxygen is placed over my face. I hear a voice: "You're going to be okay."

Before I fall away, I see a face hover over mine. It's blurry, but the eyes are full of water, face twisted in concern.

Allegra?

I blink, and the face sharpens into view.

"You're going to be fine, Bea," says Mom. I feel her hand grasp mine. "I'm not leaving your side."

Chapter 36

The lights are blinding when my eyes blink open; my retinas burn, and I squeeze them shut again. I breathe in a strong smell of disinfectant, but it only sits on top of the layer of tinged ash that feels as if it lines the insides of my nostrils.

There's a small steady beeping.

I'm in a hospital.

I open my eyes again, squinting against the stark whiteness of the room around me. My arms push against the thin bed to find leverage to sit up. I wince as a dull twist of pain racks my left side. My left arm and shoulder are completely bandaged. *Oh yeah,* I think, *I was stabbed.*

"Oh no, don't do that." A voice at my side.

"Simon?"

He stands from a chair where a blanket and his jacket are bundled up; his hair is disheveled and his eyes red. "Just stay lying down," he says softly, in a soothing voice. "You're still weak. I was so worried . . ." His mouth trembles.

I manage a smile. "Hey, I'm okay."

"I know you are." He kisses my forehead. "Oh, I need to tell everyone you're awake!"

"Everyone?"

He opens the hospital room door and disappears. I take a deep breath in the silence. Is it really over?

The door opens again, and bodies pile in. Mom and Dad come in and each hug me gingerly. "Thank God, Bea!"

After them, Allegra and Caleb enter. They stand back, but I beckon them closer. "Allegra," I say. "I am so sorry—"

She shushes me and holds her hand to her mouth. "Bea, we thought . . ."

Caleb puts his arm around her. He whistles. "It's like you have a death wish."

"Or at least a flair for the dramatic," adds Simon. Everyone laughs, the tension now released.

I grin and try to shift my weight, but I groan at the ache in my entire body. "How long have I been here?"

Dad offers me water. I take it and drink. I know it's from the hospital fountain, but it tastes like the freshest thing I've ever drunk, like it's washing away the ash that's settled in my very core. "It's only been a day, but you've been on some heavy pain meds and in and out of consciousness. You kept waking up and asking about Kelli."

Amy, I remember, her face turning to mine as she walked down that fiery hallway. Her skin, scarred from the Valencia fire, scorched again from the blast. "Did she . . ."

Dad shakes his head. "They found her and her sister together."

A new kind of pain envelops me. "And Detective Branson? She saved my life." She didn't know she'd be trading her own.

"She was a hero."

I remember the pills. "Wait, you have to get ahold of someone at the Saul Group—the heart medication!"

Simon smiles. "Already taken care of," he says. "I told the police to go check on him."

Caleb frowns. "That's why you asked me for drugs. But if I refused to get you them, where did the pills come from?"

I don't look at Simon. Instead I shrug and answer, "Just found someone selling their medication online. Random luck for me." I hope they buy it. "But how is the house?" I ask, changing the subject. My thumb finds a comfortable spot on my wrist. I spot ash still underneath my fingernails. "Is it completely gone?"

Dad sighs. "It's not good. But Caleb and Allegra say we can stay as long as we need."

"And you have your own room when you get out of here," Allegra adds. "It was Caleb's home office, but we have a guest bed in there."

"Thank you," I say.

Mom grips my hand. "We'll rebuild," she says. "It's just a house. We're just happy you're safe."

The door opens, and a nurse enters. "Well, good morning, sunshine," she says. "Let's do a vitals check."

My visitors begin to file out. "We'll give you some privacy," Dad says. Mom stays.

After the nurse leaves, Mom sits at my side. "You asked me why I never approved of Caleb—"

"It's okay, Mom. We don't have to do this now."

She sniffs, and I see tears in her eyes. She continues. "I think him and Allegra are good together, I do. But for you . . . you are my daughter. I had enough to worry about at that time! The truth is it wouldn't matter who it was—I don't think anyone will ever be good enough for my little girl. Bea, I'm sorry I wasn't there for you more. Things can be different now, right?"

"Yeah, Mom," I say. "We can rebuild."

I sleep and wake up, get poked and prodded by medical staff and fall back asleep. The time in the hospital seems to stand still and accelerate all at once. The church sends a huge bouquet of flowers, and Mom's friends supply an endless amount of food and snacks. Simon visits too. We talk and watch shows on the tiny TV in the corner of the ceiling. I ask about work, but he refuses to talk about it and insists I rest.

I've just put on real clothes—well, leggings and a T-shirt, anyway—after far too long in a hospital gown, when a bundle of hydrangeas floats into my room. Behind the blue spray, Olivia tilts her head and waves. "Special delivery from Bellingham, Charles & Chan."

My chest tightens. "Olivia?" The awful image of her fallen on the bathroom floor, blood seeping from her head, is burned into my mind. "Are you okay?"

"I'm alive." She lifts her hair and turns to display a bandage on the back of her head. "Just a slight cut and a concussion, but looks like you got it worse." She eyes my wrapped-up shoulder and arm.

"I'm alive," I say. I take the vase of flowers from her and place it on the bedside table next to a couple of others. "How did you know hydrangeas are my favorite?"

"They're your favorite flower?" she asks. "Out of all the flowers? Why?"

I touch the blooms, aggregates of tiny explosions of dreamy azure. "They're common, sure. But they're bold and resilient."

"So they're like you."

I feel the red tint flow into my cheeks. "Olivia, I want to say I'm sorry."

She holds her arms against her chest. "I was trying to help you, you know. I genuinely thought you were having some kind of breakdown." She looks down. "I think I felt so bad about Landon, I thought you were dealing with some kind of addiction too, and I wanted to do what I could."

"Well, I wasn't really acting in any kind of normal mental state, if I'm honest. But why were you trying to keep me from leaving?"

"I was afraid of what you were going to do if you left. And that if I let you, I'd be responsible in a way." She frowns.

"I can understand that feeling. I'm just happy you're okay."

We both smile, but the air is still thick between us. "Why didn't you just tell the truth?" she finally asks.

I sigh. It's a good question. "I think I thought people wouldn't believe me. Or would blame me. I'm used to just being on my own. Sometimes I forget others want to help."

"For the record, then, you can always come to me. I guess we're connected now."

"We're bonded through trauma," I note.

She puts a hand to her chin. "Well, let's just be there for one another from here on out. Friends?"

I embrace her and ignore the sting in my shoulder. "Friends."

On the day of my discharge, I meet Simon in the hospital staff parking lot to avoid the throng of reporters and cameras that has been camped out in front since the story broke. The national news has been fixated on the so-called standoff between the two "Killer Sisters" and Detective Branson, not least the sole survivor—i.e., me. Between the active investigation into the incident itself and all the old cases that have been reopened, including Landon's and Ducheney's, I have been on an endless rotation of police interviews, which has led me to needing my very own lawyer. Turns out lawyers are helpful sometimes.

There seems to be no end in sight, but at least I can continue from the comfort of the Crown home soon.

I've been placed on leave from work for the duration; it doesn't look great for me to be practicing at the moment under the BCC name. I think back to when my biggest worry was getting my promotion and I truly believed that was all I needed to make me happy. But happiness is an ever-moving goalpost, and now I know better than to pin my hopes on external motivations. Besides, the saying about getting what you wish for has turned out to be very true.

Simon helps load my flowers and goody bags with extra socks into the car. Even though the sky is overcast with soft billowing clouds, they move along with a breeze; a beam of sunshine peeks through and illuminates the world for a moment. Was it like this when I got out of the hospital after the accident? I don't remember feeling the gratefulness, the desire to live better, that I do now.

"Ready?" Simon asks, buckling his seat belt.

I hold the bouquet of hydrangeas in my lap. "Ready."

Chapter 37

Nine months later

The renovations are complete. With the fire and smoke damage, it was nearly a total teardown. But with insurance and a couple of media appearances, we got enough money to rebuild. The new porch steps don't even sag. The red door has never been brighter.

And it must have been the ash that blew into the soil, but Mom has even managed to make a small rosebush bloom in the front yard. The petals are a pale peach and soft as a baby's rosy cheeks.

We're having a small party tonight to celebrate the new house and show off the fresh-paint smell. Dad's set up in the back with barbecue, and Caleb's helped to build a firepit. Allegra and I drag the Adirondack chairs around the pit. After we make sure there are enough set out, I find Mom. "Can I help with her?" I ask.

She nods. "Yes, just while I finish putting out the plates and silverware."

She hands me the four-month-old baby, all coos and drool. Their daughter is a perfect mix of Allegra and Caleb, and she has a thick pile of black hair on her head already. "Hi, little Rosie." I rock her back and forth. She's beautiful.

Simon arrives shortly, and he, Dad, and Caleb man the grill. Allegra and I play with Rosie in the soft grass; she curls her toes inward at the little pricks of the grass blades on her feet. When the food is ready, we sit and eat and tell stories long into the evening. Simon holds my hand. He leans over to kiss my cheek and nuzzles my neck. I kiss him back.

When it gets dark enough, Dad starts a blaze in the firepit. I sit back farther in my chair while others lean toward the warmth as the cool night air closes in. Even as I try to not think about it, I see Amy's face in the dark edges of the flames. The truth is I'm haunted by her all the time. Even in the daytime, I watch her walk into burning hallways. In the shower, as I wash the angry red scar on my shoulder, I feel the grip of her hands on my body. I think about the sisters with anger sometimes, other times with empathy. Kelli's quest for the vengeance she could never have especially weighs on me.

I think about the painting in her apartment, or the photos of her art therapy from her file. It's the same bold brushstrokes, the same vivid reds and oranges struck across the canvas with the same power and hurt. I said it reminded me of poppies. Or a sunset. It was a blaze all along.

The accidents kept happening.

What did Amy say? *My sister and I were always playing with candles. We would be in the basement with those long candles you would set out at Thanksgiving, just lighting them and playing with the wax. I think all kids are fascinated with fire.*

Maybe the paintings were Kelli's way of coping with her past. Maybe they were a child's confession. My hand absentmindedly drifts to my shoulder, where a quiet ache pulses. My fingertips touch the area where I was stabbed, where a marbled scar is a constant remembrance of the piece of crystal they had to dig out of me. Funny how I didn't have any scars from the car accident; no physical ones, anyway. But Kelli and Amy—I carry them on my body now; I think of them every day.

I used to live with the guilt of what happened to Caleb and me and what he did for me. I now live in a different world, a world where I am guilty of what I had to do to save myself.

Sometimes I think I'm not strong enough to live with all of it. Haven't I seen enough already? But those days are rare now. I know my strength now.

It's all the small strengths that keep us alive, like a cup of Mom's salabat, a childhood friend's loyalty, and even the medicine that helps my brain balance its chemistry.

Looking back now, I know I lost sight of everything I had worth fighting for.

For family and fire, for the blazes that burn to ignite the buried seeds to grow, and the quiet embers we carry in our hearts for decades, maybe all our lives. Even for a firepit in the backyard and sharing bites of s'mores underneath the powder blue of a summer evening. For friends and for the loves who we lose. And the loves we lose and find again if we are fortunate.

For the future.

Some days it's astonishing to me how much I fight to be alive, but I have so much in this life to fight for.

Acknowledgments

Writing this book was a labor of love in the truest sense; it was a long process through a difficult time, and I could not have completed it without the help and support of so many remarkable individuals. My heartfelt gratitude first of all to Sophie Cudd, my agent, who is always such a source of joy, inspiration, and guidance. Thank you to everyone at The Book Group. Thank you to Danielle Marshall, who, with such grace and patience, helped me mold and shape the story into the vision it is today. Thank you to Ali for your thoughtful edits and taking it across the finish line! A big thank-you to Annie and Tristen—editors are truly the unsung heroes of publishing, and for someone like me (who doesn't actually know grammar and writes purely "on vibes"), your help is invaluable! Thank you to Carmen, Darci, Carissa, Angela, and everyone at Lake Union and Amazon Publishing!

To all of the Sogn family, especially David, Gary, Chris, Allie, Danny, Kelsey, Donna, Synova, Stu, and Sarah, and the rest of my family who always ask me to sign copies of my books for them, I couldn't wish for greater champions—thank you!

My eternal love to my Jamigos, Jami Fairleigh and Jami Sheets. I will always thank the universe for somehow bringing us and our stories together.

To my family, Mom, Dad, Danielle, and Jeff, for always being supportive and my biggest fans. And to Wyatt for being my favorite person on earth.

About the Author

Photo © 2022 Marcella Ratsamy

Jamie Lee Sogn grew up in Olympia, Washington, where she was raised in a Filipino American home. She studied anthropology and psychology at the University of Washington before going on to receive her Juris Doctor from the University of Oregon School of Law. A "recovering attorney," Sogn writes contracts by day and (much more exciting) fiction by night. While she has lived in Los Angeles, New York City, and even Eugene, Oregon, she now lives in Seattle with her son.